# The Brass Bed

Also by Alexandra Marshall

GUS IN BRONZE
STILL WATERS
TENDER OFFER

# ALEXANDRA MARSHALL

# The Brass Bed

DOUBLEDAY & COMPANY, INC.
GARDEN CITY, NEW YORK
1986

ISBN 0-385-23294-2
*Copyright © 1986 by Morrissey Street, Ltd.*
All Rights Reserved
Printed in the United States of America
First Edition

Library of Congress Cataloging in Publication Data

Marshall, Alexandra.
  The brass bed

  I. Title.
PS3563.A719S4   1986     813'.54     85–10172

FOR ELIZABETH AND PATRICK

# Part I

# One

THE DIM INTERIOR illumination displayed with effect the prized collection—as if fish were either art or artifact—of lungless creatures swimming laps. The building's spine was an enormous cylinder, a wraparound tank many fathoms deep into which scuba divers, who wore their gills on their backs, descended several times a day with food enough, one could suppose, to keep the cannibals who lived there from depleting the exhibit. The New England Aquarium was this night the implausible location of a gala.

Captain Jacques-Yves Cousteau had come to Boston to make brief appearances in person and give interviews to talk show hosts whose audiences had far longer attention spans than they themselves did, and of course to raise the money—reparations, really—to keep on exploring how great the disaster was. This "Evening Undersea" was a fund-raiser, and the journalists assigned to cover the event were the only people there who hadn't paid a hundred dollars to attend.

Duncan Jones asked the guy behind him in the press of men

and women being given name tag passes for the cash bar, "Not that I'm in favor of *not* saving the environment, but what about, for instance, unemployment as an issue to raise funds for?" He told his name to a woman dressed in sequins like a mermaid. "From the *Globe,*" he said. He noticed that she wore a choker made of half shells like the one in Botticelli's *Birth of Venus,* on which she stands looking not exactly newborn. "That's right," he said, glad there was name recognition of a sort, if that's what it was when she said, "I read the Living pages first, although my husband says it's only for the gossip. I say he can have the presidency and the terrorism and the market. At least Living's for the living." She gave Duncan Jones his name tag, adding an encouraging, "So keep it up."

It was a line he'd used himself in arguments with Jessica, his wife—his future ex-wife now—of what would have been four-teen years. "I work," he'd said, "both for the living and a living, in that order." As opposed, he meant, to her, whose clients were all corporations that did things like make tobacco and invest-ments in apartheid. Duncan answered cheerfully, "OK, I will," as if he'd just made up his mind to keep it up.

It would have been good news to Duncan's longtime boss, who'd had to say to him that morning, "Look, pal, I know what you're going through, believe me, but you also see my problem, don't you? I mean, I got space to fill with writing. How long can I keep on using bigger pictures than I should to cover up for what you say your dog ate on your way to school and similar excuses I'm not buying anymore. What I need, Jones, is copy: words, pal, stuck together into sentences and paragraphs. It's what you used to do all day long, isn't it? Christ, not so many years ago, your children-of-the-busing-crisis series had a good shot at the Pulitzer. It should have won, I know, I said so, but we got another problem now, and it's the opposite one. I hate saying this to you, pal, but you've got to get engaged or take a walk."

It was why unemployment seemed a more important issue even than clean water. What he'd done with Jessica, he'd almost said, was get engaged *and* take a walk (not that he'd done the walking), so it was a choice between two equals only in the sense that he could not do either one. He couldn't seem to get a charge, no matter how he tried, nor would he contemplate that he could be fired from the only job he'd had since graduate school. Wasn't there an insurance policy that covered crises in employees who would get it back together one of these days? He'd asked his boss this to prove his sense of humor was intact, then answered his own question, "With my luck, though, they'd say, 'This is what an act of God is, and an act of God, as we all know, is not insurable.' "

Duncan asked for a beer at the first bar he came to and went up the ramp that was a bridge over the shark pool. Ordinarily he would not want to lean over the rail and look down, but for a wish for a penny he'd look anywhere they wanted. All I ask for is a story, he wished silently, as if it were a secret. Find me something here to write up, he said as he let another penny go in after the first.

"Hey, big spender," was her greeting. As she indicated to the man who held her by the arm that if he went ahead she'd catch up, Jessica presented Duncan with a cheek.

He kissed it and said, "Of all people." It was what he'd said to her sarcastically a hundred times, but now his real surprise required he say it as it was intended to be said, with real surprise. "I didn't know you cared about conserving the earth's most important resource. Or are you here because these sharks are your clients? Eels I knew you represented."

"I'm not working tonight," she said. Jessica was dressed— unlike the women, who resembled the warm-water fish—more like the penguins, as the men were.

He was wearing a seersucker jacket and a plaid tie with a button-down shirt. "*I* am."

"I see."

"You look nice, though," he said. It was not a dress he'd ever seen, not that they'd ever gone to dances.

"Is it just this light," she asked, "or are you tan?"

"This light is eerie, isn't it?" If she persisted, he would lie to avoid saying where he'd been.

"Your teeth look so white."

"My teeth *are* white," Duncan answered, showing them off with a bitter little laugh. He also wouldn't say he'd been to Buffalo over the weekend and not told his parents they'd been separated many months already.

"You look better than you have, is all." Her smile was quite affectionate. "And tan, in this light." Now her smile revealed she knew he'd been away.

He'd lie under oath if he were asked in her presence if he'd ever been to Club Med. How humiliating to have been so openly pathetic as to go the whole week without making notes for a piece that could write itself, "Confessions of a Club Med Dropout." He had been so needy, even poor facsimiles of fun and relaxation worked their magic, and for once he'd concentrated on blues other than his own: the sky, the water.

"Nice to see you," she said.

"You too," he responded. This was no day to say anything to Jessica for which he would need self-esteem.

"I'd better catch up," she explained and pointed vaguely up the ramp to where a crowd of people plastered soft white cheeses on white wafers, shouting small talk over a jazz trio loudly improvising.

Duncan felt, as she went off to join her partner for this dance, as if he were their child and had been left home with the baby-sitter, as if they were blowing kisses to him as they backed out the door. He ought to have mentioned to her that his mother had sent something she said was a pillow she had needlepointed —it was wrapped up and tied with a frizz of ribbon—to see whether Jessica would volunteer to write his mother one of her nice thank-you cards. It somehow wouldn't be enough for him to tell his mother Jess had liked it fine but had been working awfully hard, which also was why she was never home the times his mother called. And whereas he knew he'd be forced to deal

with what the truth was someday, what he needed was still more
time to recover from the failure of their marriage.

What he'd liked about Club Med was evidence that there were
others even worse off. He'd been raised not to profit or take
pleasure from the handicaps of others, but once he declared
himself in a state of emergency the rules were different. He
hoped desperately he wouldn't have to pay by getting herpes,
but it had been reassuring in a fundamental way that he was still
a candidate for body contact. He had even been someone's
initiator into the wide-open world of multiple orgasms—he was
as surprised as she was—after multiple rum punches and a
moonlit stroll along the beach that was described in the brochure as "mile-long silvery powder sand" but was what he
would call instead the color of spermatozoa. So what if an em-
pire had been built on values he abhorred, or that with his
participation he was an accomplice to the exploitation? He
needed the reassurance, even if it came from strangers whose
names he could not recall except perhaps under hypnosis,
which explained his having brought the poster home that said,
CLUB MED. THE ANTIDOTE FOR CIVILIZATION, featuring a woman
who was nearly nude and offering him all she had and a pineapple.

Now he went to find the tanks of tropical fish like those he had
seen on the reef. His advice to would-be writers, journalists or
otherwise, was always start from what you know.

As a way to stall and because there hadn't been much to write
up the night before—and this was the consensus and not symptomatic of his own stall—Duncan told his boss it made sense for
him to go to the French Library, where Cousteau had an award
to pick up from the mayor. Since it was a photo opportunity—
the mayor's office saw to that—Duncan had the head start of
what a picture is worth, which, if not ten thousand words, as
promised in the Chinese proverb, would be a few sentences.
Now he had a few minutes before it was time to head out and
decided to risk asking Jessica for one last favor. The worst she

could say was no, and who knew better than he did what that would be like.

First he had to penetrate her law firm's switchboard, then the guard dog, Duncan called her, whose desk sat by Jessica's door and who was trained to attack. Politely he asked, "Jessica Jones, please."

"And may I ask who's calling?"

"Tell her Duncan."

"Mr. Duncan? And to what is this in reference?"

"Mr. Duncan *Jones*. Just tell her, will you?"

"Certainly."

"You called?" The flatness in the voice could not be imitated.

"Hi, Jess. I forgot to ask you something last night." He took a breath. "She's a hazard, by the way."

"My secretary? Well, as I keep saying, Duncan, you won't have to deal with her if you'll try reaching me at home."

"You're never there, I've tried." He paused. "Where are you, anyway?"

"The movies."

"Yeah, you always say that."

"Can we speed this up?"

She always said that too. "OK. I have a present for you that my mother made. I think she really would expect some thanks."

"Duncan, didn't you tell her?" The tone was parental.

"No, I didn't want to do it on the phone."

"But I thought you were *there*. Hasn't your father's birthday been yet?"

"Yes, last weekend," he admitted. "I had said already on the phone you would be working and that's why you couldn't come."

She sighed. "But so? You get there and admit the truth."

"Not easy. As a lawyer, surely you know that."

"Did you call to insult me?"

Duncan answered, "No, OK, I can just tell her on the phone you said thanks. That'd be enough."

Frustrated, she said, "Duncan, when will you grow up, will you answer me that one?"

"When did you tell yours?"

In fact it was before she had told him. "They've known forever," she replied.

"Yeah? Nice of them to write to say goodbye."

"Did you write *them*? What is this thing about if everyone would just write notes to one another?"

"Nothing. So I'll tell her you said thank you?"

"You can tell her that I said goodbye."

"And you don't want the pillow either, right?"

There was a time when this would have made them both laugh, but it was gone forever.

"No," she said instead, "and tell her not to send me Easter cards. And don't call me at work again."

"Did she send you an Easter card again this year? I'm sorry about that, I am. But how can I call you at home? You're never there."

"Keep trying."

"Yeah, you always say that. Anyway, what do your parents care if you're divorced. That's the big difference."

"No it isn't," she said, "the big difference is I don't deceive mine."

"Well hurray for you." The power she had to make him say such idiotic things as this. Did she just make him act, or was he, infantile?

"I have to take another call." Her voice revealed only the tip of her exasperation.

"Sure, you always say that too. I'm glad I'm not trying to date you."

She said, "So am I."

They hung up simultaneously.

He never thought he'd think so, but he actually preferred the times—a period of years—of his indifference to her. They had both been climbing rungs and giving work the all they had to give, and it had been enough to stay out of each other's way. But now, now he could be distracted, no, obsessed, by the sound of the absence of her voice. She had been beautiful in black and white the night before.

Taped to the stack of metal baskets labeled, as a joke, NOVEL IN PROGRESS was a clipping showing Lech Walesa having been elected the "Pipe Smoker of the Year" by Britain's National Association of Pipe Smokers. The citation praised Walesa for so ably demonstrating "the relaxing effects of the pipe despite one's troubles."

What should Duncan wish, that he smoked pipes? Or, less facetiously, that the divorce weren't still and always pending?

What he really wished was that there were still something to his marriage. Fourteen years, or almost, was a good way to begin, not end, things, given what they both had learned. The problem was that they'd been honest, as the times demanded, and had said things to each other that they couldn't then forgive, and once they realized there were things to say that should remain unspeakable, it was too late; they were already cruel. And that's what happened to their marriage: they were cruel; they said things.

In Mem Chu, the Stanford University chapel, was inscribed in stone, source unattributed, IT IS BY SUFFERING THAT GOD HAS MOST NEARLY APPROACHED TO MAN; IT IS BY SUFFERING THAT MAN DRAWS MOST NEARLY TO GOD. Duncan remembered thinking when he was a student there that he could not "relate" to that at all, which made him laugh now in a way, since it was in Mem Chu that he and Jessica were married.

Just before the ceremony he'd said to his brother, "I think charity prevailed." He was referring to the fact that because Duncan wasn't Jewish, and for having chosen Duncan neither was his daughter, Jessica's imposing father had said he would attend but wouldn't walk her down the aisle. He'd made it clear ahead of time what he could do and not do, given that he strongly disapproved of their decision to get married on a Saturday, his Sabbath, in a church, by someone they both seemed to worship. That seemed fair enough to Duncan. Jessica, however, seemed to need him to give her to Duncan (which proved her point later on when she became a feminist) and so had wept the night before (and ruined the nice dinner party given by his parents), pleading for her father's reconsideration.

But it was not yet decided, and so Duncan and his best man stood and waited. "Don't they know that charity *is* love?" he'd whispered to his brother, nodding at the angels in mosaic up over the altar: Faith, Hope, Charity, and Love.

After a long delay in which the organist had improvised but could have played another prelude, it was clear her father had decided he would do it. Jessica's small pretty mother walked to her seat unescorted. Her eyes were all shiny with relief, and she smiled up at Duncan in a way that made him feel it had been worth it. Duncan and his brother exchanged nudges there under the angels, and Mem Chu, accessorized by Mrs. Stanford with ten thousand small square chips of colored glass, suddenly seemed almost Chartres.

The feeling didn't last a minute. Overcome (this was what Jessica would call it) with emotion, she could barely walk. Their plan had been to memorize their vows, but she could barely speak. It was as if she were his widow rather than his wife-to-be. Before they'd even had a chance to promise things and give each other rings handcrafted by a San Francisco goldsmith, it was clear the most important thing to happen that day was and always would be that her father walked her down the aisle.

Of course Duncan had come to understand, since it was one of the cruel things she said, that it was not her father, really, but her own ambivalence that spoiled the wedding. Jessica, in other words—her own words—was afraid she should have called it off, was *wishing* she had called it off the night before.

So it was not her father tyrannizing the event; the tyrant was his own new bride. She'd forced her father to choose between her and his own principle, and he, good father that he was, had chosen her. That part was simple, if a little time-consuming. What her father didn't know was that she'd wanted him to say no, so she could say she could not go through with it.

And what exactly, therefore, was the reason Duncan wished there were still something to his marriage? What he meant instead, he guessed, was that there were *once* something. What he wished, he meant, was that she'd loved him.

And, Duncan admitted, he did not like change. The one time he had ventured in a way that was significant was leaving Buffalo for Stanford, which then he did not want to leave even though he'd graduated. So he stayed and got a doctorate in communications and met Jessica, who got accepted at the Harvard Law School, bringing them to Boston. On his own he probably would have stayed there in San Francisco writing for the *Chronicle*—and maybe he *had* left his heart there—and so maybe he should go back. Duncan wondered if that would be healthy in the long run and concluded—Jessica was proof—there was no long run.

Now he stuck the notepad into the left pocket of the same seersucker jacket he had worn the night before—and couldn't fail to note that this meant, in addition to all the ways he felt left out, he was not even right-handed—and went looking for Mark Otis, who had been assigned as the photographer and asked to have a ride to town. Most people didn't care for Otis, and although this list included Duncan, he knew his own reason was that he was jealous of, not just annoyed by, Mark's nerve.

He'd joined the *Globe* staff at the age of twenty-one four years before, having just won the first J. Edward Fitzgerald Award for Photojournalism with a photo essay of a rescued would-be suicide, a woman on the underside of a bridge over the Charles River who allowed herself to be brought back by a policeman. The criss-crossing of the beams made the bridge seem a trellis, and the woman—she became the flower—was plucked by the cop in the harness who'd been lowered on a rope. The composition was itself no less extreme than was the content—the policeman was a spider on a thread?—and in the judges' view it was so daring you could almost say it was a work of genius. Only someone who was immature could have abstracted; only someone who was too young to feel sorry for the woman would have seen her as a rose. In their award the judges cited Mark's bold, brilliant vision and originality of purpose. Mark was pleased and spent the thousand-dollar prize in fifteen minutes at Grand Central Cameras on a new enlarger.

He was in a good mood now. He'd put a photograph he hadn't taken over his desk, and everyone who said something about it made the same mistake. It was a woman with a round flat face, relieved by cheekbones, who was dressed in black and looked into the lens with a hard, complicated stare: Yoko Ono.

"Yoko Ono," Duncan guessed.

"Wrong, Alfred Stieglitz took this picture in maybe 1920," Mark explained, thrilled to have fooled him.

"So who is it?"

Mark replied, as if it should be obvious, "Georgia O'Keeffe."

"No kidding, is she Japanese? I didn't know that," Duncan answered blandly.

What was that, a joke? Mark wanted to say, "You're an ass-hole," but decided not to, fearing that would make the joke on him. He was fed up with the way people like Duncan Jones refused to take him seriously, resented the fact that each time he took a picture they were out so many words.

You'd think, thought Mark, the way he knew they talked about him, that he never gave a thought to human consequences, when in fact, as Cartier-Bresson put it, "In order to 'give a meaning' to the world, one has to feel oneself involved in what he frames through the viewfinder." It was one of the eight or ten quotations Mark had memorized when he was twelve and looking for ways to seem older. And here was another, also Cartier-Bresson: "To take photographs is to hold one's breath when all the faculties converge in the face of fleeing reality. It is at that moment that mastering an image becomes a great physical and intellectual joy." As if reminding himself what was in it for him, Mark repeated the last words again. Remember? A great joy. The hell with Duncan.

But it was late morning on a perfect early summer day, and

they were colleagues after all and had in common this nice weather. They were saying what a sunny day it was as they drove past the victory gardens tended mostly by old people from the old countries—two Chinese stooped over their watering cans—and Mark reminded both himself and Duncan of the human-interest-feature value in a story on the various ethnic groups and what they grew in side-by-side plots. Duncan said in that case he should wait for later in the summer, on the theory that grown plants look less alike than do their seedlings. He said, though, to be collegial, it was quite a nice idea, by which time they'd crossed Commonwealth to Marlborough Street, where, behind spiked iron fencing, the French Library was housed in what had once seen better days as someone's mansion.

Just beyond it was a space a car was leaving, which Duncan was tempted to see as a sign that his luck could change. Straight ahead was Storrow Drive and on its other side the fresh green Esplanade that banked the blue Charles River decorated with white triangles of canvas sail. Life was unfurling all around him even here in the big city, even now, and Duncan believed *even he* might possibly be carried by this natural momentum. He slipped into place. There was still time left on the meter.

Inside the French Library, Duncan surprised himself by feeling right at home—he lived in Cambridge near enough to Harvard so that nearly everybody spoke some other language—and he was glad to see they had set up a refreshment table. Neither Cousteau nor the mayor had arrived, so Duncan wandered over to see what there was. No, he was not a sherry drinker, no, no thank you, *non merci*. He'd studied French so long ago he thought this might be all he knew and didn't want it tested out. He then went to pretend to read the titles on the spines of books, and look around.

The only person seated so far was three quarters of the way back on the aisle reading the current *Match*, whose cover showed a radiant Diana in her last public appearance before giving birth to one of the next kings of England. Maybe it was because Duncan was suggestible (under the threat of having to make something of Cousteau, or else), but he thought that this woman had a cover-girl look of her own; that is, she looked quite like the Princess. Duncan stared at her until he caused her to look up at him from under those "Shy Di" bangs swept to one side of her pretty face, and they exchanged a smile with no specific content as she turned a glossy page and resumed keeping up with French press worship of royalty. Then he noticed that she wasn't only flipping pages and looking at photographs, as he would do, not knowing French, but taking long enough to read the paragraphs that passed as text. Or was she French? At Club Med he could tell the difference by the size of their bathing suits. He went back to checking titles.

When there was a stir in the foyer he went to see if Cousteau had arrived, and he was startled to see that behind the *Match* there was a baby sleeping in those arms that turned those shiny pages. Duncan could see that the story she was reading was an air crash, and that the photographer could have been helping save the victims if he hadn't had his camera ready to take pictures. Duncan said, "Grotesque," which he knew was bilingual. And she answered, "Yes."

Since the proceedings weren't requiring Duncan's full attention, he found himself wondering how young babies were when they could hide behind a magazine. Pretending to be researching this, he observed the mother hold the baby up and pat its back—with a left hand that didn't wear a wedding ring, he didn't fail to notice (not that Jessica had worn hers either these last years)—and lay the baby back down in her lap. Not many months, was Duncan's guess.

At last the prepared paragraphs had been exchanged, and Captain Cousteau had in his hands an award from a city with a harbor into which more than a little tea was illegally dumped. Just the night before, which he would mention in the article, he'd seen at the Aquarium alongside tanks of coral reefs and mountain streams a tank that showed the Boston harbor neither turquoise blue nor silver but a sort of fecal brown. The gene pool of the fish in that tank looked polluted, and Duncan knew it

would be a while before he purchased Boston scrod for dinner.
Now the audience applauded. Duncan put his pad back in his
jacket pocket and looked around for Mark Otis, who was working overtime. The mayor and Cousteau were working their way
up the aisle, and as if for the camera they shook hands, obscur-
ing from where Duncan sat the mother of the *Match*-sized baby.
He decided he would try to think of something clever to say.

"He or she is cute," he said so clumsily she'd never know he
had a light touch.

"Thank you." The reply was wrapped in a nice smile. "She,"
was the answer to the question.

"And she's good," said Duncan, "never made a peep." In fact
that was all she had made, one peep at one point.

"It was lunchtime." Now the baby was asleep. The mother
was collecting things with her free hand and stuffing them into a
bag.

"Do you need help?" asked Duncan.

"Would you put this *Match* away for me?" She pointed to the
magazine rack.

"Are you sisters?" Duncan meant of course the Princess.

"I'm her mother," came the response with a bright laugh.

He laughed too and said unnecessarily, "Your hair, I meant."

"I've worn my hair like this since college, since before Diana's
birth." She put the baby in the stroller, then she stood. "A few
people have told me that, though."

Duncan was preoccupied with the mathematics: if the Princess was nineteen—or was she twenty by now?—that made this
woman his own age more or less. You see? It cheered him to
affirm not only was his life not over, it could well be just beginning. He wished he could have a baby to confirm it.

"Anyway, thanks." For the compliment, she meant.

"Oh sure. It goes just over there?" He went to put the magazine back over by where Mark was packing up his camera.

"Got it," Mark said, "are you ready?"

"Almost," Duncan answered, as if what he meant was one
more question for Cousteau.

"I'll wait outside for you, so hurry," said Mark with a glance at his watch.

Duncan watched Mark walk to the front door and not offer to hold it for the woman with the baby. She was getting set to take off, clearly, but the door was heavy. There were two doors, actually. Duncan stepped quickly to be helpful, and got to the second door at the head of a flight of stairs in time to hold it while she backed out. As she was bending over to pick up the stroller, the breeze seemed to come up behind her, blowing open what had been a wraparound that wrapped around. From where he stood in front of her the skirt made something of a fan, as if she were rehearsing a flamenco dance.

She set the stroller back down and reached out behind her, and her cheeks turned the pink either of frustration or of a blush. "I paid two fifty for this damn skirt at a secondhand shop," she said, "and either it doesn't work or I don't understand how it works." She would never wear this sort of thing, on principle, if she were back yet in her own clothes.

Duncan held the stroller for her. He himself had often wondered why a certain kind of woman chose to wear a wraparound skirt when she could wear one she didn't have to clutch at every intersection. He laughed. What she needed was another hand, so he would say, and she would smile, "Can I give you a hand?"

She smiled.

He watched her go off toward the Public Garden one block away to be one more mother with a stroller on a balmy day and wanted to suggest to Mark that they go after candids of the Swan Boats pedaling around the pond, or watercolorists at easels, or the flowers in their carefully articulated groupings. Mark would have said, naturally, that he did not take postcard shots, and anyway, he had to print up what he had, which was, he also didn't say, a great shot of the object of this obvious interest Duncan had in older mothers of small babies. Duncan would have liked to know there was a way for him to see her again, even only in a photograph, but since there was no active conversation between him and Mark, it didn't come up. All he said was,

"Cousteau's on his way back to the Amazon. Imagine that." It made the *Globe* seem more conveniently located than it was.

Now, Duncan knew, he'd have to try to make something of his short interview with Cousteau, plus the brief appearance he had made at the Aquarium, then this quick award ceremony. Duncan wished now he'd asked one hard question—maybe something about Cousteau's son's death on one of their expeditions—so there would be something, at least, for a headline. What would happen, Duncan wondered, if all he wrote was a *haiku?*

He was much more interested in why it was that he was so attracted to the mother of a baby of another man. He was as much a sucker for the mother duck with babies ribboning behind as anyone was, but he wasn't one of those to ooh and aah on cue to strangers or to be there with a ready helping hand. It didn't have to do, he saw now, with her baby, except as the baby was the means of demonstrating what it was he liked about her. She had shown him she possessed a sense of humor about herself, which was gone in Jessica, at least as far as he could see, and which he'd also managed to lose. Or if it was not precisely her sense of humor, maybe it was her good humor. All he meant, he guessed, was that if she was in a state of stress he hadn't seen it. Duncan's own anxiety seemed so acute and by now of such long duration it had become second nature.

# Two

HER LANDLORD had brought Nina's *Globe* in on his way out, but she wasn't ready yet to skim the paper on her way to the Help Wanteds. Emilie had just gone down for her first nap of the day, and Nina decided she would shower and dress in something a little less suburban than the wraparound she'd worn the day before. An arty, lean-and-hungry look would be more what the galleries on Newbury Street would be after, rather than the nursing-mother look she still had three months after Emilie's birth. It was time to find something to provide income, now that seven months had passed since Nina's move to Boston brought her from her full-time job, but empty life, in Paris to a full-time life as her child's single parent in the city from which Nina graduated when she finished up at Wellesley (class of '63) and hadn't since thought of revisiting. She found a skirt with an elastic waist and a shirt that went with it well enough, and this gave Nina something to look forward to: accomplishing a short-term goal.

She'd spent two months short of a year now taking it just one

day at a time, the way they recommend you do after either a
death or birth. And now that she seemed to be capable some
days of taking in the news first that Jules-Jacques had died and
that his daughter had been born across the ocean in a foreign
port, Nina was ready to assume she should be ready to get up
when morning came, and not need to be near an entire box of
Kleenex in case "it all" without warning was too much. She had
some money left from having sold her furniture in Paris and
from savings put aside once Jules-Jacques began paying bills so
she could live in an apartment more conveniently located for
him than her Sorbonne neighborhood was. In the past few
years, his last few, he'd arranged to be in Paris away from his
family business, as well as his family, in Rouen, three days a
week to be with Nina in the semiofficial life they'd been carrying
on ever since she'd written to suggest they get together for a
Sunday in the country.

She had meant it too, a Sunday in the country for old time's
sake, and her impulse, not being romantic, had been cynical if
anything, since she had hoped to be invited out to meet his wife
and children if he had them to confirm that their life wasn't one
she would have wanted even if she'd had the choice to make.
She'd pictured Jules-Jacques and his family living fairly close to
his parents near Rouen, and that he'd joined the family business, which would make her grateful for her life as a free agent
in one of the world's best cities. She had wanted to be glad she'd
left after her junior year abroad to go and finish up at Wellesley
—even though Jules-Jacques tried to persuade her to remain
with him—and for all that had happened since, no matter that at
times it didn't seem to add up to that much or to represent what
most of the world called progress. She had written a nice, cheerful note to say she lived in Paris now, again—fourteen years
later—and not mentioned that she had a curiosity about her
future and her past and what they meant to one another. And
he'd answered: three weeks later Nina came around a corner
one windy spring afternoon to find him sitting in a patch of

sunlight on the sidewalk of the café that was just steps from her door, reading *Le Monde.*

The first note he had ever written to her he put on her pillow as he left her dormitory room (where he was not allowed to sleep, but had) for Rouen, where he was required to show up for a family thing. *"Puisse Paris te séduire sinon moi,"* his note said— Nina never would forget—and it was signed, "French kisses." May Paris seduce you if not me, it said, and Paris did seduce her, as did Jules-Jacques finally, to whom Nina gave as soon as she could all the virgin territory she possessed. Her own notes to Jules-Jacques were neither coy nor witty, being mostly plagiarized from various French poets of the nineteenth century —*"O temps, suspends ton vol!"* and so forth—and it was mostly embarrassing to recall what a flair she had for melodrama. Yet it was with Nina's words—or the poet Lamartine's actually—that his answer came. When Nina came around the corner and saw him in her café, Jules-Jacques stood up and made it clear it wasn't by coincidence alone he was there when he said, *"O temps, suspends ton vol!"* and kissed her on both cheeks and put the dry cleaning she carried on a chair and pulled another out for her and sat her down and held her hand and said, *"Bonjour."* And time did stop.

Because he'd been outdoors so much, she guessed—he'd liked to hunt and fish—his face reflected how the years had traced themselves in deep lines that acted as the parentheses around his features. And his teeth were stained by time and by tobacco and were more uneven than she had remembered. But those eyes were bright and brimming, and there was a clarity that made her utterly unwary. She leaned to him and kissed him on both cheeks too, and said, *"Bonjour, chou."*

That day they talked seven hours, moving inside the café as it grew chilly, drinking little, eating nothing, totally oblivious, engrossed in recapitulation. He suggested finally that they walk to stretch their legs a bit, then find a little restaurant so they could talk. The restaurant they settled on specialized in creole cooking and seemed to enjoy a midnight renaissance, no matter that the bread was dry from having been cut closer to the dinner hour and that all they could offer for dessert was mango ice cream. Jules-Jacques told her when her letter came he'd recognized the handwriting and taken it into the woods in order to escape his world, and reemerged in the good spirits he explained at dinner with a long description of the wonders he had seen at the small pond he sometimes fished.

Because she asked what wonders, he described for Nina, as he had that evening for his wife and four sons, how it is a dragonfly pair copulates, the male clasping the female from above while she curves her abdomen forward and inserts herself into the male's copulatory organ and collects his sperm. The two are locked together, flying, all four sets of wings in sync, for several minutes, then the female straightens out and the joined pair dips down and the tip of her body penetrates the water surface as the female deposits the fertilized eggs. Then they separate.

The part that Nina found the most amazing was that they could fly together, interlocked and synchronizing all eight wings, especially when Jules-Jacques told her those wings vibrate sixteen hundred beats per minute and achieve a flying speed of more than twelve kilometers an hour. Nina asked what else, what other wonders had he seen? Jules-Jacques did not pass up the chance to answer, *"Toi."*

So it was time to find their way to her apartment, she having established that he'd said he would be gone from Rouen two nights for three days of business. Jules-Jacques carried her dry cleaning home and hung it in her closet with his pants and jacket, finishing undressing quickly, sliding into Nina's bed before she came out of the bathroom. Nina hadn't thought it fair of him to smoke a cigarette and study her, and she wished now she'd said so then and pulled the sheet back to reveal what alterations time had made on him, instead of what she did, which was to take her clothes off slowly and grow quite self-conscious and annoyed at what seemed his proprietary air. Which probably explained, though, why she went on to express herself in acrobatics.

Once he had been charmed by Nina's *pudeur* (which he translated, when Nina didn't know the word, as her *délicatesse*), but this time Nina was if anything *im*modest. She moved from position to position, demonstrating what she'd learned with other men, and when they finished, it was with his clasping her from behind and above and flying interlocked and synchronized. They'd always made love face to face as students, as if to distinguish themselves by their learning from the lesser species, but it was as if now they had forfeited this bit of human adaptation for the opportunity to get it on like dragonflies and see all they'd been missing.

Nina turned the shower off, but water still ran down her face as she remembered their reunion afternoon and the two nights and the two days that followed from it, not to mention the five years. She missed him now and guessed she'd missed him all those years between what turned out to be their two love affairs. She was so grateful, even though he hadn't meant it literally, that she had taken it that way when Jules-Jacques said one morning that he wished they'd make a child together. What he'd meant, as Nina knew because she felt the same way, was he hoped they'd be together always. Six weeks later he was dead in his car driving back to Rouen for a Sunday in the country with his family.

She got dressed and went down for the paper, found a pen to circle any jobs that looked good, and worked her way through the Boston *Globe*, her one link to the outside world beyond her friend and downstairs neighbor, Rosie Lopez, who was on the city payroll as a social worker and had a home practice rehabilitating Nina. The first section of the paper was no problem. On the first page of the Metro section, though, her eyes deceived her.

Black and white, and read all over, as the riddle went when Nina was a child, were Jacques-Yves Cousteau and the mayor shaking hands and framing Nina, who was seated on the aisle and holding—nursing—Emilie. The photograph made Nina look like the Madonna with a couple of the three kings. Yes, you could call her expression enigmatic. Nina read the caption and found it did not make her feel better that at least she wasn't mentioned by name in it (not that anyone had asked her what her name was). Was it *legal* not to have asked her permission? How could the *Globe* run her picture and not wonder if she minded? Granted, she was not the subject of the photo—Cousteau held his plaque for everyone to see—but in a way she understood she *was* the center of the image. It was not for nothing that her job for fifteen years had been to do with paintings, scouting them for galleries or corporate art collections as well as for what's called private individuals: she knew what subject matter was; she knew exactly what this person named Mark Otis had in mind, for instance that he thought it cute the way Cousteau's plaque made a halo over her head. She knew just what she would say to this Mark Otis, telling him a thing or two.

The thing was, *what if,* since it was Cousteau, it got picked up? It was, thought Nina, gimmicky enough to be run other places. Nina knew her parents, who were holier than thou as missionaries, now in Senegal, and whom she hadn't yet informed about the baby, wouldn't read, say, *Match*—the sex, the violence—but did get the *International Herald Tribune* down from Paris. If you knew to notice this, you'd know, the way her T-shirt was untucked on one side, she and Emilie were joined and that she wasn't therefore simply holding her for someone else. And what about—God, *what about*—Yvette, Jules-Jacques's official widow? Nina wasn't capable of having as her first reaction *how would she feel?* Rather it was *what would she think of me?* What would her four boys think of me, of their father?

Nina called the *Globe* and asked for Otis but was told he wasn't in, or at least wasn't at his desk. When asked if she would like to leave a message, Nina said she wouldn't, having that moment decided she would go there with her baby and force him and anyone else within earshot to look at the consequences. Good, and in case Otis was off "on assignment" she'd demand to see the name that wrote the story, Duncan Jones. She felt so ripped off, the fact that his name was Jones meant that he'd stolen that from her too.

Emilie still napped in the calico-lined basket Nina had bought because it reminded her of market baskets used all over France for shopping meal by meal. She tucked a blanket in around her, phoned a cab, not living in the sort of neighborhood they cruised in, and went down to wait a moment on the front steps in the sun. She would just wait there at the *Globe* until—what *was* her goal in this, apologies? or promises?—until she got some satisfaction.

Because Mark was in the darkroom, Duncan's phone rang, interrupting only what each morning was his first assignment of the day, which was to read the competition. When asked to come down to Information to see someone who insisted on not saying what she had to talk to him about, he answered sure, he'd be right down. The nice thing about mornings at a newspaper was that there was time, as opposed to afternoons, to be glad for the unexpected.

Duncan was so glad, in fact, when he saw Nina by the desk, it didn't register with him that she'd have had no way to find him at the *Globe,* and consequently that she couldn't be there simply because he'd been charming to her. He said charmingly, "Hi, nice to see you again."

She replied, delighted, "Yes, you *can* give me a hand, in fact." Nina didn't try to explain to herself the coincidence of his arrival at her side. She was protected against thinking his name could be Duncan Jones by how nice he had been to her the day before. "I need help getting to Mark Otis. Do you know him?"

"I know Mark, yes." Duncan's disappointment showed.

She didn't see it. "Will you take me in to him?" She indicated the man at the information desk and said, "He claims Mark Otis can't be reached."

"It's up, not in," corrected Duncan, feeling petty.

Nina asked, "But will you?" When he answered with a nod, she went to get the basket Emilie was sleeping in, which Nina had set on a table out of the way. She had read the statement chiseled in the marble on the wall behind the information desk, about how the *Globe*'s founder had hoped his newspaper would bring into everyone's home a ray of sunshine—she had a ray of hope now—and she said to Duncan, "Thanks. I'm Nina Jones, and this is Emilie."

He led her to the escalator and waited for her to step on first, then he got on and said, "You're welcome." In a city in which every third name begins with an *O* apostrophe it didn't happen all that often that he met another Jones. He felt protective. He also felt he should have something more clever to say to her than, "Any relation?"

"If you mean to Davy Jones, no, I don't think so."

"No, I meant to Duncan Jones. To me." He smiled and let it go at that.

The escalator was a full two-story one, which made it endless and made Nina feel she could be underwater trying to swim up for air. *"You're* Duncan Jones?" she asked.

"Who did you think I was? You asked for Duncan Jones, I came." He hadn't thought it through, though, either.

"I don't know. I thought you were just *there,* I guess, the way you were there yesterday. I don't know *what* I thought." She took a breath and said, "You're a *reporter?"* Finally they were at the top. She contemplated getting on the other side and going down, but guessed he'd follow.

"Yes, I am. I work for Living, though, not Metro." As if that would matter to her.

"You approved that picture, I guess." What exactly *was* she feeling? It seemed something like betrayal, as if they'd had an agreement, not the mere invasion of her privacy she'd thought it was.

"I hate that picture," Duncan said, since it was true. He wasn't ready yet to turn her over to Mark Otis. She was following him to the cafeteria. "But everybody loves him. Loves his work, I mean to say."

They stood now at the head of the stairs in a room that tried its hardest to be like an ocean liner, with the effect that when Nina looked at Boston some slight distance away, she felt farther from it than she knew she was and than was comfortable. She felt adrift. "Am I at sea?" she asked out loud. All over were those colored square flags that meant something to those few who might be sailors. She felt queasy.

Duncan indicated a free table and that he would get her what she wanted from the line. "Does the baby want anything, or is that a stupid question?"

"She'll have a glass of milk." Nina laughed at the picture of Emilie tossing down a glass of milk.

"And you?" he asked.

"I'll drink it for her, that is." Couldn't he at least see she's asleep?

"Of course," said Duncan, now embarrassed. All he could think to do was shrug. "I'll be right back."

Nina sat with her back to the view of Boston trying to think what her rights were. When he showed up with two cups of coffee and the glass of milk, she thought the unsolicited caffeine might help, so she said, "Thank you. Tell me," she began, coming right to the point now, "shouldn't I have had to sign a release for you to have used my picture?"

"Cream? Or sugar?"

Nina nodded no.

He helped himself to both. "Not technically, no," Duncan answered. "Technically, you and the baby were bystanders at what was a news event." He couldn't look at her, though.

"Maybe, but I think that's stretching the point, since the picture features me. That is, I can guess he was going for an Escher effect. You know, where if you look at the dark, you're seeing fish, while in between, the light, are birds, and you can see whichever you want."

"I know who you mean, sure." Maybe.

"Well?"

"Yes, I see what you mean."

"So *technically's* irrelevant." She was correct, and knew it.

"Not if he doesn't admit it. All he has to say is you were in the way. It wasn't his assignment to get anything but Cousteau and the mayor, and he got them." He was right too, which made their talk like an Escher.

"Does it matter how I feel?" What if she wept?

"I wouldn't say to him it does."

"Would you admit it if it did to you, or were you setting me up?" At least would he say he's sorry?

"No, I wasn't, not at all. We never work together, since it doesn't do me any good to tell him what I'd like him to take." Duncan stopped. What was the other thing she'd asked? Oh yes. "And yes, I'm sorry that this happened to you. Frankly, though, because it doesn't compromise you—does it?—I'm afraid you won't get much more than this out of it." By "this" he meant that he was sorry, not the coffee and the milk, neither of which she'd drunk so far.

"It compromises me, I think, to be shown breast-feeding my baby. What business is that of his, or anyone's?" Surely this was as clear to him.

"I didn't know you were, I didn't notice that. I don't think they would show that, no." The *Village Voice*, but not the *Globe*.

"They *do*," Nina insisted, "that's what I was *doing!* Why do you think she was quiet?"

Duncan didn't know, and said so. All he'd really looked at yesterday and in the photograph was how he liked the way she looked. Today he liked her even more, now that he knew her eyes were silver.

"You even said something about how good she was! What did you think Emilie had, laryngitis?" Nina had to laugh, and did.

And so did he. "I understand, believe me, even though I truly didn't see that in the picture. Is that any consolation?"

"No. See, you don't understand." How would he know the threat it was unless she told him? "I have relatives in Manchester, New Hampshire"—who would read the *Union Leader*, not the *Globe*, she didn't say—"who could send this on to my

parents"—with whom they were not in touch, she left out—
"who live in Dakar now. Or what if it were reprinted in the
*International Herald Tribune* and they or someone saw it there? I'm
from all over. Anyone could send it to them."

She was right about his not understanding the problem. "So
your dad is in the military?"

Nina laughed.

"You said that you were from all over," he explained.

"He was a conscientious objector in World War Two."

Duncan's own father was a navy doctor in the war, and Duncan's parents' wedding portrait there on the piano in their living
room in Buffalo showed the groom in dress uniform about to
ship out to the South Pacific, where he spent the first year of
their marriage. Duncan was impressed. "Well, good for him,"
he said. During the war in Vietnam, he himself had gotten away
with a student deferment but would always wish he'd had the
nerve to live according to the higher law of conscience. He had
not dared risk applying for a C.O. status, since he didn't have
religious grounds, not organized ones anyway.

"He's a missionary—so's my mother—but we've never had
that much in common." Nina's smile was cynical. Boy, wasn't
that an understatement?

"Well, they always say a child's birth brings the family back
together, so there's hope." Speaking of sermons.

"Oh no," Nina quickly said, "who told you that? My parents
still think I'm in Paris scouting paintings for a New York corpo-
ration (which they think, parenthetically, is a violation of their
values and, they hoped, of mine), but at least it was honest.
They'd say I'm dishonest now." She said it as a fact. It was one.

"Why?"

"Because I haven't told them Emilie was born."

It wasn't as if Duncan was a great confider, since, for instance,
he had not decided yet if he would tell his parents in two
months, or wait, that he and Jessica had filed at last and turned
their great disputes to petty ones about who would get what.

But how could hers not know? "I see," he said, amazed. The baby's grandparents not *know* about her?

"Not even her father knows," Nina confided. Tears had come into her eyes and spilled now.

This made Duncan shiver. What if somewhere there could be a child of his of whose birth he was ignorant. He would agree it was dishonest, sure it was.

"It's a long story, naturally."

"It would be, yes," he said. He didn't want to hear it.

She was silent.

"Uh," he started.

"Yes, you have to go, I'm sure, get back to work and all that, and I'm sorry. Now I do feel stupid. It's pretty clear that this picture is the least of all my problems. And you have your own life."

Should he say but no, he really didn't? Not a wife and almost not a job—how did the song go?—just sun in the morning, moon at night. "Not at the moment," Duncan said.

"I meant I don't have to dump all mine in your lap."

"I meant what I said: I don't have one."

"What, a lap?" He'd made her laugh, and she was grateful.

But Mark interrupted, pulling up a chair from the next table and sitting between them. "Look who's here," he said. "Jones, you didn't say you two knew each other!" He waited to give her a chance to thank him for his picture of her and to ask for a print he'd gladly make her. He did not expect or want an explanation, not from Duncan.

"Thanks to you," said Duncan, "or I should say *no* thanks to you." Since she obviously didn't recognize him from the day before, he said, "Mark Otis. Nina Jones."

She had concluded it was not so serious after all that she'd shown up in the Boston *Globe,* but this did not mean she wanted to have Mark Otis by her side.

"You two related?" Mark was joking, having heard he thought that Duncan was divorced, or getting there. He would have had to mention something in the car if this had been his wife and child. Or Bic, or Dick Shapiro, or somebody would have pulled the picture off the front page of the section. Mark looked at Nina, serious now, "You're not, are you?"

Nina looked the other way, into the basket in which Emilie was stirring. Even though it wasn't strictly necessary, Nina picked the baby up and held her while she finished waking.

"No," said Duncan.

"Good, because there's always more than meets the eye, but that would be a little more than usual." Mark sensed he'd better not pursue it and was confirmed by the look that Duncan gave him. Getting up—this was a coffee break, that's all, while prints were drying—he tried one more time to make more favorable the impression he was leaving. "He's one of the cutest babies I've ever seen. Sorry his face wasn't in the picture more." Soliciting a bleary little smile from Emilie when he grinned suddenly at her, Mark was, however, unsuccessful at receiving an acknowledgment from Nina Jones, which led him to decide that whether she and Duncan were related or not, as far as unfriendliness toward him went, they were twins.

She waited until Mark was gone, then drank the milk like medicine and said, "I'm glad I ran into you. Thanks for being sympathetic."

He got up too but was grasping for a way to keep her there, or else to follow her out the door. Duncan recognized it as his impulse from the day before and once again was puzzled by it. What was this attraction of his? Was it that he'd been to Club Med and was now incapable of a response that wasn't somehow sexual? He offered her a tour of the place on her way out and hoped he'd come up with something less polite. She could say no at any point.

She said she'd like to see the *Globe*, especially the Classifieds. She was a faithful reader of them, she told Duncan with a smile that was both realistic and apologetic.

He would take her, even though they would be silent at this hour, by the sort of gallery onto the presses. She had said

herself, upstairs, she felt at sea, and he'd always thought, looking down into the green machinery, it was the engine of a great
ship. They could steam away together.

All she said was, "Is it noisy when they're working?"

"Everything's less noisy now; we use computers. Come on
and I'll show you Living." Duncan was prepared to answer,
when she asked if it was difficult to work in a big space with
people all around him, no, he'd never minded study hall, it
helped him to see other people going at it. He was ready to keep
talking for an hour and then to ask, in spite of the fact that her
life was obviously complicated with a baby but no husband
(unless she was married and the baby was somebody else's,
which was really too complex), if he could call her, maybe to go
swimming if she'd ever want to. He would like to reassure her he
had been abandoned too.

The fact that no one even seemed to recognize her from the
picture as they walked around the *Globe*—and who *would* read
the paper if these people didn't?—was consoling. By the time
they reached his desk, she had relaxed about the whole thing,
even feeling glad for the occasion it now represented for their
having had a gentle conversation. It had been just women so far
Nina had been comfortable with here in Boston. She was
tempted to ask Duncan if he'd mind it if she visited again once
things got settled in her life, once she had figured out the code
for Classifieds and broken into the real world and didn't spend
so many mornings reading *Match* in order to keep up her French
and feel connected. No one knew how hard it was to get through
her days, then those long nights when she needed consolation
just as much as Emilie did.

"Here's my desk," said Duncan, pointing off in the direction
then of Books and Sports and Entertainment. Maybe he could
ask her to go to a movie. Even if she couldn't get a baby-sitter it
would work, since he had often seen small babies in those hold-
ers tied to parents as a hammock is to a tree. "Here's how it
works," he said, logging on to his computer.

"What's that mean?" asked Nina.

"That I have a message. It's like being a guest in a hotel, but instead of calling the desk, here's how I ask what it is." He pressed a key and sure enough, the message came up. "It says that I had a phone call from a woman who'd tried first to reach Mark Otis."

She thought he was kidding, so she leaned in closer to see what it really said.

"The woman recognized somebody in some picture—she said it was in today's—and wanted to know how to reach her. I'm supposed to call back." Duncan looked at Nina and was shocked to see how close their faces were to one another. If they'd been more than the mere acquaintances they were, it would have been appropriate to kiss her.

"Wait a minute." It didn't seem like a joke, and yet what could it be if not one? Could it be that someone recognized her in that photograph, as she had feared? But weren't those fears unwarranted? The panic rose in her the way heat reads on a thermometer, and she thought, if she didn't get outside into some air to breathe, she would pass out right there in Living and bring Emilie down with her.

Duncan meanwhile wrote the unfamiliar name Amanda Morris, and her number, on a piece of paper he gave Nina. He could tell from her reaction it was quite important but regretted nonetheless the interruption. He would have asked Nina her own number and if he could call her twice a day until he reached her, if she hadn't run away.

That's what she did: she ran away. She grabbed the basket and dashed off and out of sight before Duncan or anyone else could say something reassuring, such as that Amanda Morris was a stranger. Her behavior demonstrated to the world what Nina knew, that she was only, only barely, hanging on, that it was taking all she had to nurse her baby and not drown her at the same time with her own tears. Whereas she had made it now ten months—a year, almost, of grieving—Nina's new life in the new

world was as fragile as if it were glass or china. She could shatter
and she knew it, and surprises were exactly what could do it.
Although Nina wasn't happy being lost, neither was it her wish
to be found.

# Three

HAVING GROWN UP in the Third World, to which Nina's missionary parents believed they were bringing the Good News in the form of their social welfare work, she'd never thought the telephone—the right, the duty to have one—was sacred. When she moved to Boston she'd assumed, as was true everywhere else, there would be a waiting list of several months and had applied to be put on it, and was shocked when she was told she'd have her service the next day between the hours of eight and five. It was as if the Constitution had provided her this linkup she had grown up thinking was a luxury, the times it worked. It had occurred to her, with winter and the birth approaching, that it wasn't an extravagance to call a taxi when she found herself in labor, or even for later when phone calls would make it easier to break into the labor market, but still she had not assumed she was *entitled*. Nevertheless, when the new directory arrived at her door after only several months, there she was in it, listed as "Jones N," of which she was the sixth.

Now Nina sat cross-legged on her living room floor with the

phone book open to the Morrises. She had the number Duncan Jones had given her that morning, but she wanted to see if there was a clue perhaps in the address. There wasn't an Amanda or a plain *A*, but there was a number that matched up, for "Morris Jeremy MD," whoever that was. There was nothing in the street name. Weston, she learned from the map on the back cover of the phone book, was a suburb next to Wellesley, but that information didn't ring the only bell it could have. Nina contemplated calling Duncan to see if he'd volunteer again to return the call that had been his in the first place, but she couldn't seem to do it. If she felt like calling Duncan, and she did, it wasn't to ask him to call another woman.

Emilie was occupied with the balloon Nina had tied onto her wrist, a helium-filled silver foil one in a heart shape Nina had bought days before and not expected to have lasted, and Emilie lay there cooing with delight as the balloon bobbed all about her. Nina, watching Emilie, decided by some special logic that Amanda Morris must have been the one from childbirth class who had been friendly and with whom she'd have been happy to exchange phone numbers and the promise to have lunch together with their babies.

But it was a child who answered. "This is Jason Morris speaking," he said in the voice of a seven-year-old politician, "may I help you?"

Nina said, "Wrong number, sorry." The childbirth class was for parents who were having their first babies, not for those with so much practice they'd already raised a fleet of older sibling baby-sitters. Anyway, it was a wild guess that Amanda Morris could be someone with whom Nina had struck up a temporary friendship. That guess was to prove there was a spring of hope in her, that's all.

More likely was that it was trouble in some form or other, either because she had failed to tell her parents of the new arrival—not so new now at three months—or because she'd allowed herself to love Jules-Jacques to that extent. It could have been enough to suffer the enormous loss of him—it *should* have been—but Nina knew even without subscribing to it in her own life, consciously, that "it" was always there to "get you," which was bogeyman theology of the sort spread abroad by her own parents and which meant that she, like Eve, would pay for her sins for the rest of everyone's life. Nina had been guilty of refusing to obey the laws of full disclosure ever since she sent the letter to Jules-Jacques and didn't say, because she claimed she didn't know, that she still loved him after all their years apart. From then on, it was true, and was remarkable after a life in which she had been faulted for truth telling, she had settled for a situation that was both a lie and quite the happiest she'd ever known. Her parents never knew that either.

And it wouldn't matter what Nina's parents knew or didn't if they weren't about to have a month of home leave and arrive on Nina's doorstep praising her for living in an integrated neighborhood but stopping there with their kind words about her current circumstances. Having chosen, on the advice of the golden sister, Dulcie, who herself had never known parental disapproval, simply to be at the airport with the baby and let them be charmed by nature taking its course in their lives, she didn't want to be preempted. It was easy to imagine a mere stranger's happening to see the *Globe* and calling up to say she'd sent that charming photo to her parents, whom she'd met once years ago in India and kept in touch with. Nina had been counting on two months' more time—her parents weren't due until July—for full-time recovery from the past year of her life. It was ten months exactly to the day since she and Jules-Jacques parted for what was to have been thirty-six hours.

Nina lay back on the carpet next to Emilie and watched the silver foil heart bobbing up against the force of gravity. It came to her that Emilie was *her* balloon and all she had to counteract the gravity of life, and death, in the big city. Every now and then, and now was one of those times, Nina nearly believed God *was* acting in her life, as all along her parents were persuaded. What made Jules-Jacques say to her one morning that he wished to make a child with her, and what made her know that he meant it even if he didn't "mean it," if not God or some force by another name with an extraordinary power? She didn't think, if Jules-Jacques knew he would be killed, he would have gone along with it, and so she wasn't saying that he'd had an apprehension and decided he would leave her something by which to remember him—it wasn't all that literal, what she believed—and yet it was *as if* he'd known. Or as if *she* had. "God works in mysterious ways," she'd heard them say a million times, and it would be just like God, Nina's parents would explain ("I am the resurrection and the life," they would remind her), to be so on top of things. She should thank God, they'd say. She did.

But how Jules-Jacques would have loved to have had a daughter, how it would have helped console her to have known that even at the very moment of his death his seed was in her. There had been no solace that first night, or week, or month, or even well into the second month (which was the third of Nina's pregnancy), given that she'd attributed the foul-up in her menstrual cycle to acute distress. By waiting so long to discover she was pregnant, Nina felt more like a teenager who hasn't been informed of symptoms, therefore doesn't recognize extraordinary change even when it's upon her, than she did the mature woman that she was. It was just that one morning, after all, that she'd been moved to forgo birth control in favor of the fantasy that they would be together always. Even their last morning, when they had been rushed, she'd run into the bathroom for her diaphragm—and how her body, six weeks pregnant, must have been amused by this—to be her shield against the slings and arrows of outrageous fortune. Jesus Christ.

From Wellesley once she'd gone to Boston and had her cards read by a large woman in a gypsy costume, and been told essentially that she'd survive an unspecific trouble she took to refer to something so mundane she couldn't now remember what it was. But so? If she'd been told instead, "In twenty years you'll have a child by this man you have loved and lost, who will not live to see the child, and that will be five dollars, please," could Nina ever have believed it? Had she been told, "Furthermore, I see deception on your part," she would have felt entitled to her money back, since one thing she'd been to a fault—the adverb her parents used was "brutally"—was honest. She'd returned to Wellesley after junior year abroad having told Jules-Jacques what the truth was, which was that she didn't know what promises to make, if any, rather than what he'd wished to hear, which was that she'd be right back and not to worry. If the gypsy had told Nina of the nightmare it would be to lose Jules-Jacques, she never would have—what? have left him? or have gone back?—been persuaded. Nina was a Margaret Bigelow Smithwick Scholar plucked from the obscurity of all over the world to take advantage of an all-expenses-paid degree from Wellesley College, and who was Most Likely to Succeed if not her? How could this same Nina Jones be so on the periphery, such the outsider, that she could attend the funeral mass at the Rouen Cathedral (whose facade she was familiar with from Monet's series but in whose interior she'd never been) and be a stranger to the family and the many hundred friends who seemed to grieve the loss of Jules-Jacques? How could life be so complex, and she, the mistress, so much not the mistress of it?

Emilie, still caroling, amusing herself still with isometric exercises, seemed to have her needs met by the shiny silver heart balloon that bobbed as if an advertisement for resiliency. She knew already it was good to be resilient, as if she knew too, already, all the disadvantages with which she had been asked to cope. To Nina, who had cried them both to sleep throughout her pregnancy and who'd delivered Emilie at the end of a labor that was overdue, then overlong and unrelenting, Emilie's embracing ways, beginning with the breath she took in just out of her mother's body, unassisted, represented their survival. As the fortune-teller put it, Nina, and now Emilie and Nina, would survive an unspecific trouble. Maybe they already had.

This time, when asked if Jason Morris could be helpful, Nina asked to speak, please, to Amanda Morris, who turned out to be "the former" Mandy Nicoletti, to whose wedding Nina had gone in State College, Pennsylvania, at the end of sophomore year. And Nina did remember now an envelope that was return-addressed "Mrs. Amanda Morris." She couldn't think what she would have given as the wedding present that provided the occasion for the note, but she could clearly see again the scripty sort of handwriting, the one *i* dotted with a circle, and the new name that looked practiced late at night. Of course she knew Amanda Morris, more or less.

"How was Bermuda?" Nina asked. What a relief it was a friend.

"Fine, how was junior year abroad? Where was it, Florence?"

"Paris. It was great." She laughed. "And then what?"

"Medical school—that is, Jeremy—four kids—that was what I was doing—and somehow we're married still, still for the first time. We go back to Bermuda every five years," said Amanda with a laugh that indicated she knew that was advertising-copy talk, "so we've been five times."

"Twenty-five years?" Five times five was twenty-five, right? "How can that be?"

"Twenty-one. It was right after sophomore year that we got married."

"That's what I thought."

"Twenty-one next month."

"I thought so." Nina worked it out again. "But five times five is twenty-five, right?"

Quite accustomed to solving math problems brought home by her children, Amanda said, "Let's see, because I'm quite sure it was our fifth trip—the hotel gave us a bottle of champagne—so: honeymoon, then five, ten, fifteen, twenty. Five times five is twenty-one, is how it works out."

"Happy anniversary," said Nina with a laugh, "and you sound just the same as always." Did she mean by "always" sophomore year? They hadn't even really met until midway through second semester freshman year, in Classical History.

"Thanks, you too. Now tell me what you're doing in the Boston *Globe* besides nursing your baby. And congratulations."

"Thanks. It was that obvious? I thought it was."

"No, just if you know what to look for, not at first glance. Only if you recognize you, is what I mean. You look just the way you did too." Amanda paused to reflect that she herself did not, exactly. She had changed, her hair, for one thing, many times. "But tell me now about the baby."

"She's three months old, and her name is Emilie, and we just happened to be there and in the way, as far as I know." Saying this, Nina felt surer it was true. For all she knew, they had already picked the photo for the next day, making it official that she was yesterday's news. "I love it, having her."

Having another was the question that had brought Amanda into therapy, and she was glad that Dr. Wolff had been successful in persuading her that she had other questions too, and some more fundamental than whether or not she felt like having yet another child: Who am I? for example. It seemed strange now that Amanda had thought it would be enough if she learned from therapy, along with the decision about a baby, something about what a doctor who tends other people's wives is like. Her husband was an obstetrician.

Nina talked about how she was looking for a job by roaming galleries on Newbury Street, and Amanda said that she was there herself now twice a week. She didn't say for therapy and asked herself, as she had learned to, what that meant, then she suggested they might meet some afternoon, including this one. She proposed they meet for coffee or a drink just after three and made her life sound easy, even with one child home from school with a stomach bug, as Jason was. Nina already, with her trip out to the *Globe* and all the interaction that entailed, had done more with her day than typically she would accomplish in a week (not that at the *Globe* she'd accomplished anything), so she was feeling energized and offered as a meeting place the Café Florian, a steamy and exotic-smelling place that provided an assortment of sexy foreign newspapers and magazines for its bilingual customers. She'd gone there many Saturdays from Wellesley and on to the Exeter Street Cinema to see a film in French whose subtitles she wouldn't read. It wasn't one Amanda knew, but she said she was sure she'd find it. Nina spelled out F-l-o-r-i-a-n and pictured Amanda's handwriting and wanted to ask if she still dotted *i*'s with little circles, but she didn't.

Amanda stopped in the shop called Knitpickers on her way up Newbury to the Florian to ask what size the sweater in the window was. It had a pelican design of the bird flying low over the water, seeing what there was, then up to plunge in after what he'd seen, his wings sharpened to points that made him origamilike, then bobbed up to sieve the contents of his pouch for food. It was what she was doing too, two hours a week—the scan, the dive, the swallowing—in therapy. In fact if this one were her size and if the background blue were just the color of her eyes, then couldn't she call it symbolic; mightn't it be fated to be hers no matter what it cost? Today she'd really worked.

Today she had brought in a dream that even her psychiatrist had seemed to think was pretty good. She'd twisted her head back after she told it to see what he'd say, to see what his expression was, and he'd surprised her with a broad smile—upside down to her from her position on the couch—and a one-word evaluation, "Classic." It had nearly made worthwhile the terror she'd experienced in dreaming it. It was her size; it was the color of her eyes; the price was what two sessions cost. Amanda Morris said she'd take it.

Then she ran up Newbury and was aware of her thirst more than anything. She'd been five months so far without a major silence, which seemed good but dried her throat out, but she always was so thirsty after talking practically nonstop like that for fifty minutes. For the first time since her first time back in January she did not stop for a Tab to go, and anyway, she reasoned, rushing, on a day that felt so wonderful and warm, so pretty nearly summerlike, she ought to order lemonade to cele-brate, no matter that it wasn't the real thing—neither was Tab—or came in a pint carton and was more than she would want. She really didn't have the time, was what it was, not after having paid a fortune for the sweater. Therapy was good and bad in making her feel like she mattered: good because she did deserve rewards too—right?—but kind of bad because she didn't know yet how to go about acquiring them.

The dream was that Amanda went in for a routine checkup and was told she probably was pregnant. Since her doctor was a colleague of her husband's—who was, it seemed to Amanda, everybody's obstetrician but her own—she didn't want to shame him (or herself) by saying it just wasn't possible; they hadn't made love once this month. Oh sure they'd tried, but both times Jeremy was beeped and never even got undressed. Her doctor might have understood, and wouldn't have judged Jeremy in any case, but still Amanda thought it was pathetic, too embarrassing to share. Instead—as if this weren't a little weird—she told the doctor that it had to be the snake.

The snake? The one that had slid in the afternoon she sunbathed naked in her yard. The doctor's face was neutral, but the nurse betrayed—disgust? fear?—some emotion that allowed Amanda to be certain it was real. She told the doctor that he had to take it out. And he refused.

He said it hadn't gone full term, and anyway how could he know what kind it was? What if the snake were poisonous? Then that's all the more reason! she replied. He told her to go home.

But she stayed on his table in the stirrups until finally Jeremy was called in, by which time Amanda was in ruins. She could feel it laying eggs inside her. Get the speculum! her husband ordered, but nobody did.

The room was full of doctors then, and none would stick his hand in to retrieve the snake. Deliver me! she kept on screaming, sure now that the baby snakes had gone into her blood vessels and would like cancer enter every vital organ. Quick! And then the vet arrived. He wouldn't stick his hand in either, but he told her husband to make the incision so he could see what was what. Emergency cesarean! her husband ordered. Then she went to sleep, or rather, she was put there. And she woke.

And she was nervous about seeing Nina and had probably

allowed herself to buy the sweater as a stalling tactic. Was she otherwise that privileged? To have bought a sweater costing more than a week's paycheck for someone who slaved for forty hours at minimum wage? And just because she'd had a breakthrough dream. Big deal.

She didn't even know yet what she'd broken through to, having only recently become aware of attitudes she was attempting to break free of. It had been at Christmas, finally, when she'd felt again and overbearingly the *something's missing* she had known—it came, it went—for all those years, and had reacted in a way that was not just familiar but predictable—that she should have another child, that what was missing was a baby—but at last she'd come to see, with help, she was already pregnant with herself and had been waiting years to give birth. Anyway, her children were thirteen, eleven, nine, and seven, and she loved them, she *adored* them and was a terrific mother, if she did say so herself. Of course she'd had more practice at it than those others who had husbands who came home. And by extension, if she was a better mother, others would be better wives for having had more time to try. So.

Anyway, the point was that she'd had the children she would have, and that was fine. So was the husband. She had grown more tolerant of Jeremy, remembering his sacrifices cost him something too. How could she criticize him for what he took from her and their children to give to his patients when what she got twice a week most likely came from Dr. Wolff's wife and their children, if he had one and they had some? Give and take, was how it worked, and it helped to remember that. The last thing that Amanda needed was to become alienated from the man she'd been engaged to since her sophomore year in college. Never mind that when they met they had both wanted to be teachers so they'd have the summers off to spend together traveling around the world. Amanda guessed that whatever it might be that she'd broken through to, it could only mean more work. She hoped she wouldn't lay all this on Nina. What if

Nina's life had been so easy she'd never been forced to ask herself these questions?

Nina told the waiter she would wait until her friend arrived, but Emilie had gone ahead without them and was nursing with enthusiasm. Even though she knew the mother-and-child look was not what they were after at the Florian, a nursing mother was *bohème* enough to make it. Nina waved. She knew Amanda was adjusting to the dark and wouldn't see her in the corner without some bold sign or other, even more because Amanda wore dark glasses. Nina dared call out hello above the meditative flute provided by Jean-Pierre Rampal by way of pairs of discreet speakers. And Amanda chirped a bird sound and flew over.

In the time they knew each other, Nina and Amanda were parallel lines that wouldn't ever intersect except by optical illusion, and they still were. But that didn't seem to matter. Benefiting from the decades of intensifying interest in what life is like for women, Nina and Amanda knew their stories mattered. In the larger sense their lines had intersected for a year, and this shared history and early affection could be counted on to carry them. They talked to one another as if they were confidantes and had been ever since Classical History.

At one point in the first hour Amanda said, "Why I think I'm so comfortable with you is because you assume about your situation that it's workable. I do about mine too, not that I'd presume to compare them—I'm an amateur and you're a pro— but you would be surprised how many friends I have who seem to be just waiting for one or the other of them to have the affair that's the excuse for putting their marriage out of its misery. Like an old dog. But you know what? We're not old." Amanda had made this discovery on her own, as if it were original. "We're younger now than we were then. I came to Wellesley with a corset that had bones that dug into my *own* bones. I weighed just over a hundred pounds and had no *flesh*, yet I assumed I'd wear that thing whenever I got dressed up for the rest of my life. Only someone who feels old could think like that at eighteen. I was fifty before I was twenty."

Nina said, "That's good, you got it over early, being fifty." She herself had not possessed an undergarment of that sort only because of having spent her childhood close to the equator. The fact that her parents preached on inner beauty being the important thing had not kept Nina from applying to her body every foreign substance she could send away for from the ads in magazines, especially depilatories. Dulcie had avoided all this, by which Nina meant not just the special creams. Her blue-eyed sister had inherited all the recessive genes that made their parents what they were, and she'd lived as successfully as they had, always the outsider with the conscience. Nina had been the outsider too, of course, but governed by a lesser law, her parents thought, than conscience. Another difference was that Nina hadn't liked it on the outside, hadn't ever been so happy as during orientation freshman year when it was clear there was a life as different from what she had known as dawn from sunset.

"Penny is thirteen," explained Amanda, "and it takes a lot of energy just keeping her from going off one Saturday to dye her hair blue." She stroked Emilie's hand and gave her a finger she could clutch the way a monkey does a branch, and said to her, "You won't want turquoise hair, OK?" Amanda made the baby laugh and display gums uninterrupted yet by teeth. "You promise? No, not purple either, no no, not pink, no, not green." Emilie laughed and laughed. "You just stay bald like you are now, OK?" Emilie came into Amanda's arms without a backward look at Nina. "Don't go wearing zipper pulls as earrings either, or you'll give us all the creeps." Emilie seemed to like the word "creeps," also "zipper," so Amanda said them both a few more times, exaggerating, isolating sounds from meaning. She must have spent months of her life, almost literally *years,* in this pursuit. It was amazing, what was actually involved in having children. It amazed her also that, when only a few months before she'd thought she envied forty-year-old women who had newborn babies to absorb them, it was clear to her she didn't envy Nina.

Emilie decided it was time to go and let them know by way of a large mustard-colored squashy discharge that was not to be contained. Amanda was kind enough to remember it was only milk and would wash out of Irish linen just as well as if she had worn a skirt more like Nina's, which appeared to have been manufactured when batiks from Indonesia were mass-marketed as bedspreads. Nina hated to admit she'd already used the last of the spare diapers she'd brought along, it made her seem so maladjusted to new motherhood, but it was pretty clear that was the case when she wrapped Emilie in a thin flannel blanket and tried coaxing her to ride home in the stroller in her mess. Amanda was emphatic with her invitation that she take them in her car, and so she did.

There was a lot of parking. Elderly men from the rooming houses warmed themselves out on the stoops, and they inspected Amanda's new BMW as if one day they'd be prospective buyers and would have to choose between the two- and four-door models, gasoline or diesel, hunter green or navy blue. "It seems my landlord is about the only one on the whole block who has a job, in the taxpayer sense I mean," said Nina, "not that there are not a lot of us employable." She smiled at having classified herself as one of the old gents—the word her landlord used was "codgers"—and at having had a lovely afternoon retrieving memories.

Amanda asked, "Where is it we are exactly?" She helped Nina pull the stroller from the backseat.

"In the South End." She had not known where to look but knew now there were better blocks than this one. Ones where there were families, for example.

"Ah," Amanda said. What she had heard about the South End was that it was in perpetual transition. Right across the street a building was all boarded up, with boards that were themselves a decade old. "Would you like me to help you?" She meant with the stroller, taking it in.

"Sure, come on up." Nina knew she really meant she'd like to see where Nina lived. "Lock up your car, though." She had three keys for the front door and another two for her own. There was mail, but none for her.

"But this is nice," Amanda said.

"Do you know why there is this niche? To get the coffin down the stairs, my landlord says." The carpet and the wallpaper changed at the first floor to an indoor-outdoor and a coat of paint. "He did the work himself, including plumbing."

"Does it work?"

"Oh sure," said Nina. Having lived with funky plumbing most of her life, what she had now was both modern and efficient.

"You go up and down these stairs?" Amanda rested. "Wouldn't it be bad for you?"

"No, good. Since I can't leave the baby, I can't jog."

"I mean I was told after childbirth not to climb stairs if I didn't have to."

"So was I. I don't unless I have to."

"But." Amanda could not believe it. "What is this, the fifth floor."

"Fourth." She was good at unlocking doors with her arms full. "And here we are," she said, "come on in." Nina gestured to the room whose furniture consisted of the carpet, a transistor radio, and two square pillows. "Make yourself at home, and I'll just go clean Emilie up."

There were paintings, but they seemed to have been taken off their stretchers and were rolled up in a corner like a bunch of travel posters. It did not seem possible to Amanda that anyone about her own age had accumulated nothing. She went to the window seat that looked out on the building that was boarded up and understood why Nina may not have been motivated to move in for good, but still she wondered where her *stuff* was. Not that it was required to have a collection of fine English china sparrows or, as Jeremy had, ships' decanters of superior crystal —they had much that wasn't strictly necessary—but where was the evidence that Nina had been anywhere? Or could it be, added to all her other troubles, that Nina's last place in Paris had burned to the ground? That happened. Amanda went to explore the kitchen to see if Nina needed pots and pans. Between the house in Weston and the one in Yarmouth on the Cape, they had too much that wasn't strictly necessary. Amanda found herself thinking of Nina and Emilie as refugees. What if, like the Cambodians, they'd had to flee? There was no window in the kitchen, but Amanda found the light switch. This was getting serious.

The sudden light had shown her maybe twenty shiny oval scurrying cockroaches, and she covered her mouth with her hand and shrieked and ran—not having had an impulse to try and kill those she could—into the bedroom, where there was nothing to sit on either. How could anyone live on the *floor*, Amanda asked as if she were somebody from the Board of Health, with *bugs?* She thought that she might vomit.

"Did you know that you have insects?" she called out to Nina. The bedroom contained a double mattress on the floor, a baby basket lined with calico beside it, a small reading lamp, and a library copy of T. Berry Brazelton's *Infants and Mothers;* that was it. Amanda felt like somebody from the Humane Society.

Nina called back, "Aren't they disgusting?" She had given Emilie a bath in the sink and came from the bathroom with a towel around her. "You should see them when you live at the equator," she said blandly, walking all around the mattress as if it were off the ground and disappearing into a big closet. "Huge. Not that that makes it—"

"These are very dangerous, you know, with babies," said Amanda. Weren't they?

Nina came out of the closet with a tiny cotton jumpsuit in her free hand. The cockroaches, she was certain, would revolt her less eventually when she could stop just leaving lights on to control them and get serious, now that she wasn't pregnant and Emilie newborn, with some heavy-duty toxins. If and when she got a job, she'd move in order to live on a block the whole of which had already been rehabilitated. Her block seemed to be an old-age home for insect life.

"Well, aren't they?" Weren't there stories of all kinds of awful things? Amanda had talked herself into being sure there were.

"But I thought this kind didn't bite. They do? I've been afraid to spray. You mean they'd bite the baby?" Nina was alarmed now too. It might be the American sort of cockroach was different.

"I don't know, I—"

Nina had once wondered if the dried milk on her dirty clothes would lure them from the kitchen, but she'd thought that she was paranoid and, sure enough, they hadn't come. Not even for the diaper pail. "You do hear stories, though, I guess," she answered. "Don't you?"

"Now and then," agreed Amanda, "frightening ones."

"Perhaps I shouldn't leave my laundry in a basket. Do you think it would attract them?"

"Definitely."

Was this an emergency? What if they were already in there? She was in no way prepared for how much laundry there would be, and urgent laundry too, produced by one small infant and a nursing mother. And the Laundromat was inconveniently located, so she hardly ever was caught up. She'd find a way to get there, though, that evening, and she said so, hoping to be reassured and reassuring.

"Let me take it home to my housekeeper," Amanda suggested. "She would love to do it."

"No thanks." It was not that Nina questioned whether or not the housekeeper would "love" doing yet more laundry—and why should she if she hadn't questioned whether her cockroaches posed a threat or were, as she'd believed, merely revolting?—but rather that she did not own enough clothes that fit her now, nor did she have spare linen enough, to send her things to the surburbs for their cleaning.

"Why don't *you* come? Really now, I mean this," pressed Amanda, though in fact she was just formulating the idea, "we have this huge house and it will be mostly empty in a few weeks. I'll commute back up, July, for therapy, and Jeremy will be in and out, nights, and we have a lovely yard I've just redone." She said this as if she'd had a chair reupholstered, and now as if she were someone from the Fresh Air Fund. "I mean it."

"Thanks, that's nice, but—"

"Frankly, you and Emilie deserve a few more comforts and a few less creatures." Very clever. "And, now really, how on earth do you expect to have your parents visit here? Or are they bringing camping gear?" Amanda laughed at her own jokes and was pleased that her impulses were generous ones.

"Well, you'd have to know my parents maybe, but they'll love it here. And then it's only for a week or ten days, since they're going on to Santa Fe to see my sister. Thanks, though, I appreciate it." Nina finished making her way back into the bathroom to the changing table so that she could finish dressing Emilie. "We'd love sometime to visit. Or at least let's get together soon again for coffee. I already feel so much less lonely." Nina finished doing up the snaps. "I'm glad you saw me in the paper, and I'm very glad I called you. And I'm sorry Emilie left her mark on your linen skirt, speaking of laundry."

"No, don't worry." Now Amanda had another idea, one that was less radical. She said to Nina, "Come some weekend. Why not this one?"

Nina's isolation had been shrinking all day. Now it was evaporating. She had been six months without the feeling she'd had twice this day, that there was a world out there she could be a part of if she cared to or was able. Rosie Lopez, downstairs, had been *it*, including having been her coach and partner during childbirth, and it would be fairer to them both if Nina enlarged her world. Here now was the motivation and the opportunity. And she had no plans for the weekend, needless to say.

Maybe it was that she had survived three seasons and was feeling confident again that there was life to live for. There were buds on rosebushes and new birds being taught to fly, and Nina had the feeling it was more or less inevitable that the year would roll to a close and that she, surprising herself, would turn out to have outlived it. Possibly Mark Otis had done her a favor by putting her in the *Globe* and back into the world from which she had withdrawn.

If Duncan Jones had not been someone she'd allowed herself to smile at and make polite conversation with at the French Library, the chances were she'd never have received the message from Amanda. She would have told Duncan—probably there in the lobby, since what inspiration would he have had to be helpful?—to tell Otis she had seen it and was angry. If he had returned the call himself he would have told Amanda he had no idea at all how to reach anybody unidentified in photo captions. No, he would more simply have referred the message back to Mark, who'd have ignored it. In effect, then, it was because she had shown a willingness to be involved, to play a part in her own life, that there was progress. In this way this day marked her arrival, finally, here in Boston. That Nina had Duncan Jones to thank for this, for having smiled first, struck her as beside the point, since she had other and less clumsy reasons for some future meeting. She would call him. In the meantime, here was her past and the chance to have some continuity. The invitation from Amanda represented one thing more.

Nina asked, "Would you mind, in that case, if I brought my laundry?"

# Part II

# Four

IT WAS THE NEXT TO LAST morning of July, a Friday, and as Duncan packed for the weekend in Buffalo, he planned the conversation with his parents. Now that his divorce was final, it was time to break the "news" to them. He knew his mother would protest not having been informed when there was something for her to have done to help, but Duncan's answer was that there would have been nothing for her to have done, and he anticipated saying this in such a grown-up way they would both treat him as if he were a contemporary. If he'd told them six months earlier, by contrast, when the future seemed more hostile even than the past, his pain would have permitted them to rush for the first-aid kit. Now they would sit—he knew in which chairs—that evening after the rehearsal dinner for his cousin's wedding the next day, and they would have a last drink and a first chance to be honest with each other. He almost looked forward to it.

Out in Weston, the midsummer light seemed green, so leafy were the trees around Amanda's house, so plush with health the perfect lawn. The day was getting under way with sit-ups performed to the music, something classical, that spilled into the yard from speakers in the living room below, and to which Nina's father danced a two-step in his bare feet on the grass, a cheek-to-cheek with Emilie. Amanda's task was to get through the morning and to her last session before the long month of August without the commutes to Boston from the Cape for Dr. Wolff. She had been dreading his vacation since being informed he took one—Jeremy took days, was all—although it would be a relief to have her parents take a break from asking her exactly what the struggles were that she discussed with Dr. Wolff. Each summer for the twelve preceding, her only task was to be mother and daughter (and on Saturday nights, wife), and she was breaking with tradition, taking off and showing up at what seemed odd hours. She'd enjoyed the variation, and her marriage, like her children, had a growth spurt in July. She dreaded August.

Nina, on the other hand, was in the neutral gear she always coasted in when with her parents. It was her goal to get through this day and get them to the airport for their plane to Santa Fe to visit Dulcie, *then* to relax and enjoy the progress they had made together. For the first time in a decade she'd kept to herself the details of her life and simply offered Emilie to them by way of explanation. Dulcie had been right about that as a strategy, as had Amanda been with her idea of bringing them out to the suburbs for fresh air and more space than they could use up in ten days' time. They had approved of Nina's spare approach to comfort, and had disapproved of the "consumerist mentality" Amanda's lifestyle represented, and, that clear, were more than happy to be out in Weston for the rest of their stay. After all, it was vacation.

In the kitchen Nina's mother, Vivian, sat reading the *Globe*, drinking from a bowl of coffee in the French style. As Amanda came into the kitchen, Vivian offered her hand for a good-morning shake (as if she no longer remembered it was not the custom here in the U.S.), and said, "Good morning, dear

Amanda, did we wake you?" She took off and then replaced the
reading glasses she had been applying to the morning's *Globe*.

"Oh no, I slept quite well, thanks," said Amanda, amused to
be feeling like the guest in her own house. In her hand was the
list in progress of the numbers Nina might need, for the
plumber, for example. Nina would be staying in the house all
month, and at the moment it was not clear who was doing whom
the favor. "I hope you did," she replied.

The implied question wasn't heard.

Then Nina came in and said to Amanda, "Hope we didn't
wake you." From her smile it was clear she had overheard her
mother. She glanced at the kitchen clock to see how far along
they were in getting this day over with. Not very far. She looked
over the list Amanda had made and said, "Electrician?" It was
not as if Amanda would be going very far, although she surely
seemed to think so. "Who's the one who does the sprinkler
system? Does he have a number?" It was walking distance to
their country club, but otherwise, what could she get to on her
own except by phone? "Oh never mind, it's not as if they won't
be coming twice a week, I think you said, right? Everything will
be just fine here." Who was doing whom the favor?

"What's the population here?" asked Vivian.

Nina asked what she meant by *here*.

"Why, here, in Boston," said her mother, folding the newspaper, folding up her glasses, and putting them in their case.

Nina looked to Amanda. Population was one thing she never
knew, no matter where, it always having seemed enough to
know whether a place felt crowded. Dulcie, on the other hand,
was something of a specialist.

"A million?" guessed Amanda. She had no idea.

"And what percentage would you say is black?" pressed Vivian.

"I don't know. Ten?"

"And what would you guess?" *You* meant Nina.

"Fifteen?" She'd lived in the South End, after all.

"No wonder, then."

"No wonder what?" said Nina.

"Just no wonder," answered Vivian disdainfully, "there is a problem."

Nina felt the heat rise in her and could have screamed something ugly and just might have if this weren't the last of their ten days together. Nina merely left the kitchen.

"I know what you mean," filled in Amanda blankly.

"No you don't, dear," Vivian said kindly, "but isn't it nice that you and Nina met again? You've been so very sweet." In fact she'd had not one nice thing to say about suburban life.

Then Nina's father came into the kitchen. "Well, good morning," he said to Amanda, "isn't it a lovely one?"

"It is," Amanda said.

"I think she may be hungry," he suggested helplessly about the fussing Emilie.

"Let me ask you the population, Mike," his wife said.

"Sure, of what?"

"Of Boston."

"Oh, say—OK, honey, I'll go find her in a second—something like six hundred thousand?"

"What percentage black?" persisted Vivian.

"Say, twenty-two or -three? Where's Nina?"

"That's my point exactly," Vivian said. Nina, having heard Emilie's crying, had come back to get her. "Nina," said her mother, "and you too, dear, for that matter, how is it that when as Mike just said a quarter of the population's black you don't have any sense of that? I mean, where are they?"

Nina said, "I'll take her now, Dad."

"Can you tell me?"

"Weston doesn't have that many blacks," Amanda didn't need to say but did.

"No, Weston is Johannesburg, I mean down*town*. We went to Quincy Market, for example, and they are all white."

Her husband then suggested, "Tourists."

"No, that wasn't my impression. I thought they were office workers, school kids."

Nina left the kitchen.

"Filene's Basement," Vivian continued.

"Oh, you got there, good," Amanda said. "Did you find anything?"

"You should remember, Viv," said Mike, "you're coming from a culture that *is* black, and so you're used to seeing only blacks."

"Of course. Excuse me, dear, I don't mean to ignore your question about Filene's Basement, but it seems a hopeless situation here. I bet Atlanta's ten times better, for example. Don't you think so, Mike?"

It wasn't that he disagreed, but that it was too early in the morning, and too late in their short visit, for a close discussion of the world's injustices. "I see you like our continental coffee," he said to Amanda, then, his sadness audible, "I'm going to miss the baby so much."

"I know what you mean," Amanda said, "me too. I'm going to stay down there a month now without coming back to Boston. Not," she added, "that I mean that it's the same thing." She thought Mike was very sweet and could have watched him dance with Emilie all morning.

"Obviously, I'm the only one who cares that Boston is a throwback." Vivian got up to leave. "It feels more like the nineteen-fifties around here."

"No, this is our last morning, that's all," Mike reminded Vivian. "Of course you're right about all that." He paused, then asked, "Do you think *this* could be our work now?" Wasn't it that charity began at home?

"What, Boston?" She could not believe it.

All Amanda could distract herself with was what Nina answered when she'd said that Mike and Vivian seemed nice, which was, "Yes, nice to visit, but I wouldn't want them living here." Amanda smiled. She knew what Nina meant now.

"Winters," Vivian went on to say. There was no way they could come back from life abroad. He couldn't have been serious. "What time's our plane, again?" She had been looking forward to their Southwest week with Dulcie, then to stopping off with friends in Honolulu. Vivian liked being as far as she could be from whatever was once home and people who still called her "Vivie." "I'll go check." It seemed reactionary to her, the way Nina seemed to keep on coming back here. And it was disorienting, seeing the way Mike was with this little baby. He was—was she *jealous?*—acting like a man in love.

Amanda said she thought she ought to go, although (she didn't say) there were no blacks at all in Yarmouth. She had to get back to her completely unprogressive parents. What would Dr. Wolff say if she told him that she'd rather have a mother who from time to time said "Negro" but who knew how to hold babies? What would he say if Amanda said, to paraphrase (she thought it had been) Unamuno on his deathbed, what the world needs more than light—someone had lit a candle—what the world needs more than light is warmth.

American had two departures side by side, to Buffalo and Santa Fe by way of Dallas. Nina and her parents had been at the gate an hour already and had watched the Buffalo flight board and joked that anyone who had a chance to go to Santa Fe or Dallas and chose Buffalo was crazy. Buffalo, for one thing, or so Mike informed them, had officially the worst climate of any-where in the U.S. They were amazed to see the passengers file on and that, when the man in the ruby blazer closed the door to the boarding ramp, none tried to get off at the last minute. "Help! I've seen the error of my ways!" they joked.

This last hour of their visit had revealed high spirits that had been like petticoats beneath the skirts of other feelings. Vivian, her boarding pass securely in the pocket of her husband's shirt, relaxed her standards and seemed for the first time in ten days secure. She hadn't interrupted once or said for the ten thou-sandth time how she was looking forward to seeing the work that Dulcie had been doing for the human rights of Indians. About Amanda all she'd said in this last hour was how her generosity of spirit was a gift to treasure (rather than that she was shallow and/or pampered), and she'd even told Nina to make the most of high-rent living, most of all the housekeeper who would continue to come in three days a week. The only reference she'd made to the unexplained identity of and the role played by the absent father, about whom she had not asked directly but about whom neither was there any information given, was that she could not help but regret the loss to Nina of a wonderful relationship like hers and Mike's. She wasn't criticizing Nina for the loss to Emilie, but for her failure to have found a boy just like the boy that married dear old Mom. She wished that everyone could have a marriage as great as her own, and she had said so. In this hour she hadn't found it necessary to repeat this.

Nina was viewing herself as lucky for not having had to justify the birth of Emilie. They could have lectured her about how she had violated church and state, or used the kind of terminology —like "out of wedlock"—that had been invented by their generation for this purpose. She wanted to thank them for that but decided not to risk it. Mike's eyes had been filled up since early morning, and he seemed exhausted by his wishing they would stay the month to try it out, and then forever.

Mike had not known how he'd longed to have a grandchild until this one had been put into his arms at this same airport. Here, it seemed to him, was God at work in the world in the form of one more chance—he'd missed the other opportunities presented by his own two children—to be his own instrument of peace. He'd spent his marriage serving God by serving others, by which he meant Vivian and the forgotten of the Third World, in that order. Vivian's devotion to him, without which he never could have dedicated himself to the miserable of the world, required of him acceptance of her need for exclusivity, and in exchange for this she'd met his every need, at the expense, he understood now, of their children. Now the problem was, he had needs that could not be satisfied by Vivian because they had to do with continuity. They had to do with getting old, with preparation for a future in absentia. He was dying, he could see now that his daughter had a daughter of her own, and for the first time he was homesick.

Consolation for Mike was that he would have another week before leaving the continental United States, and that if these thoughts persisted he could talk to Philadelphia—headquarters —about a transfer or retirement or whatever it was he might have in mind. It was that something had been born in him when Nina gave him Emilie to hold, and something died, which were illusions he'd had that they were a family in the real sense. For example, when once during this time he'd asked Nina if she wished to tell him who the father was and why she chose to raise the child alone, and she had sighed and answered only that it was such a long story—dot-dot-dot—and he'd admitted to himself they didn't know each other well enough to presume intimacy and she had rights to this privacy of hers, he'd seen her hurts and, more important, hoped to heal them, given time. He'd seen that something awful happened to her, recognized he didn't know about it either at the time or now, but wanted to. He *longed*, in fact, for consolation of this true kind.

"See now, Mike," said Vivian, persisting with their joke, "there's yet another who wants on that plane, apparently." Then she and Nina shared a smile and listened in.

"I'm sorry, sir," the man was told, "that flight has gone."

"But it's right *there*," argued the man, and he was right.

They nudged each other and laughed softly.

"No, sir, that flight's gone."

"But I can *see it!* Look!"

"Yes, sir, but think of it as gone."

"I *can't*, because it *isn't!* Look, please, let me on it," he appealed, "the traffic is a mess, it's Friday, I spent twenty minutes in the tunnel sitting going crazy, and I had to park my car. I got here as fast as I *could*, I mean, and I have got to get there for a wedding." He nearly decided to lie and say it was for his own but didn't think he'd be believed. "Please, you have got to let me on it."

"Sorry, sir, I can't." The gate clerk picked the phone up,

which made it seem he was going to call Security, and said, and it was broadcast to the waiting area, "We're ready now to board American's flight eight-thirteen to Dallas, with continuing service to Santa Fe, starting with rows one through five and those traveling with children or who are in need of special help. Then we will board rows twenty-eight to thirty-nine, rows twenty-eight to thirty-nine, please."

Nina's parents were row six, so there was time to watch the Buffalo plane pull away and the Buffalo passenger resign himself to having missed it. When the clerk said, "Sir, could you?" and indicated he could use the counter space, the man said, "Sure, OK," and moved to one of the free chairs to rest and reconsider.

"Well, there's always Santa Fe," Mike told him sympathetically. If this were Senegal there might not be another plane all week to Buffalo's equivalent.

He'd never been to Santa Fe, although at Club Med there had been that woman whose first name began with *J* and who'd said it was either Santa Cruz or Santa Fe she either came from or was going to move to. He smiled at Mike because things had improved in his life since then, at least. And he would ask the guy in the red blazer when this flight was boarded what else he could get to get him to his cousin's wedding in time. "Have a nice flight," he said to Mike. When he smiled to indicate the same went for Mike's traveling companions, he was reimbursed by Nina, grinning. "Well hello," was what he said. He'd tried to call her once or twice but hadn't reached the right "Jones N" and given up. It was too late then anyway, he had assumed, afraid she wouldn't have remembered him even if he had found her. Evidently he would have been wrong about that.

She had recognized him only when he turned to face them, but her pleasure showed.

"Now rows eighteen to twenty-seven, please," came the announcement, "rows eighteen to twenty-seven."

"And that's Emilie?" Duncan surprised himself, remembering the baby's name as well.

Nina nodded. Emilie was asleep in the pouch called a Snugli, strapped to Nina's chest. All that could be seen of her was her tiny perfect profile.

"How's she been?" What a dumb question. More to the point, "And how've you been?"

"Fine." Nina smiled. It was true too, more or less, even though progress had been slow. "And you?"

"OK, except I missed my plane."

"Rows six to seventeen now, please, rows six to seventeen."

Vivian had gathered up her carryons. "You keep in touch this time, dear, will you? And give Emilie a kiss when she wakes up." She leaned toward Nina and kissed her on both cheeks.

Mike bent down to give Emilie his own kiss. He said, "I want a picture every week."

" 'Bye dear."

" 'Bye, Mother. Sure, Dad." Nina hugged her father around Emilie. "I promise. 'Bye, Dad."

Mike kissed Nina on both cheeks and one time extra, and he said, "I love you, I love you both." He pulled a bandana from his back pocket and flapped it open like a flag, and blew his nose and stuffed it back into the pocket, then he smiled and took a few steps backward. His wife took his arm, and he turned and walked forward with her, taking the two boarding passes from the pocket of his shirt and waving with them in his hand.

Nina could see her mother say, "She seemed to know him, didn't she?" and Mike ask, "Who?" When he looked back at Nina for the last time before disappearing, he looked puzzled. It was an expression of his Nina loved, and so she laughed. It was so easy to imagine Vivian saying, "What do you mean you missed it?" all the way to Santa Fe.

She'd called him once or twice when he was not at his desk, but she hadn't left her name or any message, and the time when she thought it appropriate to call him had expired without her having reached him. Then there was a story in the *Globe* he'd treated sensitively, Nina thought, and she had contemplated calling him to say that but decided it would be embarrassing—a month had passed—if she had to remind him of their having met.

"So tell me who Amanda Norris turned out to be," Duncan said. He was himself amazed at how that name slipped into place for him.

"Amanda *M*orris," Nina answered, "—very good—turned out to have been Mandy Nicoletti, and we were sort of good friends in college." Then she had to laugh, and ask, "Are you sure you're not an investigative reporter?"

He hadn't noticed—probably because she hadn't laughed that morning at the *Globe*—how pretty Nina's teeth were. And she'd cut her hair or something, or lost weight. She didn't look the same at all in all the small ways. And since the man in the blazer had checked the computer for him, he knew to relax about that too. He answered, "If I were—I wish I had been—I'd have found you." He would have tried every "Jones N" in the phone book, for example. "I did try, in fact," he told her.

"So did I, somewhat," she replied. "Did you get another plane, I hope?" Because she laughed again, she said, "I'm sorry, we were joking about who would want to go to Buffalo." What a relief it was to have the visit over, after all her apprehension. There they went, as 813 backed away from the terminal to taxi into takeoff; they were Dulcie's issue now.

"No, no one *wants* to," Duncan answered, "which is why, I suppose, they don't run another plane until tomorrow morning."

"Oh too bad. I mean the inconvenience."

"It was worth it to run into you." The conversation with his parents wouldn't be the same if he arrived when the rehearsal dinner was all over, anyway, and now he would reschedule it for the late morning before going to the lunch before the wedding, and they would sit in the yard—he knew in which chairs there too—and be grown-ups. In some ways it would be better, because none of them would yet have had too much to drink. And in the meantime, in between time (as the song says), it appeared he could have fun. "Is she asleep?" he asked.

Nina stepped closer so that Duncan could see what he could of Emilie.

"She's lovely," he said. He remembered that about her. "She has your mouth. Her lips look like little dragonfly wings, don't they?" What made him see this, or say it, Duncan really didn't know. It struck him as a bit familiar.

Startled, Nina told him that the word in French for "dragonfly" was *libellule*. Jules-Jacques had called her Libellule as one of the most private of his nicknames for her, since what it referred to was their making love that first night they were back together, interlocked and synchronizing all eight wings and staying airborne. *"Demoiselle* is what you call a little dragonfly," said Nina, then, "I'm sorry," as she wiped the tears from her eyes. She offered no explanation, though she did smile, she thought, bravely.

Duncan wondered what would happen if he were to put his arms around her. But he didn't dare. "Can I buy you a drink?" he asked.

"I'd love it." Yes, she really would.

He could have kissed her, meaning both they stood that close together and he was that pleased.

His ticket was rewritten, and they walked across the bridge that led from the main terminal to a small elevator that went, as if Duncan's secret, to the tower, where there was a cocktail lounge with a view that was wraparound. It never failed to thrill him on a clear night to see Logan Airport as a simple problem in geometry, and it seemed to please Nina also to watch planes come in and take off as if they were dancing to the song— "Raindrops Keep Fallin' on My Head"—that slid like fingers down a keyboard from the ceiling speaker just above them. They got a carafe of white wine.

Nina removed Emilie from the Snugli and placed her down on the empty swivel chair beside her. It could be a cradle until she woke up and wanted feeding. Plus, she was too hot and heavy, now that Nina had recovered and was feeling light again, and open. It had been so long since anyone had paid attention, it was not hard to abandon for the moment feeling sorry for herself, in favor of the pleasure it was to have run into an old friend. Would he find it funny, or pathetic, if she were to say he was an old friend as far as she was concerned? She hadn't made a newer one since meeting him.

He touched her glass with his and said, "So bon voyage to Mom and Dad. And now what?"

"Cheers," she answered. She had stopped herself from saying, *"Santé,"* to avoid his thinking she was a French-English dictionary.

*"A votre santé,* it goes, right?" Everybody said this all day long at Club Med.

Now she touched her glass to his and said, "That's right. Who's getting married?"

"What?"

"You told the guy you had to get to Buffalo for a wedding."

"My cousin's getting married, but I got divorced. A double feature. Maybe if I'd said I had to get to Buffalo to get divorced, he would have let me on the plane." Why was he telling Nina this? "The papers just came through this week," he said in order to explain it, "so I thought I'd tell my family."

"So they wouldn't read about it in the paper first, you mean?" Or was that so oblique he'd miss the reference to the circumstances of their meeting?

"Yes, I guess you know the feeling." Duncan sipped his wine. "How was it?"

"Fine," she answered, "easy, though I'm sure it helps they live halfway around the world. We don't talk on the phone and hardly ever write. I hadn't seen them in a year. Or more." She'd seen them in the spring, and in the summer Jules-Jacques died. In fact her visit to Dakar, which was one of the few times they were separated not because of Jules-Jacques's other obligations but her own, had been much harder for Jules-Jacques than he'd anticipated. In *fact,* Nina thought this three-week absence—one with Mike and Vivian and two with Dulcie, who was working out of Algiers, worrying about the drought and famine in the sub-Sahara—was what in some way prepared them for conception. Emilie had been conceived on one attempt, the one time Nina ever in her adult life went unprotected into sex. They must have wanted, both of them, insurance against loss. This wine was working on her like massage, relaxing knots.

"That's nice," said Duncan. She was staring out the window at the lights, and so did he. "There's something to be said for censorship; what they don't know won't hurt them. That's how I was raised at least, not knowing what was going on, if anything was."

"Was it there," asked Nina, pointing to the black of Boston's outer harbor, "that the ferry crashed? I very much admired your story."

Duncan answered clumsily that he would have thought Nina might not read the *Globe,* but thank you. He could show her how it happened, and he did. "It left from the Aquarium," he said and pointed that out, "and would have come back in over there at the commercial ferry wharf." He pointed. "See the channel? That's the tanker's route."

"And where were you—oh yes, at the Aquarium—but why were you there?"

"I just happened to be," Duncan answered.

Nina said, "Your specialty," and smiled.

"I'd come in—" Duncan stopped to smile at that, at her "—because the fog came in. I had one of the Boston Harbor Sailing Club boats, which are moored right next to the Aquarium. The fog had come in so fast I was grateful I had made it in. I don't know if I heard the crash or not—of course we all were sure we had once we learned what was happening—but, God, the sirens out there in the fog. I never will forget that sound."

Now Emilie was waking up and sputtering like an old engine. Nina asked how he had found the sister of the missing woman, changed Emilie's diaper quickly, and offered her breast for nursing. She had learned to be efficient because, as in libraries, in cocktail lounges also Nina didn't want to draw attention to herself.

"That's it?" asked Duncan. How capable.

"But I'll be here for a while, so it's good you've got a long story." At some point, and for the record, she would have to make it clear that everything she said to him was off the record. Said and did. She wouldn't want to read his version of her sitting in a swivel chair in a dark cocktail lounge that looks out on the runway lights of Logan Airport, drinking with a transit passenger and, when she cries, pulling her shirt up for her baby daughter. Nor to see it in a photograph, no matter what the "purpose" of the picture was.

He guessed it was all right to watch but thought he shouldn't when he understood that just as Emilie was stroking Nina's breast, so did he wish he could. "Where was I?" Duncan had to ask.

"I wondered how you found the sister."

"Right. She had it wrong and thought the boat was coming in where it had left from and was waiting there, where, as it happened, the Coast Guard brought in the other passengers. We had been talking and I knew her sister was on board with someone—Gary, was all she knew—she herself had never met, and that the plan was they would meet after the ride and go for dinner. She asked every man there was, 'Is your name Gary?' "

"I remember that. How awful." Nina took a sip of wine. "Did she know you were a reporter?"

"Yes." He looked at Nina and said softly, "I had nothing to do with that picture, you know. I'm a feature writer. I don't go around exposing people."

"I believe you," Nina told him, "but so it's in words, you don't have any interest in me for a story, do you?" This was probably presumptuous—or at least she hoped it was—but still, a yes or no would let her feel a little safer, she thought. For some reason she was feeling quite exposed.

"No, for a story none at all. My interest in you never was professional. My interest in you," he embroidered, "was—is—

personal." He thought he ought to ask, "Do you find that acceptable?"

"How personal?"

Duncan admitted, "Very."

He was charming her, she recognized. "How interested?"

Duncan repeated, "Very."

"Yes, in that case," she replied, "it is acceptable. I'm very drawn to you too," Nina said.

"Good. That's settled." Duncan filled their glasses and they drank. To think that he could be just landing if he'd flown. Instead they were just taking off.

She sat Emilie up and rubbed her back until a bubble burst, then offered her the other breast. "She'll drink almost again that much, however much that is, and that's it for the night."

"The night?"

"Well, until three or four."

"Still, that's terrific." Was she saying she was free to be with him?

"But anyway, go on about the woman."

"Joan?" He guessed she wasn't saying that.

"Yes, Joan. I wrote to her, in care of you, in fact. You made her very real."

"She got a lot of letters sent to me to forward."

"Did you think they'd find the body?"

"Yes, I did."

"They could, still?"

"I'm afraid not. I don't know, but everyone I talked to said the current would have taken it real far real fast. The tide was going out too."

Nina said, "How awful, not to have the body, even. How did she find Gary?"

"I did. He had a bad head cut, and they'd taken those who needed first aid to a different place. Gary was standing at the urinal when the crash happened."

"He cut his head on the paper towel dispenser, I remember. You didn't say 'standing at the urinal,' I don't think."

"No, there is no better way to say he wasn't hanging on to anything, but no. The *National Enquirer,* but not the *Globe.*" He gave a shrug that meant that's show biz.

"Hadn't he been told that all were present and accounted for?"

"We all were told that. Are you interviewing me?" he asked. She answered, "Am I?"

"Do you want to talk about this?"

Nina said, "Well yes. You don't?"

"We could think of another subject. We could talk about, say, us."

She wasn't quick enough.

He pulled back. "All I mean is, aren't you hungry? How about if we go somewhere and get dinner?"

She considered: light brown hair that wasn't either straight or curly, glasses that recalled John Lennon's, eyes behind them that were bluish, good clean teeth and pretty lips, what she would call a decent chin, a truly lovely neck—he'd taken off his tie and undone buttons—and a tennis player's forearms, wonderful long-fingered hands—no jewelry—resting on a crossed leg, jeans that were just good old Levi's (perfect fit, she'd noticed in the terminal), a blue shirt that was too loose to say much about his torso except that he wasn't fat, and then that lovely graceful neck again, and—now he smirked—his head was cocked.

"So would you like to see my legs?"

She laughed and said, "I'm sorry. Yes."

"Which question did you answer?"

# Five

IT WAS NINA'S SUGGESTION that they go to Weston so she could put Emilie to bed, and when she said there would be food enough, he knew that Nina understood he hadn't necessarily meant dinner when he'd asked if she'd like to go somewhere and get dinner. He was further pleasantly surprised that Nina hadn't driven to the airport, which meant they would not have to go out to Weston in two cars, and was delighted when she let him know Amanda would stay at the Cape all month and that her husband, Jeremy, had plans to join her for the first part of this first week. Duncan thought it all seemed perfect.

He had never been to Weston, though, and because Nina didn't drive she hadn't paid attention to the route, and they got lost. Her plan had been to take a taxi from the airport back to Weston, and she realized nervously how easily she'd have been taken for a ride. It also hadn't registered how far out, meaning far away, from everything was this place she'd committed herself to for what would seem forever if she came to feel marooned. How would she find a new apartment or a job if she

could not say where she lived? Her parents had a car they'd
rented, and they hadn't made it seem too hard to get to Logan
Airport, but for Nina learning how to drive would never be an
option. Since college she'd had to explain that in the rest of the
world driving a car wasn't automatic and, besides, the trains
went everywhere you'd want. And now too she would qualify,
she thought, as phobic. She'd been told Jules-Jacques had been
crushed like an insect underfoot, the force of the collision in
which he had died had been so great, and Nina had vowed never
to possess a driver's license, ever.

At last something looked familiar, and they made their lefts
and rights and lefts again and came to the end of the driveway.
Duncan noticed there was a blue plastic tube up on a stick that
indicated *Globe* delivery didn't mean some kid who tossed the
paper in the pachysandra, also that the cars out this way were all
sporty models he would gladly trade his Saab in on if only he
could come up with the thirty-thousand-dollar difference by
some other means than winning Megabucks in the state lottery.
Swimming pools in landscaped settings seemed to be the specialty of every fifth house, and he wished the Norrises or Morrises would qualify and he and Nina could unwind by swimming
sidestroke as they got to know each other. In his suitcase was a
bathing suit he'd either wear or not wear, as she chose.

He left his suitcase in the car and followed her into the dark
house. "Look at this," said Nina, turning on the outdoor lights
first and revealing spotlit trees and bushes and the lawn whose
bald spots had been patched to make a seamless green. The
lawn was where the pool would be, and Duncan felt ridiculous
having to hide his disappointment at a yard that could have been
designed by the best set director in the business. "Maybe you
could go around and open windows," Nina suggested, "and I'll
go put her down upstairs and be back in a minute." This was not
quite true, since she would take a shower and be back in ten or
fifteen.

Duncan had been running for the plane he missed since early
morning and, if he would not be swimming, thought he ought to

clean up somewhat. "Houses like this always have too many bathrooms," he began, "so since I have my suitcase in the car, would you mind if I used one?"

If Nina had entertained her parents in this house, would a towel be an imposition on Amanda? More to the point, if they were preparing to have sex, as they both knew they might be, what was the point being coy? If nothing else came with advanced age, surely this did. "Not at all," she answered quickly.

She brought Duncan to the third full bathroom on the second floor, which was the children's, off the room she'd put her parents in. And it amused her now as she showed Duncan where it was that it no longer mattered to her that they'd moved the beds together, whereas on their first night there, after they'd gone to bed and she could hear them changing the arrangement of the room, she'd felt so *angry,* felt so—she could never quite admit—left out. And what had caused the change, the past few hours? The next few?

Nina thought about not changing Emilie's wet diaper but decided that was selfish—if she woke, she woke—and anyway it wasn't as if anyone was in a rush at this point. Emilie obliged by dreaming getting a dry diaper and resuming dreaming about whatever it is that pleases babies who are almost five months old. Then Nina put her on her stomach for the night and tucked a blanket in around her, then pulled up the side of the crib that came well used from Amanda's attic store of baby items. Having made herself at home in this and other ways, Nina decided she would take a shower not in "her own" off the guest room but down the hall in Amanda's more exotic—there were orchids not just on the wallpaper but in clay pots—designer bathroom. What if, Nina reasoned, she might feel like singing?

This house had such comforts as she'd never seen in any of the decorating magazines Amanda seemed to have subscribed to all her adult life, and it went without saying that she'd not herself lived in this style to which she could become accustomed without undue effort. The appliances, so all-American, all worked, and this was saying something. And it had what if it were a painting she would call *élan*, a vital energy related to impetuosity but focused and creative and creating. In this house, as unlike anyplace she'd lived as could be, Nina was inspired to sit back and relax *and* to begin to make up for the lost time she'd accumulated. It was not as if, until the summer Sunday morning when Jules-Jacques died, her life was everything she wanted. Were she to be truthful, Nina would admit that being someone's second wife, but simultaneous with the first, was not her idea of amusing. For five years she'd been alone on major feast days.

Thus she ran the shower hot enough to fill the room with steam, the way Amanda had asked her to on occasion for the orchids, then got in to wash away the day's accumulation of spilled milk and leaking baby. Frosting herself so with soap and shampoo as to be a cake, it rinsed away and revealed her a golden color tinged with pink that disappeared when Nina ran the water cold in honor of the summer evening. She was looking forward to this looking forward for a change, instead of back.

What she could use was obvious: a little well-intentioned body contact with somebody who was not a stranger, not a baby. Pregnancy was body contact on the grand scale, as were childbirth and now nursing, so Nina was not complaining. She could not imagine how she would have done it if she'd been, as she thought she was at the time, alone, with nothing to soothe the particularly jarring pain of raw, exposed nerve. Nina understood why some, to deal with grief, to rid themselves of it, performed what functioned as a root canal job on their central nervous systems and went on to live, but brain-dead. Emilie had spared her this, and gratitude was not a big enough word to express her thanks, but Emilie was after all—it was her purpose in life still to be—a baby. It would help to have a man.

She had a brand-new diaphragm for which she had been fitted at the six-week checkup after childbirth. The nurse had insisted on it, as if Nina planned to be a welfare mother and have more kids without fathers. By the calendar it was nine days short of a year ago that Jules-Jacques died, and that long therefore since

she'd had sex, which would hardly put her in the "active" folder.
For whatever reason she could barely even get the thing in-
serted right and had to make a second try. Only the jelly was
improved in her long absence—colorless now, it no longer had
the personality of what had been coughed up in a flu season—
not the instrument itself, which remained stubborn for her.
Surely there was something out there in the pile of ideas as yet
uninvented to replace this safest means with some device that
didn't ask you to be double-jointed. Lucky for her she'd decided
she would plan ahead rather than wait until the moment was
upon them. Duncan would attribute a long absence at that point
to an ambivalence on her part that seemed quite unlikely. When
would she be freer than after she'd seen her parents off, or
readier?

So she dressed in a caftan from Morocco that was of a soft thin
cotton in a soft thin blue and was, the way it fit her, not what
you'd think would come from a Moslem country. There were
tiny crocheted buttons that continued to the waist, and Nina was
inspired to fasten less than half of them. As soon as she stopped
nursing Emilie her breasts would shrink from view no matter
what she left undone. For this night she could let them show.

She found him on the flagstone terrace sitting on the low
stone wall and looking out. The automatic sprinkler system had
come on, and it was like Versailles, he said, which made her
smile because it wasn't. Versailles is all gravel paths, she said. He
knew that, so they both smiled. He said he now understood why
people lived here in the suburbs, it was for the oxygen. He held
a hand out to encourage her to join him, and he kept her hand in
his while she described the shock it still was to see water wasted
like this, after growing up in places where the gardens, and they
were much more impressive, got their water plant by plant in
order to conserve the resource. She told Duncan how she had
been teased at Wellesley for her inability to leave the water
running while she brushed her teeth, and how she made a point
now not to leave it running, even though it had been more than
twenty years since she'd lived where there was a shortage.

Where had he grown up? she asked, and then remembered Buffalo before he said it. There was silence after that because, since it did not seem necessary to them to say how glad they both were that Duncan hadn't made his plane, they merely kissed. "That's what I mean about the oxygen," said Duncan.

What he liked about her was how much there was unsaid between them. Now that he no longer trusted telling all, and hoped he never would again, the more loose ends there were the more that seemed to promise. Jessica had told the truth too often, as the times required, but she had left him with a limp he'd always have. He much preferred imagining, no matter that it made him a reactionary of the sort he used to say those people were who argued against nudity in films as being less erotic than when it was left to the imagination.

Arguing and leaving were the theme songs of his marriage, as a matter of fact. Was it his bad luck, or what, that he had married someone who could be her own defense? There wasn't that much to contest, or property to fixate on, but he'd been sure he would get screwed. He'd bought a handbook, *Your Guide to Your Own Divorce*, but hadn't found a section on what you should do if your spouse went to Harvard Law School. No, there wasn't someone else, his wife had said, it was just that, and she was sorry, she no longer cared enough to justify her time with him. And unlike work, where it would pay to spend time on a case whose subject matter wasn't vital, it made no sense in a marriage, and no, she'd said, old time's sake was not enough. It was here she'd encouraged him to be glad they'd have split up in time for their anniversary. Imagine going to the Harvest restaurant with empty barns, was what she'd said. "Speak for yourself," he'd answered, but she'd said, "I am."

He was the victim; this was what he had concluded. For a while he'd been convinced it could be No Fault (in deed as in name), but no. They'd both said things that turned out to be what should have remained unsaid, but Jessica seemed to enjoy it. When she'd said, "The morning of the day I married you I almost called it off and wish I had," he'd seen what he would call a smirk, a facial gesture of such cruelty there was no responding to it with a "So do I!" or "Do you think I ever wanted to get married? It was your idea, you bitch!" It was so cruel, that littlest smile, it knocked the wind out of him like a blow between the shoulder blades. She'd almost called it off? How could he not have known, how could their marriage have contained a secret of that size for fourteen years? That was more demeaning, even, than her saying she could count on one hand all her orgasms. At least he'd known that was a problem area.

He hadn't lost his sense of humor even if he'd lost his pride. Just now he had made Nina laugh by promising to tell her all he knew about the natural world in two seconds. "Oxygen," he'd said again with one of his endearing smiles, "now you tell me about the Third World."

"When we lived in Tanzania," explained Nina, "I once saw a woman who was many miles from any village, walking on the road but not attempting to flag down the public bus my sister and I rode on, who was carrying on her head, as if a huge load of laundry or a bale of beets for market, a gigantic patent leather pocketbook."

He put an arm around her in a comradely, appreciative way and told her, "I wanted to be in the Peace Corps, as a doctor, but my problem was that first I had to get accepted at a medical school. My sophomore year I was having trouble with organic chemistry and, panicked, I went over to the med school for a little conversation with the dean, who was a classmate of my father's. He was frank and said he disapproved of this, nevertheless it was no longer good enough to want to heal to get admitted, not at Stanford anyway, and he advised me to look into other possibilities than medicine."

"And there went the world's chance to have another Albert Schweitzer," Nina filled in.

"It *was* Schweitzer," Duncan said, impressed, "and Kennedy of course. I guess for everybody it was Schweitzer." He had felt unique at the time, and dramatic.

Nina nodded. "Then what?"

"Then I wrote a story for the Stanford *Daily* on a freshman who, on his way to his senior prom, had been forced off the road —it was a little Sprite he was in—into a tree. He went on to Stanford anyway, only a whole year later than he'd planned to, but was blind now." Duncan liked how Nina pulled his arm around her then more tightly, as if to protect her against this sad story. "I discovered easily all the ways this guy fed on and was nourished by his bitterness—he called himself a cannibal—but also how to get him to describe for others what it was to lose his sight. And when it turned out that the story moved his classmates to set up a network to help out with class notes and assignments, I learned then about the power of the press. And I decided my desire to heal could well be satisfied without having to go to med school, for which I was grateful, since, as my own doctor-father had been trying gently to persuade me, I had simply never had the aptitude."

She didn't want to ask about the accident. She didn't want to hear about it. "Were you in the Peace Corps as a journalist, then?"

"No, I went to graduate school, in communications, stayed at Stanford, got a doctorate." Met Jessica, got married, moved to Boston, started at the *Globe*, he didn't say. "By then those of us who would have gone in the Peace Corps were against the Vietnam War and were busy here at home." First Bobby Kennedy was murdered, then he and his bride stopped in Chicago on their way back East, where during the Democratic Convention Jessica saw friends while he was learning to hate cops. And fourteen years had not dimmed Duncan's memory of sixty-eight, Chicago, cops in helmets colored pastel blue advancing, dancing, bringing caveman clubs down on the heads of a whole generation. Mayor Daley was the chief, Imperial Wizard for his pale blue hooded clansmen. Nixon won. What Duncan learned was it was order, only order, not the law, cops were in charge of. Law and order were two separate spheres, one governed by enforcers of the other—cavemen, clubs—the other governed by

the likes of Jessica. Some system. Duncan said, "Some system."
What he wanted was a drink.

"So what year were you?"

"Sixty-four."

"And I was sixty-three, so I was gone already by the first
assassination."

"Gone to?" he asked. "Pasture?"

"England, yes, at first, where I learned drawing for a few
years. Then I lived in Greece, and painted, and I was back here
that summer, when my parents came on home leave. We
watched the convention with my aunts and uncles, who already
were of the opinion Democrats were all barbarians. My father
almost never came back after that—I think I told you how he was
a pacifist—and maybe he would still not have if Nixon hadn't
been impeached. I kidded him he went back just to watch the
hearings televised, to rub it in." Her fondness for her father
showed. "You'd have to know my relatives," she said and shifted
her position slightly. "At the airport I was wondering how we
would do as people, like these relatives in Manchester, who
lived together day to day, and realized we'd all be different. If I
had felt insecure my whole life about where I fit in, I could
contrast that with knowing and decide which would be worse.
My cousins know where they fit in and deal with it by overeat-
ing."

"As opposed to us," said Duncan, "undereaters."

"I was just about to say that. Aren't you hungry? Let's go see
what we can find." The sprinklers for that part of the yard would
come on soon anyway, which Nina knew from having had a
conversation with her father rained out. There was chicken that
would taste good cold with mayonnaise made by Vivian and
ruby red tomatoes that were local. On their tour of Quincy
Market they'd bought cheeses—cheddar to take on to Dulcie—
and a huge black bread Mike picked out. There were grapes to
feed each other if they felt like putting fingers into one another's
mouths. The grapes were russet seedless, hybrids, sweeter-tast-
ing than the green.

He squinted at the light from inside the refrigerator but was glad there was wine being chilled there. Looking where he was directed, he found the corkscrew and glasses, silverware and napkins, plates, a bread knife, trays to put it all on. Nina had thought they could picnic in the living room with the sand-colored carpet, if he wanted, as he did. It would be nice to see the outdoors from within and feel quite sure they were alone.

He was a stranger not to Nina, whom he felt already close to, but to Weston and this place that neither of them would have known of had it not been for Mark Otis. He felt foreign, or else it did. When he said it was hard to believe Amanda and he were the same age, Nina knew what he meant. How could anyone have put so much time into making an environment just so and not be on the old side? This house represented countless hours spent shopping.

Once he had committed a real act of bravery, and he contemplated telling Nina about the time, in an elevator in Filene's department store, two adolescent venturers with the wide-open freckled faces of St. Mary's altar boys baited a black kid who was shopping with his mother. Duncan told them to shut up—the other shoppers having stiffened into silence—to which they responded by intensifying both the racist and the pornographic in their taunts. The black kid stirred, his mother pressed herself against him, and the other shoppers, men and women but all white, edged back into the corners. Duncan grabbed the two toughs by their shirtfronts.

For a second he thought he'd be able to do something from the movies, maybe smash their heads together, let them slump onto the floor, the other passengers stepping around them to get off at six, Home Furnishings. But they were used to fighting for their lives, and so after that second it took them to get it clear, they creamed him.

Someone pressed the button for ALARM and as the doors opened at two on Women's Shoes those who could get out did, some stepping over Duncan's legs to flee into the arms of anonymity and Intimate Apparel. Duncan's rescuers-after-the-fact, the fact being a broken collarbone, were two shoe salesmen and a guard—a woman posing as a shopper—who had handcuffs in her purse and who led the toughs off to prosecution for shoplifting merchandise found stuffed into their jackets.

Duncan was led to a chair and complimented on his instincts if not his intelligence. He'd never broken anything but knew he'd broken something now from how it hurt, oh how it hurt. In a mirrored display he saw that he was not just white but chalky, and that blood ran from his nose. He leaned his head back and looked at the sprinkler system on the ceiling. Could somebody call his wife? Duncan was lucky being married to his lawyer, but for once he envied friends whose wives were doctors.

"So I went from Filene's to Mass. General's Emergency Room in a taxi that pulled up to where the ambulances make deliveries. I went through the electric doors behind a stretcher with a tiny baby on it—like a Cornish game hen on a turkey platter, was how wrong it looked—and stood at the desk to give information, mostly about my insurance. Shall I bring this salt and pepper?"

Nina said yes and picked up the other tray, and wondered whether all his talk about disasters was so she would fill him in about Jules-Jacques, as if he knew her red-flag words were "ambulance," "emergency," "dead on arrival." But she had survived ten days not telling Mike and Vivian, so why start here? If he persisted even when she changed the subject, as she did in asking him to bring the candles from the buffet, she could tell him all about how well it went at Emilie's birth. It was only as the pediatrician said, "You have a daughter," that she fell apart completely.

"But where was the blood, I wanted to ask," Duncan went on, "or the stabbing victim with the butcher knife still stuck between his ribs? Where were the gunshot wounds? The kid electrocuted on the third rail? Where was someone struck by lightning? 'Migraine,' was what a woman in line ahead of me had said when asked why she was there, but how could migraine be *enough*? Shouldn't her brains need to be spilling out? Where was the panic in the air? Why wasn't anybody running?" Duncan had to laugh at his imagination.

Nina didn't.

"All they did was x-ray it and put me in a figure-eight sling that made me feel like I was a parachutist all the time. They told me I could wait there for my wife to pick me up—my wife at the time, that is—but I'd already read the big sign on the wall like an eye chart: 'WE WANT YOU TO KNOW CHARGES FOR EMERGENCY SERVICES START AT 75⁰⁰. LAB WORK, X-RAYS & SPECIAL PROCEDURES ARE EXTRA.' I was ready to leave, though it made me wonder what it said under the paper pasted over the old fee, or what it had gone from to seventy-five, and why they didn't get a whole new sign. I've always hated restaurants that change the menus by putting on little stickers with new prices. Isn't the inflation rate enough without constant reminders of the fact that nothing is what it once seemed?"

She lit the candles, poured the wine. There had to be a better subject for a dinner conversation. Not inflation either, though.

"Well, cheers again," he said and touched his glass to hers. "I'm sure I've bored you."

"No."

"It's even in your face by candlelight. I must be nervous," he admitted.

"No, not boredom. Hospital talk makes *me* nervous." She put pepper on her slices of voluptuous tomato. "Aren't you hungry anymore?" If he'd been trying, he'd not have been more successful in capping the energy that had existed. She wished they were back on the wall. Then, at least, she'd felt like eating.

He had hoped to tell her one last thing about Mass. General, how the main lobby looked to him the way he thought a movie set would, with these extras in their wheelchairs waiting as if for direction, smoking between takes. He'd ask, "Who wouldn't smoke, if you were playing someone who had been explored and told he had ten weeks to live?" He wished he had a cigarette for right that minute. "Less than I was," Duncan answered about hunger. What had happened? "Tell me something."

"What about?" she asked.

"More about you. I'm doing all the talking." What an under-statement that was.

"I still read the Classifieds," said Nina, "only now I'll need a place to live too. And a job." It seemed, instead of simplifying her life, she was complicating it. It seemed the same had happened too with Duncan. All she'd wanted, honest to God, was a sexual encounter that was as impersonal as it could be without being unfriendly. Nina didn't want to be reminded of the struggles and the effort that went into day-to-day. The point of *night* was a vacation. "Don't remind me," Nina added.

He would have asked, "What kind of job?" figuring he might know someone in whatever field it was—his work's advantage was the way it let him meet a lot of people—but he didn't.

Nina let the silence last until she thought of what to say, which was a long time. "I hope you won't be insulted, but can't we be superficial? Do you have to talk about emergencies and prejudice? That's all my parents talk about, and when I put them on the plane I thought, OK now, for a few hours I won't have to *worry* about how the underdogs are doing. I just spent ten days not having my needs taken care of because my needs aren't extreme enough to even *mention* when what we're concerned with here is river blindness and starvation. Jesus Christ." She stared at the flame as if she were one more of her mother's moths attracted to the candlelight—her mother had a moth collection for which she was somewhat known among some lepidopterists—and was reminded that she'd meant, at least, to ask her mother about dragonflys, but that she hadn't. God, this was discouraging. She felt like a fool sitting there so unprepared for talk and well prepared for sex, when neither one was working out and maybe wasn't what she wanted.

Duncan did the absolute right thing at that point, which was to pretend that the sand-colored carpet—sand the color of ground glass—was the mere desert island they'd been ship-wrecked on. No problem. Worse would be if he were there alone.

"I'm sorry," Nina interrupted.

"No, I was just trying to think what to do first. Should I wade out and catch a fish with my bare hands or look for some vines that I could make a net with? Do you like fish?"

Nina's smile was promising. "Fish?"

"Or should we discover fire first? We could be here for a while, and that's a lot of sushi. How are you with sushi?"

"On occasion, fine," said Nina.

"Should I shinny up that palm tree and knock down that coconut? We can't just wait until a speck appears on the horizon, can we?" Duncan stretched out on his back. "Around here it could be a whale."

She laughed. "Did you say whale or while?"

"Both." Then he turned onto his side and propped himself up on an elbow. With his free hand he reached not for Nina's breasts, though they were at eye level and he had to work to resist finishing uncovering them, but to get his wineglass. Two steps forward, three steps back, was what this game was. Luckily it was one he had played his whole life.

"Cheers again," she said and touched her glass to his. She also touched his face with her hand and felt that thing tugging in her belly indicating hunger that would not be fed by food. She wanted him to touch her back—no, not her back; she wanted him to touch her *too*—to put his face against her breasts.

And so he did. "I'm looking at these little buttons," Duncan explained, "on your dress, without my glasses." Actually he'd put his contacts in upstairs and could see everything he wanted. "Did you knit them?"

"No, I don't knit."

"Is this superficial enough?" He was fumbling with the buttons Nina hadn't left undone. "The talk, I mean." He hoped she would at least allow herself to be teased. More and more the women he met wanted to get down to basics right away and skip the get-acquainted aspects, as if they were in this dreadful hurry for whatever reason. "How old-fashioned of me," he apologized, "to think to tell you who I am, as if that mattered any-more."

"No, I'm old-fashioned too," said Nina, running her hands over his chest as if putting suntan oil on. "It's just that—"

"I know, it's complicated. That's the trouble these days, there's so much more background than there was. I'm thinking maybe we should write out memoirs, all of us, and hand them out ahead of time, you know, like guidebooks you read before going someplace new." He had just three more buttons. "Even pamphlets would do the trick, outline form, you know, just lists, like things to see and where to eat but people you've been married to and good or bad things that have happened, any-thing especially outstanding, you know what I mean." He got the last one and took her breasts in his hands. "I—"

"Do you always talk so much?" She pulled his face to hers and kissed it.

"I was going to say how beautiful I've always thought you were. And do you always talk so little?"

Nina couldn't answer because Duncan's mouth was sealing hers off. They leaned backward to lie down beside each other in the space between the coffee table and the sliding glass door open to the yard. Yes, she was in that hurry Duncan meant. It was a good thing now that she had planned ahead. It had been *so long* and so far away; but Nina forced herself not to refer back to that last time. He had found a way to slip her arms out of their sleeves and pull his own shirt up over his head, with her help, and there was this pleasure to distract her. Duncan's hands were very knowing, and she couldn't get over how nice it was, this being kissed, and what a consolation it was, pressing him against her. They undressed each other as if it had been rehearsed.

"How should we—" he asked.

"I already have," she answered.

Duncan hoped she didn't mean the old wives' tale even he knew nursing as a form of birth control was, and he was relieved to find as he explored her what she meant was his old friend. He'd noticed that her fingernails were short and rounded, not the perfect painted ovals Jessica's were. He had joked, in fact, that his wife was the only woman since the Chinese revolution whose hands had become vestigial organs. Jessica had said she grew them to prove that she didn't type, but Duncan knew it was because she really wanted to have claws. At first he'd teased her and pretended that he liked them in a way, until the day one night she'd claimed to be unable to insert her diaphragm for fear she'd break one. That night he had said, "Good, now let's have a child," not realizing—not for months, the pack of Trojans he'd bought the next day untouched in the drawer of his bedside table—it was over.

"Or did I misunderstand you?" she asked to acknowledge his preoccupation.

"No, you didn't, not at all." He felt like telling her he loved her but made do with more sign language. Now it was he who was rushing, anxious, needy.

Nina took him in with the sharp intake of breath she associated lately with her checkups and the hand of a technician. Something about Duncan's belly pressing on hers made her think that she could cry. They were so *close*.

"Are you all right?" he pulled his face away to ask.

"Stay close, I'm fine. Are you?" She closed her eyes to isolate the feeling of his filling her with his flesh. "Duncan," she said. She was calling him by name for the first time.

And he said, "Nina."

# Six

AS IF THEY were Harvard's visiting professors, cars seemed to park there on Irving Street by the semester, so it wasn't ever easy to get home. Today it was made harder still by the commotion in his head. He hadn't been in love in years. His joints had lost their tension and he wondered if he might collapse, or if he might throw up the flutters in his belly. He had slept in Nina's bed and canceled in his mind his plan to go at all to Buffalo, to spend instead the day with Nina and the baby being thrilled with one another. It was only when Amanda showed up like that before seven in the morning, and there was the scene that was resolved by Nina's telling him he'd better leave but she would call as soon as she could, that he'd thought he'd leave at all. He wished when he walked in the door she would be calling to tell him that everything was fine and she could see him every day from now on. He would be a new man or a shadow of his former self, depending on the outcome of these runaway affections. He was set for life, in other words, he felt, or done for.

By his door a neighbor had left brownies for him, as she often did on weekends, but he had no appetite at all for food. He fumbled with the locks and brought the brownies in for later on, to share with Nina on their picnic or to eat in bed with milk, of which he'd seen her drink three glasses for the baby. Duncan sat down on the couch that was, though it was bought with wedding-present money from his parents, still quite white, a tribute to the years he and his ex-wife spent not entertaining, and he put the plate down on his oak cube of a coffee table. Once there had been two, a pair, but Jessica had taken hers as one example of an item jointly owned that could be equally divided. Fifty-fifty was her way of doing things in matters quantifiable. He'd tried to get her to go fifty-fifty in the area of human needs, but with no luck.

He waited. How long would it take Nina to call, and what should he do in the meantime? This was why he ate a brownie, then another and a third, which brought him to the kitchen for a glass of water and the sense that she could maybe *not call*, or, since it was not yet eight, not call for many hours. So he asked himself whether he ought to go to Buffalo to pass the time and went to lie down on his bed to find the answer, which was yes, he ought to get it over with, since she might not call until evening, which was not it. Duncan started over and concluded that a good idea for going was that Nina made it more and more a good idea to get his slate clean.

When his parents asked him what the matter had been with his marriage, he'd say on the left wall of their bedroom were two closets side by side, but whenever they'd dressed for something they were going to do together, they would never come out looking like a couple. He would not have worn a tie and she'd wear silk, or she would put on shorts and find him in a turtleneck and long pants. They'd perceived things differently no matter if the issue was whether the so-and-so's gave formal dinner parties or what kind of breeze there was out on the water. One of them was always wrong, and it was always quite clear which, which gave the other one a way of being right. They operated—this was what he would try to communicate—at each other's expense, the entertainment being finding out who had been wrong and by how much.

His parents wouldn't understand this, probably, since they tended to disbelieve in a relationship existing between motive and behavior. Why not just decide ahead what you'd both wear? Or let one person choose for both, and then take turns? You always make so much, they'd say, of *explanations* of why this or that is what you see it as; why not devote your energies instead to looking at *solutions*? Duncan saw that it might not be too creative to go into detail with them and decided when they asked him what the trouble had been he'd be better off if he said sex. They wouldn't want to know about that and would come right out and say so, A, and B, it would be true.

He looked around his bedroom and felt the relief it was to have reclaimed as his the space they'd occupied together. For a long time after Jessica's departure, now that she no longer could insist on closing drawers and making the bed neatly so that the electric blanket's wires would not be bent back on themselves, the bedroom always looked as if it had been searched for drugs. If he had not in truth enjoyed the mess, he'd loved the freedom, which led Duncan to discover one spring Saturday that he was as free to bring order to his life as chaos. He'd gone to the hardware store, bought yellow paint, and painted over all the blue of all those years. He'd bought a rug and several posters of exhibits he had liked at the Museum of Fine Arts. He'd bought a plant that seemed to get enough light through the matchstick blinds and gave him the security of knowing that no matter how bad the air was outside, here was a creature who could turn it into oxygen and keep him going.

Duncan pulled himself up and went down the hall into the bathroom, where he'd put the Club Med poster, as if to prove he still had a sense of humor, of the woman offering him all she had and a pineapple. Her pinup breasts, chorus-line legs, and blue regulation eyes did nothing for him, as opposed to the pineapple, which seemed absolutely real and made him thirst and hunger for it. When he'd pointed this out to an architect friend,

who was also his best tennis partner and his oldest friend in
Boston, he was told he was a pervert. Duncan laughed and
zipped his jeans and flushed the toilet. It was likely he would
take the poster down before the first time Nina came there.
There was no comparison, but still he made one: Nina's silver
bullet eyes, the way they flashed, the breasts that fit into his
hands and filled with milk while they lay sleeping, skin with
contours, skin with resiliency, skin he knew like his own already;
there was no need for her to be holding fruit.

He'd tell his brother about Nina on the way in from the
airport, and Skip would tell his wife, Cathy, who would ask him
while they danced at the reception what if anything he planned
to tell his parents. Duncan would sense in them both a little
thrill that once again it was complex, as if he were the family
entertainment, this latest announcement starting a new season
of a show they'd watched for years. It was nice not to disappoint
them, though he thought he wouldn't mind at all the day that
Skip's life volunteered itself in some small way. Not that he
wished them harm, but it would be a change if once his mother
said that Skip and Cathy's nine-year-old had been arrested in a
drug bust at her elementary school, instead of that she loved her
figure-skating lessons. How he envied Skip his, well, his stunted
growth.

Rather than the seersucker suit he'd packed to wear, Duncan
dressed in the newer tan one he was saving for something more
sexy than a family wedding. With it he put on a shirt he thought
looked English and a tie that was Italian and cost more than
what he used to pay for shoes. They would believe him when he
said he had to fly right out again for an appointment and would
never guess he'd called Nina when he got there to say that he
wouldn't be at his home number and ask if the coast was clear
(since he was inland) and report schoolboyishly how much he
missed her.

Duncan's nieces—Heidi, Dorothy, and Alice—wore organdy
pinafores over their matching gingham dresses and appeared to

have come from their storybooks for the occasion. As adorable was Cathy, who had made her own dress of the same pale blue check as those she'd made for her daughters. Duncan marveled at the fact that Skip's tie wasn't of the same material—his theme was golf, though, and his tie had little greens and flags and sandtraps painted on it—and at what his life would be if he'd been born his younger brother. He decided that the word for it was snug. Or was it smug?

The band played "Mountain Greenery" and Duncan felt like dancing to it with his willing sister-in-law, who was dying for the chance to ask him, as he knew she would be, about Nina. Skip had not asked any questions when he'd told him on the way in from the airport that he had met someone special, so he hadn't answered any. Cathy said it was just so she wouldn't blurt the wrong thing out to Duncan's mother that he'd better tell her two things: everything and then what he had told his parents.

"Nothing," Duncan answered with a laugh. He had decided it was plenty to tell them that he and Jessica were final, so he hadn't gone into detail with them about what else he might be up to. "Nina Jones, her name is."

"How convenient!" She was thinking, he knew Cathy well enough to know, how easy it would be to change her name if they got married. "Tell me more. When did you meet her?"

"Yesterday." He grinned.

"Oh, you're impossible."

"This is the one, though, if you want an inside tip." Duncan performed a Lester Lanin era twirl she followed easily. He never danced at all now anymore and wondered how much Nina liked to.

"How old is she?"

"About forty."

Cathy was exactly Skip's age, but they'd married practically right out of grade school, profiting from arrested development. "Well, that's too bad."

"How come?" he teased.

"I don't want to sound like your mother, but what about

having children? You'd be a terrific father. Ask my girls." He was
by far a better dancer than his brother, and she found it effort-
less to follow him. The lucky girl, thought Cathy.

"Nina has a baby five months old." He twirled again, and she
stayed with him, so he pulled her in a little closer and tried
something fancy, using up a lot of space on the square platform
of a dance floor in the tent in the backyard.

"You're kidding, right?" asked Cathy, laughing in his ear.

"About the baby?" Since the song was ending, Duncan made
three turns and leaned them both into a dip. They were both
dizzy. "No," he said and smiled and shrugged, "why would I
kid?" He guided her back to the table Skip and several of their
cousins occupied, around which they'd been swapping jokes like
in the old days. Har-har-har, laughed one of them, an old man's
laugh that sounded inappropriate from someone who was
young enough to not wear socks and not look stupid except
maybe to the help. It was too bad the way the men were boys and
then one day the old farts they would be until they died. There
seemed to be no middle range, as if there were no longer time to
have a prime of life. Duncan was grateful that he had recovered
from his slump and vowed—he always did on his trips home—to
not act old before he was but neither to be boyish longer than
was healthy. Duncan promised himself he'd thank Jessica for
having told him once a day for fourteen years that he should
grow up.

Then he went inside to use the telephone, to try again to get
an answer about whether everything was fine again after
Amanda and if he could come to her straight from the airport.
No one answered for the fourth time. When he overheard one
of the caterers telling another the bride's mother had said they
would cut the cake now, Duncan seized the opportunity to van-
ish. He felt sorry for the groom, whom Duncan's cousin had met
on a dude ranch in Wyoming and who was a good sport in the
rented wedding clothes that fit him poorly because they weren't
made of denim. Duncan had said to his mother as they danced
that it was nice of Aunt Bea to have let him wear his cowboy

boots, which Duncan meant to be ironic, since the boots were obviously custom-made for the occasion, but his mother's answer had been, "Yes, they're *snake*, of all things!"

He went through the house and down the front steps to the street and walked along the line of cars and guessed he could be in Grosse Point or whatever that fashionable suburb of Detroit was. "Buy American" was what they'd done, as if Japan and Germany were military powers still and it would be not merely bad for the economy but seriously unpatriotic to have gone for value or for craft. Still, he wished that he had some car keys in his pocket and could take off for the airport on his own. He'd had the dreaded conversation with his parents, so all he had left was to wait for his cousin to throw her bouquet to her assembled bridesmaids, after which she and her husband could light out, like Huck Finn, for the territory.

The talk he had been postponing for a year had gone well in that they'd been honest and admitted the divorce was for the best. They'd sat not in the living room chairs, as he'd first envisioned it, but at the little kitchen table, which enforced an intimacy. Both his parents had said, for example, that they'd seen it coming and had wished for his sake, as one wishes for an alcoholic, only that he had hit bottom a lot sooner. Then they'd both exclaimed how well he looked now, Duncan's mother asking if his suit was new and saying that she thought his tie attractive. Neither one had asked if Jessica was well or if he'd give her their regards, though Duncan's mother did say she'd write Jessica a little note.

He knew that Monday morning she would take down all the photographs of Jessica, revising history as they do in the Soviet Union, and that his ex-wife would be the Khrushchev of the Dr. Raymond Joneses. The relevant silver frames on the piano would be emptied, now that the news was official, and he wondered how it was that keeping current was a value in home decoration when it didn't seem to be in global politics, space exploration, or the arts. There was nothing like visiting his parents to make Duncan realize why he'd loved her, and he was aware of feeling, even in the midst of his discovery of Nina, a nostalgia for the good old days when he and Jessica were giddy with potential. Walking back now toward the music—the band played the tune he had learned as "The Farmer in the Dell" that doubled unexplainedly as "The Bride Cuts the Cake" at these things—he recalled with fondness what a good time they had always had at family weddings, his and hers, attending as if they were anthropologists who had been hired along with the photographer to keep a record.

Jessica would have found out without his mother telling her that the groom's boots were made of snake. Not only that, she'd know what kind, and whether snakes were grown like mink just for their skins, and how they killed them if they were. She would have done a little study, and they would have danced to "Mountain Greenery" and twirled the champagne in their blood up to their brains and giggled uncontrollably at what she'd learned. He wished they would be friends again. He wanted to apologize for having parents who could not ask how she was, who didn't even have the common decency, which was one of his mother's favorite phrases, to ask how she was.

On his way through the house he tried the number once more, but again there was no answer. Silly as it was to "miss" someone he hadn't even "met" at this time on the previous day, he did and couldn't wait to tell her. There was nothing about which he should be worried—when Amanda blew up like that at him it was only because she'd expected Nina to be at her service in order to help her through this first rough day, not entertaining overnight guests—but he wished they'd stayed around the house at least to pick the phone up when it rang. Instead they probably were swimming in one of those neighbor's pools, which made another reason why they should have had their own installed instead of all those costly bushes. Duncan checked his watch and saw he had enough time to get to the airport for the earlier plane of the two he had a seat on, so he called a taxi and ran off to kiss the girls goodbye, including Cathy and his

mother, who would talk about him as he flew to Boston in terms
of the kind of girl—their kind—who would do wonders for him.

Logan Airport was deserted, and he was depressed that Nina
wasn't waiting at the gate, or anywhere. That settled it: he never
would go home again. He crossed the lobby and walked past the
elevator occupied by people going to the cocktail lounge, and
he wished he could be with Nina now and riding up to do it over.
This time they would go to his place, where Amanda wouldn't
find them, and he'd never fly again. He found his car, which had
been freshly gouged, and paid the parking fee, another gouge,
and it was settled.

But he hadn't called her from the airport, had he? There was
traffic in the tunnel from the airport to the city, and he sat with
static on his radio and all the windows shut against the awful
fumes and came to the conclusion that since Jessica lived right
there where there was light at the end of the tunnel, it could
make sense to stop and say hello. Their conversations on the
phone the past few months had been progressive, and he could
call Nina later. Even if he'd wakened up in Nina's bed, in more
important ways this day was Jessica's.

He parked his car, not easy on a Saturday at Union Wharf, and
used both names when through the speaker by the main door
Jessica asked who was there. "You're still the only Duncan I
know," she replied and buzzed him in, a good beginning, given
that he hadn't ever rung her doorbell and had half expected she
would call back, "Who?" He'd noticed she was up on three and
took the little elevator by the ficus tree that flourished without
an apparent light source.

"Down here," she called from the left as the doors opened,
and he stepped out and looked left to where she was framed by a
doorway, brightly backlit. If she'd known the outline of her body
showed up through her dress as every bone would in an x-ray,
she would never stand there like the Leonardo man inscribed
within a circle, unless—and Duncan admitted he did not know

which it was—she knew full well. She had lost weight, that much he knew.

"Come in," she said. She smiled and offered him a cheek.

He kissed it lightly. "I hope I'm not interrupting."

"No, in fact I'm bored to death. I stayed home from a Vineyard weekend and regret it. Want a drink? Come in."

He did. She looked right out on Boston harbor. "You just saw my plane come in," he told her in amazement.

"I was in the shower. Want a drink?" She closed the door and nudged him forward. "Haven't you been here before?"

Duncan said, "No, I haven't, only to your office."

"But the new one, right?" It was familiar somehow, his reaction.

"Yes, it has the same view, higher up."

"That's it. What can I get you?"

As up in her office, Duncan looked first out and then around, and as up there he was surprised to look around and see nothing he recognized. He wondered what she had done with her fifty of their fifty-fifty. "Water," he answered.

They sat on porch chairs on the small balcony that overlooked a strip of boat slips. On the far side smaller boats were parked as at a shopping center, but on the near side were yachts tied end to end. "They look like circus elephants, except not wrinkled," Duncan commented, then said, "and not so cheap to feed. How much, would you guess?"

"Do you mean to feed?"

"To buy."

"Half what I paid for this place."

"Are you boasting?" He'd forgotten that this was a condominium.

"No, not at all." She laughed. "And this place doesn't float."

"It's beautiful."

"Yes," Jessica said. "Thank you."

Duncan looked back through the open sliding glass doors at the furniture that was all new, that was all hers. It hurt him that she had no souvenirs around of all the years they spent together, until Duncan forced himself to think of them, himself and Jessica, as college roommates. Would he hope to see felt pennants on the wall, and pictures of the Beatles? Wasn't the whole point that since their separation they'd grown up? "So did you have a decorator?"

"Does it seem that foreign to you?"

"Frankly, yes. I like it, really. Did you?"

She knew she would gross him out—the old expression came to mind unbidden—if she said yes. She was tempted. "No," she answered.

Duncan looked at Jessica now. "This is the real you, then." Tailored, well-coordinated, clean, not quite original, and not too welcoming, but nice. He liked her. That they had been married once and for so long seemed very odd. "I like the real you," Duncan said. He raised his glass.

As she leaned forward to touch hers to his what she replied with was, "How unexpected." It was just like her to be a commentator when the moment called for tears or "cheers!" or just the clink the glasses made. She recognized that. "Here's to you," she added.

"Thanks."

The little silence yielded when she asked, "Where were you flying in from?"

"Buffalo."

"Ah, Buffalo." She laughed and took a very big sip. "Buffalo, God. And your parents, they're OK?"

"They're fine. It's nice of you to ask."

"Well, no it's not, it's nothing. It's the very least." She sipped again, again laughed. She had not missed them, and wouldn't.

Duncan almost said from habit, "They both send their love." Instead he told the truth, "Dr. and Mrs. Raymond Jones regret that they're unable to accept the kind invitation of their son to wish his ex-wife all the best."

"Oh dear, no needlepointed pillow?" Jessica feigned hurt, then smiled. "And tell me, what did you do with the other one?"

"You mean I didn't tell you?" He put his glass on the table. "I

assumed it would have chipmunks on it or some other shit like
that, or strawberries at least, and it was wrapped in little chickie-
duckie paper, so I took the tag off and gave it to Mrs. Brown for
her new grandchild.''

"Good idea. How is she?"

"Fine, and she does ask about you every time I see her. She
still makes me brownies. Anyway, she made a big fuss, how I was
so thoughtful and it was wrapped up so beautifully and on and
on, and I thought, Great! Now I don't have to be pissed off at
Jessie for not taking it." He took a sip but indicated there was
more. "The next time I see Mrs. Brown she says how nice her
daughter thinks it is for me to give her kid a present, on and on
like that, how much the little girl adores it, on and on, but she
asks, all apologies, if J.K.J. means something special."

"J.K.J.?" It took a moment, then she burst with laughter and
cried, "J.K.J.! That's very funny. Then what?" She could not
stop laughing, though it wasn't quite *that* funny.

" 'Jessica Katzenburg Jones,' I said. The bitch my mother is, I
thought, the first time in her *life* she needlepoints initials!"

"No, you didn't say that! You said Jessica Katzenburg *Jones?*"
She had to hold her stomach, wipe her eyes.

He said, "I couldn't say that, no. So I said it means 'Just Keep
Jumpin'.' "

"Just Keep *Jumping?*" She could not contain herself.

"No, Jumpin'," Duncan deadpanned.

"How I wish I'd been there. I would have been on the sidewalk." It was true. Jessica said admiringly, "You're good,
though. Quick. You always were." It made her laugh again a
little, then was over. "Are you?"

"Jumpin'? No, I wouldn't say so," he admitted. "On the other
hand, I think I fell in love last night. And you?"

"No, no one. Some guy with a summer house on Martha's
Vineyard, but as you can see, I didn't go this weekend."

"Well, your real estate's not bad."

"You know what's bad? The sex." She meant in general.
He didn't want to touch it. So what else was new?

"I'm sick of having sex with men my age who've rediscovered it. They think of nothing else."

She'd cut her fingernails, he noticed. It seemed years ago, but wasn't two, when she had said her nails were too long and she wasn't going to risk them putting in and taking out her diaphragm, and they had not had sex again, not once.

"I mean, I *like* it, it's not that at all, but."

Maybe she was running too. Her calves were more athletic-looking.

"But you know, it's not the most important thing," she said.

"Sex isn't?" This was far too threatening. "What is, real estate?"

She frowned, and then she smiled. "At least it's real."

"OK, I shouldn't be sarcastic. I don't want to hear about your sex life, though."

"You brought it up."

"No, Jess, I said I think I fell in love last night. I never mentioned sex."

"It was implied," she countered.

"No, it wasn't."

"Do you mean you didn't have sex?"

"Well, I don't—"

"That's all I'm saying, see? You did, admit it."

"So what if I did?" This was absurd. Now they were going to have a fight about sex. So what else was new?

"So nothing."

"Let's not argue, Jessie."

"I don't want to hear about her."

"Fine." He meant it. "I'm sorry I brought it up."

She drained her glass. "Now let's get out of here and go do something."

Duncan hesitated. "Sure, OK. Like what?"

"Like dinner. Since you're all dressed up—you look nice by the way—why don't we try the Langoustine? It's good. I know the owner." Jessica did not say that he was the man on Martha's Vineyard. "I just mean we could get in without a reservation."

"Sure."

"So shall I call? You seem ambivalent."

"I'm not, no."

"You had plans already." It was not a question.

"No, I didn't, no, I don't. Go call." Why not. Or else go home and call and not have Nina answer?

# Seven

THE NEXT MORNING, Sunday, Duncan picked up breakfast for two and found his way to Amanda's. He would have called first, but he had called and called already all the previous day, and—this was the real reason—what if Nina answered now and said she wasn't free to or was not inclined to see him?

He looked in a kitchen window and saw the *Globe* spread out like a deck of cards for solitaire, then walked around to the front door and rang the doorbell. Since the flagstone path seemed to suggest to him he walk around the house to find her, Duncan did, and found her on her stomach on a beach towel on the grass and sound asleep. He knelt and touched her shoulder lightly. "Nina?"

She rolled over and said, he thought, blandly, "Hi," then checked her watch and asked him, "Did you hear her as you came through?" She was almost never wakened other than by Emilie.

"Her car is gone," he answered. One side of Nina's face and her thighs were textured by the towel, as if she'd been asleep a while. He wondered if he should have let her stay there. It did not appear she had been dreaming about him as her Prince Charming.

"Emilie," she said from deep inside a yawn. Again she checked her watch.

"What did you say?"

"No, Emilie, I said. Amanda's at the Cape."

That's what you said on Friday, he could say, but Duncan left Amanda out of it and answered only, "No, I didn't." He produced the shopping bag and offered it: warm bagels, salmon-colored cream cheese, fresh-squeezed orange juice, and coffee.

"Wonderful," said Nina, nodding yes it was. It was disorienting having multiple starts to the day—it wasn't nine yet, and she had been up at four and back asleep since seven-thirty—but this day seemed promising. She had assumed when she'd called Duncan and found him gone that he'd be away all weekend. Now he wasn't. She stood and shook out the towel, stooped to pick up the novel she'd been looking forward to beginning, called *Celestial Navigation.*

Inside, Nina went to respond to Emilie's summons and suggested to him that he get the water going. Duncan was reluctant to sit at the table with the *Globe,* since that was what had caused Amanda to appear the previous morning, so he walked around and looked at what he'd missed the night before that. He was also interested to see where they'd made love together, as if to prove it had happened. Frankly, he'd expected she would kiss him at least. He felt foolish having gone around announcing to the world he'd found his woman. Was this an example of what his mother meant by an overactive imagination? She had always said he had one.

Nina came down with the baby. Emilie's plump bare foot dangled, and because it looked to him like marzipan, he pretended to take a bite and made her giggle. "Here, why don't you hold her while I—" Nina suggested, intending to complete her sentence by unpacking Duncan's shopping bag. The kettle steamed. But she watched and took pleasure in the way Emilie smacked her pink lips at him, and the way he took it personally and kissed her half a dozen times, which made Emilie laugh and laugh. He hadn't held that many babies but knew from his brother's how important it was to keep moving. Nina complimented him on not having the impulse to talk goo-goo to her, which he answered saying no, he had the impulse, he was merely too self-conscious.

They sat in the dining room at gingham place mats that seemed girlish, as opposed to what he would have called Amanda's personality, based on their briefest meeting, when she'd functioned as a bouncer. "Out of curiosity," he said, "would you mind telling me what's going on here? I'm not all that comfortable for fear she'll show up and ask who said we could use her best china, and tell me to get out again."

"She won't," Nina assured him with a laugh. She chirped a birdsong, whistling single notes whose wind brought laughter— bellsong—from her baby's open mouth. "She loves this, watch," Nina said, turning Emilie onto her stomach. Emilie's legs were like beaters frothing air.

"Should I relax, then?" he had to ask.

Nina leaned across to him and kissed him warmly. "Yes, please do, and eat." The colors were her favorite golden pinks, and sun streamed in to light the painting it could be. What a day to wake up to, when at first she'd thought the Classifieds were her companion for the morning. "Did you go to Buffalo and come right back, or not go?"

So he told her, and about his telling Cathy all about her. He left out the parts that had to do with Jessica and let it seem he'd arrived back too late to call. "But where were you?" he asked, "I tried a dozen times." It wasn't true he'd worried, or not literally true, but he told her now, "I worried." Now it seemed to him he had.

"I'm sure she startled you," said Nina, "and she's sorry she was rude, she said to tell you. So am I."

"What was her problem?" Duncan took a bagel now and sliced it open.

"Panic. In the middle of the night, she said, she woke up needing reassurances she'd make it through the month. The night before, I gather, Jeremy, her parents, and her kids all said as a joke but not kidding they were glad that for a month she'd be her old self—daughter, mother, wife—and let it go at that. She didn't want to be that old self, for a month or anymore, but saw this as the first time she'd had to confront all the discomfort she was causing other people, people she loved, and she wondered what to do. The only person she could ask was on vacation."

"Who's that, you?" he questioned. What it sounded like was that she needed someone more—what was the word—available.

"Her doctor."

"That sounds better."

"But he's not around," said Nina, "so she tried me."

"And she found me."

"And she got upset. I tried to tell her that's what's good about it, her getting upset, but that it was her family she was mad at and she ought to deal with them. This took almost all morning to get her to admit, and by that time they were frantic, since she hadn't left a note. By then their houseguests had arrived, so I guess it got pretty crazy. She'd planned to just drive up and have breakfast with me and feel better about everything, then get back down there in time for the houseguests." Nina put a spot of cream cheese on her little finger and put it in Emilie's mouth. Emilie's need was more for the finger than the food, so Nina handed Emilie a teething ring and turned her over on her back again so she could work her gums. Communication was so simple when nonverbal, Nina noticed.

"So you mean it wasn't me?" It surely had been Duncan she had told to get out of her house.

"No, she just thought I would have told her if I'd met someone I would be having stay the night, so she was feeling left out, used. That's what she said, that I had used her."

"Used her house, you mean." He would have told Amanda how nice her house was if she had given him a minute.

"Anyway, you get the picture. There was lots of talking. She said what she felt when she saw you there at her kitchen table reading her newspaper—so I told her it was *your* newspaper, to be accurate—was envy. I'd just put my parents on a plane and there I was with a new baby and a man in a house for which I was not responsible. It seemed ideal."

"It did to me too," Duncan said.

"Me too." She smiled. That was the word—"ideal"—exactly.

She had spent the first hour of the morning on the Classifieds and come to the conclusion that, as she and Duncan had pretended with success, it *was* a desert island she'd been washed up on. And although it had been nice thinking she could use a man, it was clear now to Nina what she needed was a boat.

Now that her parents had gone on their way, the thought of spending August phoning out for groceries as the need arose, and walking to the country club to swim, or using the housekeeper as a baby-sitter if she had the urge to take up tennis or learn golf, made no sense to her. Now that she was on her own she wanted to get on with it and learn how to find Somerville and Brighton, which were listed in her price range. Where exactly was East Boston? She remembered wondering that the first time she searched the ads for an apartment, and was sorry to have made so little progress.

Maybe she could call her landlord? How should she deal with her longing for the old men on the stoops, and even for too many locks on every door, for sidewalk jump ropes, cooking smells of different ethnic origins, car radios you could hear with the windows closed, gay couples renewing their buildings alongside developers who'd found a way to turn a profit renovating for the low and middle income, even for the bugs and drugs of which there were far more than people, if she didn't call to ask if by some chance the guy who'd moved in after her had changed his mind? What was she doing in the suburbs? Now instead of just the problem of a job, she was both unemployed and homeless.

And why *were* there openings for Glaziers and Upholsterers,

Nite Broiler Chefs and Donut Makers, even Grassroots Activists, all with experience required, but not for someone who knew art? She was too old to be a Person Friday and too soft to be a Loan Collector, and Masseuse Trainee, well, everyone knew what they meant by that. No, she was serious. Even if she'd worked as much as possible on a free-lance basis, she had credits. For example, for a few months she had scouted for the Chase Manhattan Bank, whose art collection was the first and best in all the corporate world and was presided over by one of the bank's vice presidents, and they had bought an artist Nina had discovered on a houseboat in the Seine. Now was that nothing?

"Are you better than Amanda about the neighborhoods?" she asked. "All she knows are the streets she shops."

"Which one of you is moving?" Duncan asked her in return.

She had to laugh. What a thought. "I am," Nina answered. "Or at least I hope I am. Do you know where Jamaica Plain is?"

Duncan knew where everything was.

"Should I live there, is what I mean?"

"Sure, that's one place. You don't want to get a car, though, do you?"

"I don't want to get a driver's license. Tell me someplace I can walk to from my job." She laughed again, but cynically. "This is depressing."

After having done the dishes Duncan asked if Nina would like to go out to Walden Pond to see the markers for Thoreau's shack and to swim. He noticed that it was a theme, this fantasy of swimming with her, and he wondered what it was a metaphor for. One thing he had done at Club Med every chance he got was float in sky blue waters.

But she said no, she had to find a place she could move to at the end of the month. It was not what Duncan would have thought of as the way to spend the first of August, but he offered anyway to take her on a guided tour of all the Boston neighborhoods she could afford. He would have started with the job, then found the place to walk to from it, but it wasn't as if August was a good time for a job hunt either. What seemed premature to him, he knew, to Nina must seem overdue. He wondered if to Nina it was also inappropriate, this other fantasy of his that they would live together somehow. Maybe he should show her his place.

They began with the apartments she had circled and continued until they had made a circle of their own, and had found nothing. Duncan had been lucky, having paid his rent to the same landlord for ten years, and he was shocked to learn that for more money he could have a smaller, less safe, noisier, dark, dirty home sweet home, that he could pay rent to a landlord who would rather go to Small Claims Court than fix a faulty furnace, and, though there was legislation, that it obviously was cheaper than to replace lead paint to discriminate, and break another law, against prospective tenants with an infant who would grow into a toddler who might gnaw on windowsills and get brain damage. It made Duncan wish he were a columnist. No, it made Duncan wish he were litigious.

Nina was good-humored, in spite of the first-of-August heat and all the stairs and buckling Emilie into the infant seat and taking her out, putting her back, buckling up, as long as Emilie could cope. But when the baby snapped they both did, then they all did, and it seemed to Duncan and to Nina that, as Duncan put it, there was more erosion than there was soil to erode. They should remember that they didn't really even know each other except in the biblical sense, which was how he would have put it if he'd thought she would have the capacity to find it funny.

Emilie had tumbled from hysterics into baby slumber, but they'd had to pull off to the side of the road for Nina to nurse her. Nina had refused to let him drive with Emilie not in her car seat, and he found this, and he said so, quite extreme, since two miles off there was the Arnold Arboretum and a thousand lovely trees in whose shade they could sit and attempt to recover. Even Buffalo seemed better than a side street where they clipped their hedges Sunday afternoon with whining, buzzing, vibrating hedge trimmers on the ends of long electric cords, the sort of thing you would expect to send away for to Drawer G, Grand

Central Station, with a money order or a certified check. Duncan wondered why on earth he'd rushed away, when right then he'd be playing tennis if he'd stayed in Buffalo, and winning at it. Nina was successful putting Emilie back in the car seat after having nursed her to sleep, but neither one of them knew what to propose next. Duncan headed back to Weston.

And though this could have been enough to make Nina cry, what did make her cry was that Emilie woke up when she tried to remove the car seat. And Nina could not deal with the consequences. She blamed Jules-Jacques, she blamed Duncan and Amanda and Mark Otis, she blamed Mike and Vivian and Dulcie, she blamed everybody else for making it impossible for her to have a life and be a single parent both. She blamed herself for having tried.

When Duncan realized tears were streaming down her face like rain down windows, he regretted feeling he deserved somebody easier. He told her he would not be leaving, but since Emilie was screaming so, he doubted she'd have heard him. All he could do then was wait, was sit and wait.

While Nina sat and rocked Emilie, milk rushed to her breasts unbidden and leaked out in two wet discs the size of cocktail coasters. Nina offered herself to her daughter, but Emilie wasn't hungry. Nina in the meantime couldn't stop her tears, not even after Emilie's peaked and subsided and the only other sound was the crunch of the rocking chair. Nina imagined telling Duncan, as if he were interested, as if he would be even *there*, about the way she rests and mutters, sort of chants—her hands in little fists, though—and then suddenly, as if she were an, I don't know, an airplane taking off, she's airborne and at peace. Her hands come open, they unfurl like ferns, and there's no tension in her body anymore; the only motion's in her chin. It quivers, she imagined telling Duncan. But her own did too. She felt not only just unequal to the task, she felt the task had already consumed her and she was like Jonah in its belly.

Duncan had joked earlier, with Emilie up from her first nap of the day at nine, that she must be on European time. An awkward silence followed in which Duncan seemed to have remembered something about Paris, though they'd not discussed Emilie's father beyond Nina's mention at the *Globe* that it was a long story. She had not known what to say then, and now in her feeling sorry for herself it seemed enough to make her think Amanda might have something there. She'd joked that Nina should be glad she wasn't Catholic, because she'd have to consider paying for her sins as a good explanation of what happened in her life; and she was kidding—she did not believe it either—but what of it? It made sense to Nina now to believe in conspiracy instead of chance. You couldn't prove it either way.

But why was everybody *joking* all the time? Was it so funny? Nina's parents had exhausted her with their ability to find fault, whether or not they had used it, and in her relief at their departure she'd let her defenses down. And maybe she was lucky it was Duncan she had gone to bed with, not some salesman, but that hardly worked for her as consolation. She had been about to say a dozen times she thought she loved him.

Putting Emilie into the crib, Nina knew she would sleep too for that hour she wished could be longer. First, though, she went downstairs for ice water and was not surprised to see him sitting at the kitchen table. It seemed every time she came around the corner there was either Duncan or Amanda waiting, wanting something. Before she could ask him, "Now what?" Duncan asked how he could help her.

"Sleep," she answered, "let me sleep when she wakes up next. Baby-sit, please." It seemed such a simple answer to a very simple question, but as a solution to a problem it was radical. She showed him how and what to try and filled a bottle for him to coax Emilie to take, and then she took two aspirins and went to Amanda's room and drew the heavy curtains. In the artificial night she slept forever.

Evening brought her back reconstituted, and when Nina came around the corner this time she stopped in the doorway to admire his work. Her daughter's entertainment was the mirror he had brought in from the dining room and propped up so that Emilie could watch herself dance in her Jolly-Jump-Up to invigorating music from the radio that was Nina's companion on another station and at lesser volume.

Duncan held the empty bottle up because it was a trophy he had worked to win. "We went for a long walk," he said. "I changed her diaper three times. She got up a little after four. She ate some applesauce like you suggested, and I hope it's all right that I gave her ice cream, since she loved it. And a bath. I just used Joy here in the sink for bubbles, which she liked, because I looked upstairs and couldn't find the bubble bath." His nieces never took a bath that wasn't bubbled by some beads or crystals he had given one of them for Christmas.

"No, she's never had one," Nina said.

"No? Well I hope—"

"No, no, it's fine, it's just, I never thought to," she admitted, "and I never would have thought of Joy." How else, she wondered, had she been neglectful? But the answer was too obvious.

Duncan was grinning, thinking of *The Joy of Sex*, imagining her saying that she never would have thought of joy, of sex. He wondered how soon they'd be back again to where they were on Friday night. At this time then they were already in the tower and had been cleared for takeoff.

It was then that Emilie lost interest in the Jolly-Jump-Up and without transition decomposed from a whole being to a mere sum of her parts. Nina had been about to take three steps to Duncan and, in romance terminology and style, take him into her arms and press her lips to his, and he could tell this. When she asked him, "You don't have to leave yet, do you?" he said, "No," and added, "not at all," and meant it.

Nina retrieved Emilie and, soothing her, suggested also, soothing him, that after she nursed Emilie to sleep she get the teenager from next door to come do her homework here while they went out for dinner. They'd have to be back early because it was a school night, but, and, if he wanted—Nina laughed at herself for her if, and, but—he could consider staying over.

The teenager came, glad for the job, and they took off like rockets. In the car they both felt the exhilaration of a team that narrowly escapes a loss and turns the game around to win. The fans were going wild in their enthusiasm. At a stop sign they reached for each other and kissed, celebrating their persistence. At a traffic light they kissed again and filled each other's mouths, and had to be told by the car behind them that the light had changed. They both felt that if it were not for seat belts they would, as the Beatles once suggested in a lyric, do it in the road.

Instead they went to his apartment and got out of traffic and their clothes. She didn't even seem to want to look around, as if she'd been in Duncan's bed a hundred times in her imagination and knew absolutely where she was and why. She hadn't been so eager since, as they say, she could not remember when. From Duncan's point of view, the sleep had made her so responsive, so *awake* it seemed like morning.

Since the summer evening had dressed them both in a coat of perspiration, after their gymnastics they lay on their backs to feel the air along their lengths and let their breathing be less quick, and Nina's stomach rumbled like a storm approaching. She smiled and said, "Do you think we'll ever eat? It's twice now we've done this for dinner." She rolled to face Duncan and traced on his chest a question mark.

"What was the question?" All he was aware of was his relaxation and the shadow on the ceiling made by philodendron leaves illuminated from below, and thinking it a nice idea to make love in a room whose light source was a grow lamp.

"Aren't you hungry, was the question." Nina traced another, larger question mark. She'd eaten nothing since their bagels that midmorning.

"No," said Duncan, sitting up and looking down at Nina and not wanting to get out of bed, "but I'll bring something." Had he eaten all the brownies?

"No, I'll help." She came to her knees and stroked Duncan as involuntarily as if he were a puppy squirming for attention.

"That's not helping," Duncan warned her, rocking back and bringing Nina with him. He had learned about her that in kissing, Nina talked and told him without speaking words enough to make him certain she was kissing *him* and not her baby's phantom father, not some mystery guest whose true identity he could intuit but knew not enough to name, not any other man but him. Because he thought that she was telling him she loved him, he tried telling her the same thing.

Finally Nina rolled off to one side and took a deep breath and let it go slowly. She was wondering how it was—she knew, but she meant how it could be possible—that she had come here by way of her life in Paris. Then she wondered if they could have met without her having gone to all the trouble of having a baby. Where had Duncan been her whole life, was the question; or was it instead the case that Nina-before-Emilie was not the Nina he'd have wanted? She tried to imagine Duncan before whatever it was that made him what he was, and couldn't.

He was very lightly touching Nina's breasts. When she had wakened from her sleep they had been firm as fruit and decorated with a network of blue veins that made them seem to be batiked, and they were full of the milk Emilie had taken off to her sleep. In this pale light, without knowing what he knew, he never would have guessed the secret life they led, the tidal pools they really were. Hers made the breasts displayed at Club Med seem to be of simple flesh, of very modest intellect, of minimal ambition, very little interest. Duncan smiled. He knew that he was rationalizing. What was he supposed to do, though, with the fact that it confused him, bothered him that this, her past, was current. Duncan was afraid it was unfinished.

"You asked me this morning, indirectly," began Nina, "to tell you about her father." Nina took his hand and held it. "Do you want to hear?"

He had to say yes, even though he'd pictured it quite differently, in daylight, dressed and able to walk off if need be. Since his question was What made you want to have his baby?—which he didn't want to know but had to—was he ready? Duncan said, "Yes."

"I first met Jules-Jacques my junior year, in Paris," she began the story, "and I thought of staying. He was my initiation sexually and, as I learned, but later—it took me a long time after he wrote to say he was getting married to let anyone get close—it was miraculous I hadn't gotten pregnant. I spent the next fourteen years, like any convert, overarmed, and transferred all I hadn't known about the art of contraception into its deliberate practice. I felt at the time it was my one free throw and compensation for my hurt at his having rejected me, but that I mustn't ever think I'd get another. Why I'm saying all this is to let you know that it was not an accident that I got pregnant, even though it might have been an accident the countless times that junior year when I did not." She shifted off her side onto her stomach but kept looking into Duncan's face.

"And all that time passed like a movie from the forties, months and years like pages of a calendar the wind disperses. I'd been back in Paris for a long time, years, and things were fine. One day it wasn't that they weren't fine, but something was different. For six months or so I'd been in a relationship with someone with whom I could not see spending my next birthday, I could not see telling him how I felt, and I couldn't see him understanding if I could have told him. It was nothing personal in some ways, only that I needed some perspective on my life. I probably was feeling that I'd forfeited what chance I'd had to have a baby, and that Jules-Jacques represented one last opportunity, but not that I knew at the time. All I knew then, I thought, was that if I could see what might have happened to my life if I had not gone on with it the way I did, I wouldn't worry anymore about the future or the past. I wouldn't worry anymore, I thought." She laughed and didn't interrupt herself. She turned onto her back and hoped that this would make her comfortable.

"My parents' marriage was too close, especially out in the

world, where Dulcie and I were so different and apart from life around us. Now there's slack between them, but there wasn't when I was a girl and coming in a distant fourth after my mother or my father, their ideals, and third, my sister, who was younger and more cheerful and was better suited to them. Anyway,''— she tried to hurry—"I was never much aware of wanting to get married and/or have a family. I would not have minded finding someone with whom I could be as close as they were, but if I had found that person I would not have been inclined to have a child who would have had a life like mine. This is just background.''

Duncan nodded.

"There's so much to say." She seemed lost.

"What about what it was like to see him again?" Not that Duncan couldn't guess. He'd had the same experience at Logan Airport.

"Very sweet," she answered. "He was waiting for me one day and he stayed for three, and that time it was pure recovery. After that, though, it grew harder in both senses, difficult and dense— *c'est dur*, one or the other of us said so many times—but still we had five years together.'' She touched Duncan's face, and when he kissed her fingers she felt better. "One day it was true," she said, "it was too hard." She wished he'd hold her, knew he wouldn't. This part was the answer to the question he'd asked.

"Maybe I can tell it this way," Nina tried. "Once when my parents lived in Mombasa and I was visiting them, I was sitting in a café and struck up a conversation with some people who were touring, kids. I had just finished Wellesley and had gone to Kenya on my way to London, where I had a scholarship to study art. The group was French, and we were speaking French, and this guy from another table heard us and came over. He was French too, off a sailboat. In a while the group got up to leave, and they exchanged addresses, promising to rendezvous in Paris. He and I stayed talking, and we talked for, I don't know, ten hours or something. The next morning he was leaving, sailing up, imagine this, into the Gulf of Aden, through the Red Sea to Suez and Port Said, into the Mediterranean, and back to

France." Nina knew how to get around the world by map, without one, and she didn't mind giving her parents credit for that.

Duncan couldn't picture it. In Buffalo, geography meant New York State. He might not have known where Mombasa was if she had not said Kenya—he would have guessed Tanzania—but the more important point was, where was *Nina* going with this, not the sailor. He was restless and smiled a neutral smile to indicate that sounded like some trip.

"He said," Nina explained, "it was absurd for him to give out his address to all those people and then not to me, when I'm the one he'd like one day to see again. We knew we wouldn't—at that point I'd vowed I'd never go to Paris, ever—but I got his point. He wrote it down and gave it to me. Do you see what I'm about to tell you?"

"Tell me."

"With Jules-Jacques I had that feeling. The whole world was filled with people,"—now it sounded flimsy and capricious—"whereas here was one I would remember. If I were to have a child, Jules-Jacques seemed somehow worthier than all the others I had met, or anyone I didn't know yet." Nina left a little space for silence. "I'm not saying," she continued, "that a baby was what I was after, merely that if I were one day going to open myself to the possibility it would be quite absurd to do it with someone who wasn't as important in my life. Do you see what I'm trying to say?" What she meant was Emilie was, in the good-old old-fashioned sense, a love child who had come not as an answer to a question, but rather as a statement of fact. Emilie was word made flesh, was the fact of a durable, frustrated love but testimony that this love had someplace to go. Emilie was and would always be the product of a union.

Duncan said, "I see, I think, although I don't agree that an address equals a baby, A, or B, see why you thought you wouldn't—or is this self-serving?—find—"

"Find you?"

"Well, yes. Find me. Why not?"

"I hadn't, had I? What I'd found was someone I'd already

loved once. At the time that seemed terrific, even if more than a dozen years had intervened and he was now somebody's husband and the father of four children."

Duncan wondered if this was good news or bad. For him, he meant. He found it shocking, never himself having had an affair with a married woman. Did he want to be with someone who had done that for five years? He sounded scared when he said, "Jesus."

"No, it's different. Life is not so linear there as it is here, not so one-dimensional." Did she sound like a travel agent?

"So they don't say things like, 'If his marriage had been good, he never would have been there for you?' What *do* they say? What's the two-dimensional way?" Obviously Duncan was identifying with the wife. What was the French word for "rejection," Duncan wondered.

"No, they don't. In fact his marriage was a good one."

"But your conscience bothered you," Duncan suggested.

"No."

"You mean it worked? You were one big happy extended family?"

"No—don't be sarcastic—no, it had its problems. Basically it worked *and* had its problems."

Like life, he would have said, but that would have been sarcastic. Now he was identifying with Jules-Jacques. "What was the reason, then, you left him?"

Nina sat up. "You're not listening. This is a sad story, Duncan. You act as if it's about you."

"Mine's sad too. They all are." God, how he wished he had never asked.

"So one day, one bright morning fifty-one weeks ago, Jules-Jacques and I finished breakfast—it was Sunday, like today, and August, like today is, just—and we made love although there wasn't really time, and he drove partway to Rouen." She said this in a whisper, almost. "And he died."

He didn't think he'd heard her say that. "And he *died?*" he asked.

"He was killed. He was speeding. Everyone was." Nina took in a deep breath, and they both heard it tremble out.

Unlike his own, about divorce, hers was a story about life and death, and Duncan wanted to say he would not presume again about her, ever. Now he understood the saddest look that flickered on her face when Emilie did something precious. It was one thing being left by someone who lived across town and with whom it was possible to terminate things over time, but she'd been left behind in life by a man who'd gone on to die. This was the big time. Duncan felt inadequate to Nina and the task he had of saying something. "I'm so sorry," was what he said. It was all there was to say and was enough.

And in a moment he dared touch her on the hand. "I used to think," she said in that still quiet voice, "that I was haunted as a house is by the ghost, not of Jules-Jacques, but of our love, haunted all those years. I used that ghost as an excuse that kept me from having to make attachments to a place or person. No belongings. Emilie now keeps that love from being that ghost. Emilie is living proof the love existed, still exists. I don't feel haunted anymore, I feel attached, alive." She shivered even in the evening heat. He placed his warm hand on her back as if to cover up the tracks, and she said, "Thank you," formally, as for a service rendered.

What he then said was, "I know who you mean when you say you feel attached is Emilie, but—"

Nina interrupted with, "No, bigger. More."

"But my attachment is to you." He'd made his own share of excuses over the years.

"What I mean by more is *living.*" If it was true less is more, what did that make more? Certainly not less.

"Did you hear what I just said?" Duncan asked.

"And loving," Nina finished.

"Yes, I guess you did."

"You said you love me. That's what I heard." Nina took another breath that this time didn't flutter out. "I said the same thing to you."

Duncan hadn't been in love in years, he'd been reminded just the day before, and here was love at fourth sight—first at the French Library, then at the *Globe*, third at the airport, and now fourth here—here and now. He hadn't been in love in years, or really, he'd say, in fact, ever.

# Part III

# Eight

BY LABOR DAY, Nina had joined the workers of the world. Through someone who knew someone Duncan knew at the Museum of Fine Arts, she'd been given an interview and then the job as an assistant curator for contemporary paintings. She had followed Duncan's wisdom in first getting that and then the place, and sure enough, once she knew where she'd have to get to every morning it was clear which neighborhood she ought to live in. She was used to cultures where the housing market was more difficult than jobs were, she'd explained, although she was smart to have found a place before the student hoards arrived to start school in order not to prove her point. She was in the middle of Northeastern University, which made her feel young and inquiring in addition to providing baby-sitters.

She had borrowed from Amanda the crib and the changing table she had found to come in handy during her month out in Weston, and, over the more than two months since, she'd bought enough more to avoid appearing to live in a place that was robbed only moments earlier. The paintings she'd kept rolled up off their stretchers in her South End place had been reconstituted and hung all around and brought life and fond recollection rather than the painful memories Nina had been afraid of. She was so at home in Boston, now that she was on her own and as they say adjusting nicely, she'd bought goldfish and at a suburban yard sale an enormous tank with a filtration system and a castle carved of coral. Emilie, she vowed, as she and Dulcie never were allowed because it was bourgeois, would have pets.

Nine months old now, Emilie spent workday mornings at home being "grandmothered" by one of Nina's older neighbors, and her afternoons in daycare learning with her peers how to applaud herself and vocalize the pleasure she took in the discovery of locomotion, feeding, music, toys, and other people. The only bugs in the new apartment were those viruses she caught with this her first daily exposure to the world at large, but they lived not far from the office of the pediatrician Nina trusted absolutely because she had been on duty during Emilie's birth and had been the one to say, "You have a daughter."

And Duncan had been encouraging in every way, including the aquarium, and they had spent an autumn that was as bright in its coloration as the land was in its trees. They'd been to Walden Pond and Salem, reading aloud to each other from Thoreau and Hawthorne, and they'd been whale watching, reading Melville. They had climbed Mount Washington, although by car—and Duncan had bought Emilie a tiny T-shirt that said the same thing as did the bumper sticker he did not buy: THIS CAR CLIMBED MT. WASHINGTON—and then Mount Mansfield, by gondola. They went out to Provincetown to roam the dunes Eugene O'Neill had and were pilgrims to the former site of Henry Beston's *Outermost House* on the Great Beach of Cape Cod. They'd come to count on one another four nights out of seven, and they seemed only to benefit from regulation. Two weekday nights he would come from work to her place and give Emilie a bath and a warm bottle before putting her to sleep, while Nina cooked; on weekends they would leave from his place for their outings, Emilie content to travel in the backpack and be bathed when they returned in Duncan's tub and put to bed with Nina's lullaby in a crib he had borrowed, while he cooked. It was such a stable arrangement, Nina had a standing date with a Northeastern student who was happy for a place to study, leaving Nina free after the baby was asleep to see a foreign film, and once a week she went to bed at eight and slept eleven hours, which was a consolation prize for being forty and having a baby and a full-time job. Their time apart was useful to them. He had bought a season ticket to the Celtics for the first time in fourteen years.

Now, though, coming up was a real separation for the five-day-trip Nina and Emilie were taking to New Mexico to visit Dulcie. How could she have turned down Dulcie's invitation when it was accompanied by a free airline ticket made available by Dulcie's contacts, and when leaving Tuesday and returning Sunday only took a day's vacation because Thursday was Thanksgiving and she had been given off either the next day or December 24 four Fridays later? Dulcie hadn't yet met Emilie, who was only a first trimester fetus when last Nina and her younger sister were together, and it ought to be well worth-while, reasoned Nina, even to upset the patterns to which she and recently the baby seemed to have adjusted. She had not been anywhere by plane since coming on from Paris pregnant—airsick—and alone, with all she owned aboard in baggage, and this trip would be a big improvement at least over that one.

Nina's phone rang. It was Duncan. "I'm at Newark Airport and about to take off," he explained the change in plans, "so I can meet you now at your place." This meant they would have some time before her plane left, rather than the plan they'd made to rendezvous at Logan as if they were tag-team relay racers. Since he'd had to be in New York all the previous day and night and out at Princeton early on that Tuesday morning to interview Carlos Fuentes, it was going to be a week they'd be apart. "I miss you," he gave as his reason. He had wished they'd spend this family holiday, their first, together as a family, not for him to be in New York, her in Boston, her in Santa Fe, and him by default back in Buffalo. What Duncan loved about their life was that there wasn't anything abrupt about it. This plan of hers to go to New Mexico had seemed to him to come from nowhere.

"I miss you too," Nina told him. "How was Fuentes?"

"Fuentes went well, but the other story of another afternoon in the life of a former Boston TV anchor gone to put his polish on the apple isn't necessary. I spent all of yesterday that way, a day arranged to look both hectic and exciting—you know how New Yorkers live—and I'm exhausted. There's nothing there anyway." It seemed to Duncan the lead story at six and eleven, arson, had been perpetrated by the network for the news team, wrapped and tied up like a thigh bone for a special client's pet. There was no substance there, and he'd told Bic this the day Bic assigned it.

"That's good news for us," said Nina cheerfully. She had been looking forward to the cocktail tower they'd not been back to since the time he missed his plane to Buffalo, but not more than she would a chance to reassure him. He seemed so uneasy, Nina wondered if there weren't more to it than that she and Emilie were buckling up and taking off into the dark. These late November days it got dark earlier and earlier, but still.

"How's Emilie?"

"She didn't sleep that well. I hope she's not getting a cold."

He realized his hopes were for an ear infection in time to prevent their flight, and he felt mean. "I hope she'll be OK to travel," he politely lied.

"She will be, although I remember having awful earaches as a child when we would fly." Nina was still surprised that after all those years of dreading getting seated on a long flight near a woman with a baby, that's who she was.

Duncan said, "They pressurize the cabins now."

She laughed. She'd told him how they'd flown with goats and chickens in wood cages in the aisles, and how the runways would have to be cleared of bony livestock that would graze the airfields. "What time will you get to my place?" Maybe they were both uneasy.

"Soon. In fact I better go, they're calling my flight." He was calling from a pay phone near the gift shop and could see they had for sale a T-shirt with, in his opinion, a preposterous slogan. It said, I ♥ NEWARK.

She got home enough before him to insert her diaphragm, it being clear the purpose of the change in plans was conjugal, for which she was as glad as he was, and put its flat plastic box into the open toiletries case she'd left on the bathroom counter to be packed at the last moment. It struck Nina as ironic that she'd be retrieving it in Santa Fe and therefore that it would be with her on this visit after all, when she'd made the point to herself that this was to have been the first time in the relevant parts of her adult life that she'd leave home without it, by design.

He had two T-shirts in his briefcase, souvenirs of Logan Airport, he said were for them to wear in Santa Fe to reassure him. I ♥ BOSTON was their message.

"I love Duncan," Nina told him reassuringly.

He'd had a night of nightmares in which she had disappeared a dozen times, and he had not been able to stop thinking of what his friend Dan had told him once. The woman Dan lived with had been killed in a plane crash, and he'd said he never would recover from his regret that they'd not made love both more and better and, specifically, that the last time before her death he'd met his own needs more than hers. Dan said he wished he'd memorized her like a poem he could recite his whole life long. Already Duncan felt that heat behind his eyes the way he did when he might cry. "I'm memorizing you," said Duncan as he kissed her.

"That's good," Nina answered him, "since 'memorize' means 'learn by heart.' "

A plane crash! "Come with me," he said and led her to her mattress, "we need to be closer. I've missed you so much I don't think I can make it five more days." He smiled to let her know he wasn't asking her to cancel her plane reservations, but how happy he'd be if it happened that she didn't make it on in time. It didn't make sense to be threatened by a visit to her sister.

"I know, me too," she said, and she took his glasses and his watch off, and her own watch and the gypsy earrings she was wearing.

Duncan grew impatient with the buckle of her belt and said, "It's faster if—" and so undid his own. It was less ceremonial, but this day, as if he'd been burned, his body needed the balm of her nakedness more than it did the pleasure of uncovering her. That it was her sister she was visiting was not the problem.

Nina hurried for his sake and rushed her skirt off, shrugged her shirt off, popped the latch on her bra, opening it like a window. She had lost that fluid and was thinner, now that she'd weaned Emilie completely. Her breasts were her own again, now his.

"But I'm afraid I'll lose you," he admitted. He meant either that she'd die or that she'd stay in Santa Fe, which didn't seem that different to him as disasters go.

"You won't." She thought he meant she'd fall in love with someone else and tried to kiss him better than she ever had kissed anyone, or could.

"I know. I'm still afraid."

She kissed him more.

"What if you get out there and find how small and boring Boston is? What if our life seems too routine, so you decide to get a horse?" What wasn't possible, if this was?

"How would I get a horse back here, on a bus?" Now he was only flirting with her, Nina thought, so she would too.

"That's what I mean, you wouldn't *come* back. It will all be too exotic out there, so available and independent, all that Western restlessness." Or was he thinking of his cousin on the dude ranch riding off into the sunset with her cowboy of a husband in his snake boots?

"Kiss me," she said, "you're not kissing me."

He did.

"That's better."

He would never understand why Jules-Jacques didn't leave his wife to marry Nina, all those years. He'd never understand a setup that complex, or tolerate it in his own life. Luckily for him, however, and this was what Nina told him whenever he brought it up, he wasn't Jules-Jacques.

"What's the matter?"

He admitted to wishing insanely Emilie were his child and told Nina of the picture on the anchorman's desk at the TV station in New York that showed a woman and a child on a boat in foul-weather gear. Their faces shone out of the yellow oil-cloth like a pair of headlights in the night, but he had noticed only how the child's face was an exact copy of his father's, and he'd wished that Emilie looked just like him. He was afraid of losing her too.

"Hold me," Nina told him.

He did. "All I mean is that I love her, and I love you."

"Tell me," she said.

He did that too. And were she to die that evening in the plane crash, his grief would have to take other forms than a regret that in their last time making love he'd met his own needs more than hers. He knew she had been satisfied because she said so.

When it was time to get Emilie from daycare, Duncan said he'd like to do it. He got up and went into the bathroom while she lay there feeling fortunate. He came back, and she watched him dress and wondered what was wrong. He sat on the edge of the mattress putting on his socks, and when she touched his back he straightened it to pull it from her reach. It seemed an adolescent gesture of hurt feelings, so she asked, "What?"

"I'm quite the convenience, aren't I?" He was working on his laces.

Nina couldn't think what to say. "Say more," she asked.

"Pick up Emilie and take you to the airport, be there when you come in Sunday, bring you back here." Duncan turned to face her now. He was all dressed. "I never asked, although I've been preoccupied by it and still am, if we have a policy for or against sex with someone else. I decided that for the—quote—good of the relationship, in spite of my fears, evident as I've just made them to you, I would trust you wouldn't."

"I won't," Nina said.

"No, you *might*, is I gather what the truth is. Why don't you admit you might be?"

"Having sex with someone else? Because I won't be." She was slow with this transition, but now she could feel some anger. "What's the point here? Are you just expressing fears, or are you making accusations?" She was running out of patience.

" 'Just' expressing fears—thanks for your condescension—so why not admit you might be?" It seemed further proof she might be that she had, in fact, with him. "Is someone you know going to be there, or will you see what you can find at the airport?" She'd found him and brought him home, no questions asked.

Nina sat up now. "What the hell are you trying to do? It's insulting enough that you've brought it up, but since you have, and gotten me to tell you I will not be having sex with anyone— not the copilot, not a traveling salesman, not my sister's boyfriend, not the Indian chief—why do you refuse to believe me? Why don't you believe me, Duncan?"

"How can I *believe* you," he said with all the authority of an attorney prosecuting, "when the only thing you've packed in there is, not shampoo or toothpaste, is your *diaphragm!*"

"My diaphragm case—"

"How am I supposed to feel when I see that?"

"It's just the case." She turned away to keep from smiling. This one was ridiculous, thank God, but Duncan didn't seem to know it yet. "I'm wearing it, it's just the case for when I take it out." She laughed now with relief that this one turned out to be simple. "Which I can't do for at least six hours." Now she touched him and he didn't pull away. "As you know. Right?" She touched his face and leaned toward him.

"Yes, right, I know that," he affirmed, "at least six hours." He put his arms around her, and the tension streamed from him like tears. "Do you think this may be a touchy subject?" he asked with a laugh. "Two things I just can't do are sharing and good-byes."

She fogged the lenses of his glasses with her breath, to tease him. "So who told you that this was goodbye? It could be only the beginning."

"Just don't tell me if it's over, please don't tell me. And don't tell me if I've shared you."

Nina knew he wasn't either serious or kidding, but was in between. "And why don't you stop counting on it?" she asked, trying for the same tone.

Duncan stopped and thought. "All right," he said quite seriously, "I will."

"So let's exchange phone numbers, then, OK?" Now she was giddy, reaching for her address book and looking up the penciled entry that was Dulcie—Dulcie started out in ink but moved too often, and now Nina just erased her every eighteen months or so—and telling Duncan, "I don't know exactly where she'll have us staying, or, frankly, whose number this is, since somebody answers half the time in Spanish and appears to know no English."

"Don't call me, in other words, I'll call you?" He put the small piece of paper in the pocket of his shirt and smiled.

"I'll let you know tonight, I mean." She was ready to write his parents' number on her ticket folder as proof that she wouldn't lose it, then decided she may as well write it in her address book, in ink. She knew he knew it by heart. She'd been shocked to realize his parents' number was the same now as it was when he was three and they moved into this same house, and that he still remembered the phone numbers of the parents of selected friends whom he'd not seen for twenty years except at weddings but with whom he had played soldiers every schoolday afternoon through the fifth grade.

He gave Nina the number and immediately looked forward to her calling. Otherwise the weekend loomed like a house with too many rooms and too few lamps.

From the gate, Nina and Emilie on board and the plane having backed off from the terminal, Duncan went to the cocktail
lounge up in the tower for a drink and to make sure Nina's plane
didn't crash on takeoff. He felt stupid and pathetic—he would
have said pathological, but no, he knew he wasn't that bad off,
yet—for his fear that Nina wouldn't want to come back to him
and their life together. If he weren't so insecure, by which he
meant if he had not been left already by his ex-wife, he would
surely have been able to see Nina off and not make her feel
guilty that she had a sister with an airline ticket. He would not
have had to ask at the last moment why it was that Dulcie hadn't
used the ticket to come East, meet Emilie, and have Thanksgiving. Nina hadn't had an answer, but her eyes had filled with tears
of, he thought, probably, frustration. He'd felt stupid and pathetic.

From the airport he went to the *Globe* to write the story of the
TV anchor he could tune up the next morning, and to transcribe
notes from having breakfasted with Carlos Fuentes. It was typical that though the story he could write on Fuentes would be
both fun and substantial, what he had a deadline on was something on the pretty face who didn't even write his own material,
whose day was jam-packed but seemed empty when compared
with one hour's lecture to a room jam-packed with Princeton
undergraduates. The Carlos Fuentes idea was his own, the other
Bic's, who said correctly that Thanksgiving was a day for television for most people.

Mark Otis stopped by Duncan's desk and elicited from him a
toneless "Hi." Duncan was not in the mood at all to see Mark,
although involuntarily he'd come to mind just now at Logan
when it came to Duncan that Nina and Emilie could well have
left for Santa Fe without his even knowing of it. Without Mark to
take the picture that brought them together sympathetically,
and gave them something they could work with when they met
again for good, she'd simply be the woman with the magazine
whose wraparound had fanned wide open as he helped her out

the door of the French Library one day. It made him feel resentful that he should feel grateful to Mark Otis.

Mark picked up the small framed photograph on Duncan's desk, of Nina holding Emilie, who didn't look the slightest bit like Duncan. Neither one of them was in foul-weather gear. "I heard you're dating her now," Mark said, recognizing Nina, though the baby had changed.

Duncan wouldn't call it dating, which he hadn't done since college. "How old are you, Otis?"

"What's that got to do with anything?"

"Just curious."

"I'm twenty-five."

"That makes you six the day John Kennedy was killed, and only three at his election." On page one of that day's *Globe* was a Mark Otis photograph taken the day before that showed a group of Brookline schoolchildren placing a wreath of flowers on the porch of the plain clapboard house that was Kennedy's birthplace. The kids were of course too young to understand the loss, but what had struck him was the teacher's little-girl looks and the fact that she would have to be too young too. As was Otis. Duncan wondered what emotional content the picture had and would have asked except, he thought, the photo caption said it all: "Marking the anniversary of JFK's death, Brookline schoolchildren and their teacher, Joanne O'Hara of Jamaica Plain, place a wreath at the birthplace of the slain president, as part of a unit on presidents."

"So?"

Duncan answered, "Nothing. No, I like your picture, Otis." He took back the snapshot Mark was holding and said, "But it's not your business, is it, who I'm dating?" If he were on top of things he'd have said *whom.*

"You think I give a shit, Jones, *who* you're dating?" Mark's long day was showing on him all around his eyes, and he was suddenly not boyish. He'd spent hours that day trying to get Bic to run his pictures for tomorrow on page 1, not where the story was continued, even if it was a whole-page spread inside. He'd been upset when Bic had said the story was more serious without the pictures. Duncan's story, to which Mark had been assigned, was black and white about the city's failure to attempt to solve the racial crisis.

Duncan wanted to ignore Mark, so he did. He took his notebook from his jacket pocket and logged on to his word processor. He told Mark what was obvious, "I've got to work," and wrote a paragraph about the newscaster's arrival at the station in a company-driven Chrysler.

"Screw you, Jones." Mark had been planning to tell Duncan Bic had put him on page 1 above the fold, but screw him. Duncan could come in to work the next day and find it out for himself. Mark hadn't read the story, and now he decided that he wouldn't. He crossed behind Duncan's desk and walked the corridor that went eventually to the real world.

When Duncan was again alone he looked at Nina and Emilie in their hammock in the snapshot he had taken in their living room not all that long ago, the hammock being one of the new household items she had bought to try and make a house a home. It *was* a home. And it was in that hammock after dinner one night, listening to Tina Turner, that she'd asked her mother's question—how can it be that the only state to go for George McGovern against Nixon also goes for segregation?—and inspired him to ask questions of his own. He should have asked Mark, Duncan guessed now that he was reminded of it, if he'd finished up the pictures for this story. He had turned it in to Bic on Friday, but for having been in New York had missed the reaction. Duncan hoped that Bic agreed it was his best work in a long time.

For the last big story he'd done on this subject, profiles of the children caught in cross fire during the Boston busing emergency, he had read sociology and child development. But for this story he'd done history. This time Duncan thought he ought to know the model on which Boston's institutions had been built.

And what he'd found was no surprise: that Boston's tone was

set, and not since varied, by the Puritans, whose Christianity came from the law-and-order Ten Commandments, as opposed, say, to the Sermon on the Mount. The "Thou Shalt Nots" contrasted very interestingly with the Sermon on the Mount, where the intent of Jesus was not to replace the Law but rather to complete it, to explore the mercy in it. Puritans were men of minds, not hearts and minds, and men of means not prone to giving except to their institutions. They were preachers; they were statesmen; they were tireless in setting the good example and assuming space in heaven as reward. They intermarried, concentrating their genetic assets in the sons who were no longer named for saints, instead for forebears.

Was it a surprise, then, that the colony they founded prospered? Was it any wonder that they never would do well with strangers?

What Duncan interpreted from what he read was that the Puritans equipped themselves with built-in colanders for draining off the cooking water, which was good, as well as juices, which removed from certain foods not just the pleasure but the purpose. Harvard was their best creation. Then, as now, mind triumphed over matter there, and Harvard College, then as now, fulfilled its charter when it made all those who hadn't gone there feel inadequate. But matter was the stuff of life, and wasn't it first Harvard's loss, and then the city's and the country's, that just 2 percent of Harvard's full-time faculty was black?

But then it wasn't Harvard's *fault* exactly; Harvard was simply a good way to describe the problem. Boston was a city set up by the few who were elected antidemocratically—that is, by birthright and a version of divine right—and who governed those who all along and for the most part still accepted their authority. No Irish Need Apply? No blacks? The people haven't yet recovered.

All five interracial couples Duncan profiled told him Boston was a place they wouldn't choose to move to. Five blacks, men and women both, told Duncan they'd made their adjustments way back to life in a culture whites presided over, and yet there were still adjustments. They had to live in one culture at a time because there was no overlap. Their children had to be instructed by their cousins who lived elsewhere about music, about books, about their history and the heroes they could have they'd never heard of. It was work to keep the input equal when their all-white classmates wanted only to absorb them one by one or two by two. It could be really quite exhausting.

Then the city seemed to tolerate, if not endorse, such hatred in the lower middle classes, in the poor. The Little Rocks and Birminghams of twenty years ago lived on in the mean spirits of the Irish in South Boston and in Charlestown. Children carried guns and used them on each other if they trespassed; kids pursued by other kids with sticks and broken bottles couldn't count on adults intervening even to the mere extent of telephoning the police. There were no jobs; there was no hope.

What jobs there were, what hope there was, went to the whites. The Irish first, then the Italians, took for their own people the police and fire departments, the trade unions, and the city and state government work those with power could create. They shut the blacks out as the Yankees had shut them out and assumed with reason they were playing by a set of rules that sliced the pie for everyone eventually. But they were wrong; there were no slices left for blacks.

In sixteen years Boston's ambitious liberal mayor, who won with black support against the racist candidate, built her to "world class" status but gave jobs to only half as many blacks as were on New York City's payroll with a nearly equal percent population. Boston's soil—and most of it was fill—was poisoned. Boston's soul, with more than half the city Catholic, flourished in a state of sin.

The *Globe* would report all this, to be sure, and also to their credit the fact that their own hiring performance—2.9 percent black—was worse even than the city's, was worse than the New York *Times* or Washington *Post*, managed to look good only if you compared the *Globe* and Boston's other newspaper.

So *why*, the question might be asked, when marriage isn't easy in the best of times or places, why would anybody choose a partner from the other race? He didn't need to ask it. Duncan knew the answer from his own experience, first that Jessica was Jewish, now that Nina was the mother of another person's infant. He had married Jessica and he would marry Nina, if he did, for love. That was the answer to the question.

He would marry Nina? That was news to him. He thought he had agreed it would be best to be sure he'd recovered from his first before he went back in the running. This was why, he'd analyzed, he was attracted to her in the first place: because of her complications, her responsibilities, Nina was no more free than he was to get serious. He and she both needed friends, and he and she both needed lovers, and he'd thought and so had she that they were lucky to have found a friend and lover in each other.

But it would explain the trouble he was having with her leaving for Thanksgiving if he feared his love was unrequited, or it would be once he mentioned marriage. Nina had avoided marriage to the point of having herself heavily insured against it with a long affair with someone who would never bring it up. And obviously Emilie was not sufficient motivation in a culture leaning toward the single-parent family, if you go by numbers. What he didn't need was more rejection by a woman he seemed to love more than she loved him. He'd rather spend the rest of his life at Club Med.

And it was dumb to think he could write up the story of the newsman's day tonight, when he could do it in the morning and still get it in for Thursday. He had nothing left to work with, even if he hadn't really put a day in. Duncan logged off his computer and from habit locked his notebooks in a drawer. He was exhausted. What he needed was a shower; what he needed was a drink.

On his way out he recognized that hunger was another problem and remembered that he'd had no lunch or dinner. When he found the Milky Way bar in his pocket—he had bought it back in Newark—Duncan tore the wrapper's end off and filled his mouth with the nougat, caramel, and chocolate candy. On the escalator down he wondered if he might not puke. But no, he walked across the lobby on his way out and, as Duncan often did, stopped to ask the night watchman if he'd heard the score— the Celtics were at Philadelphia—and was glad to hear that at least *they* were winning.

Then a strange thing happened. The night watchman, who was one of the *Globe*'s 69 black employees (out of 2,339), had just read the next day's front page, which he showed Duncan and made Duncan feel not only that he'd done a day's work after all but fully justified in his vocation as a journalist. The feeling was familiar from that first time back at Stanford after he had done the story for the *Daily* on the freshman who was blind, and changed his life and thus his own. And several times since, he had known he'd made this difference and had been rewarded with this feeling that he was engaged in work that mattered.

Work that mattered meant to Duncan what his father did all day, which was save lives, which made it God's work. Work that mattered was this piece that was so strong they had to put it on page 1, that told the truth about the city. Duncan scanned the story to see how it had been edited—it had been scarcely altered —and was filled with pride. But so was the night watchman proud. And friendly as they'd always been to one another, this was the first time they'd had a real occasion to shake hands.

# Nine

FALL MORNINGS on the waterfront justified her investment in the condominium, she felt, and Jessica was often late these perfect mornings, lingering to read the paper on the couch that faced the view. This Wednesday it was seven-thirty, and she sat there still, unable to get moving. She'd read every word of Duncan's and then almost every word of nearly everybody else, and it was clear now she was stalling until it was clearer why she had reacted as she had. She never cried.

It wasn't for the blacks or for the failure of the city; it had to do with success, either the marriages that he described or Duncan's own success. This first piece was a masterwork, and she would not fail to congratulate him once she understood if what had made her cry was a nostalgia for their good old days together. Jessica had not indulged this fondness in so long she barely recognized the feeling.

She had to start over on her face with water, cream, and blush and on her eyes with the light brown mascara she used on her lashes. And though she did not give too much thought to clothes, when she checked herself in the mirror on her way out she decided she should take another minute and go change from brown to honey. She might not have kept the honey-colored jacket except that it was of cashmere. It was one of his last presents.

She decided not to ask her secretary to get Duncan on the line, even though Duncan's line was busy when she tried it and she hated busy signals. Jessica knew how he hated being told to hold, especially by what Duncan called her guard dog.

"Duncan Jones," he answered. Sometimes he joked and said, "Dunkin' Donuts," but today there were already a lot of calls from a lot of people he had only heard of. Someone from the office of the governor-elect had phoned to mention there would be a task force set up on inauguration day, for instance.

"Hi."

"Hi," Duncan answered neutrally.

"It's Jessica."

*"Hi,* Jessie." It was a relief it was a friend. He wasn't sure they could get through.

"Congratulations."

"Thanks. Sorry I didn't recognize your voice." He didn't have to tell her that, did he?

"That's OK." Though it wasn't, Jessica decided to ignore that feeling. Otherwise, she'd get defensive and they'd argue. "It's terrific."

"Thanks a lot."

She wanted to say it was the first good strong work he'd done in years but couldn't think how to make it sound like a compliment, not insult. "Good for you," she said instead.

"Yeah, thanks. How are you?"

"Fine, I'm fine."

To fill the little silence, Duncan said, "Me too," and kind of laughed.

"I was about to ask." She laughed too. "And I was about to ask if you're free for Thanksgiving." Because Jessica always corrected men who did that when they meant to ask her out—

"Say what it is you're offering. I won't tell you I'm free if it's not something I would like to do."—she quickly added, "I'm having a few friends over for Thanksgiving dinner."

"Old friends? Anyone I know, I mean." Just out of curiosity, he meant.

"Yes, some. Did you hear Bruce and Marilyn are back together? They'll be coming. Esther. She has a new husband named Joe Williams."

"Esther Williams?"

"Gordon, still, but I thought that was funny too. And Martin—"

"How *is* Martin?" He had rather liked him.

"Fine, his new job is in cable television. But his father died."

"Oh, sorry." Duncan had heard Martin talk about his father once, he thought, but had no recollection of the details. "Were they close?" It wasn't something one could just assume.

"Yes, very."

"Too bad. Will you tell him?"

"What, that you said it was too bad?" And she laughed.

"I think it would sound better if you said I said I'm sorry. And I'm sorry, but I'm going to Buffalo tonight."

"Too bad. Now *that's* too bad."

Where was this light touch all the years they were together? Was she flirting? He did not think she approved. "I'd love to, otherwise." He meant it.

"Just a thought. Perhaps another time, or year. Or time of year." It wasn't true, but Jessica said, "It's just a last-minute thing." Who would be free the day before? She hoped he hadn't thought her rude. It wasn't like her. What she meant was that it wasn't like her to care what he thought of her behavior.

"Are you free to have a drink?"

"Yes." Jessica then asked him, "When?" and realized it almost didn't matter when.

"Whenever. Or lunch? I can't make lunch, never mind."

"Me neither."

"After work?"

"At six? What time's your plane?"

"Nine-thirty. Six, then. Cricket's?"

"Fine." She reconsidered, since it was the night before a major holiday. "Or five? I think I can get out by five."

"At five, OK. At Cricket's?"

"Fine." It was nice she had worn his jacket. He would like that.

"See you then, then. Thanks for calling."

"Sure," she said and hung the phone up. It was an old affectation begun in law school that she never said goodbye. It made every conversation seem like business, was his theory.

Duncan put down the receiver and immediately his phone rang. This time it was Duncan's mother wanting to know if he'd gotten on the early plane he must have said he'd try for. And why was his phone so busy? She told him she'd tried two hours.

He said it must be the circuits, and the early plane was booked. She would misunderstand if he said the last call was Jessica, and if he told her what he'd written she would very likely reply with something that would offend him, such as, "That sounds fascinating." No, it wasn't fascinating, it was shameful that this story could be written on the city on the harbor into which the tea was dumped and war declared against the King's injustices, and where there was one of the great centers of learning in the world, in history.

"But the Barneses hoped to see you for the drink they're coming by for," whined his mother. "Are you sure?" she asked. "They'll be so disappointed."

Duncan didn't think he ought to have to say again that no, he wouldn't make the early plane, and so he didn't. Nor did he say what she also knew, which was that Duncan couldn't stand the Barneses. Geoff and Julie Barnes—Dr. and Mrs. to him—were, and once he'd told them they were, fascists. *Sure* they'll be so disappointed not to see him. "Yes, I'm sure," he answered.

After telling her he had to get back to work and he'd see her that night, Duncan went back to the TV anchor story for which he had written a first paragraph about the guy's arrival at the station in a midnight blue Le Baron. He stared at the screen and read his notes for quotes and knew all he could write was satire.

Bic waved Duncan in and listened patiently to Duncan's reasons, then said with impatience, "Presto, now he's got a reputation to protect? From now on he'll write only sermons? Look, pal, I'm glad for your stardom, but I've got my space to fill. I'm figuring a half a page and need the copy in two hours."

"But don't you think it undermines this series if the next day there's a piece by me on how they make his hair look fluffy?"

Bic wanted to tell the truth, which was that only a few readers noted bylines. What he said was, "Make it serious. Just because you happen to be prejudiced against your colleagues in TV doesn't make what they do a joke. The story's perfect for tomorrow, all those people waiting for the damn parade to end and get on with their football. It's New York, for Christ's sake, and who wouldn't want to get promoted? You can do it, Jones. If you can get the mayor's office calling up to tell me all the things they've done for blacks, then you can write me three hundred lines. Make it two fifty. Now do we have a deal here?"

Duncan was impressed with himself to hear that the mayor's office called, although the mayor's office called the paper most days and he knew that. "I just haven't got it in me," he explained.

"What is this *in me?* What are you, a movie actor? Jones, look, you're a grind-em-out guy. Don't go prima donna on me." Bic answered his ringing phone with, "Bickford," put his hand over the mouthpiece, and said, "Do we have a deal, or not?"

When Duncan nodded, Bic swiveled his chair around and looked out his large window at the traffic Duncan could see too on the expressway. It was building up already for the holiday. Either he'd write a piece so flat it would be diagnosed as brain dead and put to sleep, or so charged it would be obvious there had been editorial error in assigning such slight subject matter to a major talent. Or he could do Carlos Fuentes.

Duncan walked across the newsroom to his desk deciding to do Carlos Fuentes calling on the President to alter course—the

President was going to "stay" it in Latin America—and realizing
Bic would kill him, A, and, B, it would be worth it. At some point
in his career, it would be his turn to say no. Why not a high point
like today?

Amanda gave them each five dollars and dropped her three
younger children at the Copley subway stop near Dr. Wolff's.
She told them to meet her in front of Faneuil Hall at Quincy
Market in two hours and knew she'd worry the whole time and
blame herself for waiting for the dishwasher repairman, who did
not arrive, instead of leaving Weston in time to be sure at least
they got there. She did not trust Boston's subways and admitted
that she didn't have a reason.

Unavoidably the session was concerned with her anxiety
about her children's safety in the city, which led naturally to her
own obligation as a parent to instruct her four kids wisely, to
make them alert and self-assured, and therefore whether she
and Jeremy had made a big mistake settling in the suburbs,
where there wasn't anything to practice on. She asked where Dr.
Wolff lived. He said in a suburb.

By the time she finally settled down, the hour was almost
over. She decided not to bother feeling guilty, though, for having wasted his time and her husband's money, and she said so.
Dr. Wolff asked why she didn't think of it as *her* time too, *her*
money. There followed a longer silence than Amanda ever
thought she would be capable of tolerating, after which she said,
"Good question."

She had walked the two blocks to her car before Amanda
realized that on her way out she'd neglected to wish him happy
Thanksgiving, and she took that as a good sign, whatever its
meaning. He had put his finger on the problem, and it should
have shaken her to understand that after ten months not only
was she not "all better"—nor "almost all better"—but instead
just getting going.

She parked in the lot behind Bill Roger's Running Center and
cut through the north side of the market, hurrying in shoes with

heels that made it hard on cobblestones. She half expected, having done so poor a job of raising them, they wouldn't have been able to negotiate the distance between Copley Square and Quincy Market. It amazed her that she saw them standing there exactly where they said they'd be, the boys at least. But where was Gail, but where was *Gailie?* The boys were across the circle of spectators watching the magician and enjoying the fact that it was still warm enough to be outside in late November in the last light of the day. She searched the faces of the children all the way around the circle and was going to scream her daughter's name repeatedly, hysterically, when the magician said it for her. "Pick a card, Gail," was what he said, "and don't show me what it is."

Amanda calmed herself because she felt she had to. Look at Gail: her shy nine year-old daughter wasn't scared to death! On a toy bugle the magician played a flourish and called, "Take a bow, Gail, and let's hear it for her!" Everyone around the circle clapped for Gail, who took a graceful little bow and then withdrew in just the right way. The magician took his bow while two assistants passed his hats.

"Mom, Gail did *tricks,* and she tricked the *magician* even," shouted Jason.

Scotty had his arm around his sister's shoulder and wore an expression that said, "I'm her agent, speak to me, I handle bookings."

Gail said, "Thank you," when another girl her age said she was great.

"Mom, did you *see her?"* Jason screamed.

Amanda nodded. It took all she had to keep herself from saying to the crowd as it dispersed, "I'm her mother." She kissed her children as if they'd been separated for a week and suggested a drink so they could sit and tell her all about it.

They were at a table in the glassed-in outdoor part and telling how they'd spent their time and money and asking if they could do this every Wednesday, and Amanda wished only that thirteen-year-old Penny wasn't cheerleading that afternoon and

Jeremy knew where to meet them. She was jealous of the woman several tables off whose husband waved to her from outside and came in and greeted her enthusiastically. The woman had a bottle of champagne already at her side on ice and with a napkin draped around its neck like a silk stole. A wedding anniversary, Amanda guessed.

But it was Duncan. He seemed to have found himself another woman, and Amanda thought, Poor Nina. She would run home and call Nina and ask her and Emilie to come to Weston for Thanksgiving.

He was at her side then, and though she vowed she'd be cool toward him, Duncan was warm and sounded sincere when he said he'd hoped he'd meet her kids one day. He told them, introducing himself, he was Nina's boyfriend, just in case they might have heard of him, and that Nina and Emilie were in Santa Fe for Thanksgiving to visit her sister, to which Amanda responded with an invitation to him for Thanksgiving dinner. This was cool? But when Duncan identified himself as Nina's boyfriend, he was absolutely charming. As he left the table, saying thank you anyway but he'd be with his family, Gail whispered that she'd seen the cute picture of him Nina had and he was even cuter in real life.

Duncan explained to Jessica how he had met Amanda. "Maybe you remember how in August that night I told you the night before I fell in love with Nina Jones? It was at her house, at Amanda's," Duncan said.

"What you said was you thought you fell in love," corrected Jessica. He hadn't said her name was Nina, and she'd surely have remembered if he'd said her name was Jones.

"Well I was right, I did."

The waiter had released the cork expertly and was pouring champagne into tulip glasses. "Do you mind if we don't drink to that?" she asked. The waiter backed off.

Duncan was embarrassed for the waiter as well as for himself and tried to recover with a joke. "Of course. What would you like me not to drink to, Martha's Vineyard?"

Jessica had a perplexed look, then said, "Oh God, him. God no, he's long gone. All I meant was that I asked you for a drink to celebrate your work. It's wonderful. I'm proud of you." She raised her glass.

Part of the reason he was smiling was that she seemed not to notice he'd asked her to have this drink, but never mind. It had been years since she had celebrated anything about him. "Thank you," he said simply, "I appreciate the invitation." The champagne was excellent, as far as he knew.

"And where did you get those couples? Are they real or, as they say, composites?"

"Real," he answered, "very real. You didn't see their photographs?" That meant she'd only read page 1.

"I thought they might be models."

Duncan forced himself to disbelieve her insult was intentional. "The *point* is they're real people," he said, but the irritation showed.

"I'm paying you a compliment," she argued.

"Oh?"

"The way sometimes the scenery's so gorgeous what you think of is a postcard, that's all. What you wrote so moved me that I thought you had to make it up. Am I making it worse or better?" This was not the way she'd planned it.

"Worse. A journalist thinks real life's good enough. If you don't know that, you weren't paying much attention all those years." He felt he could be with his mother.

"I know that. All I meant is they seem too perfect."

"Well they're not *too* perfect, they're just *perfect.* Why can't you just say it's wonderful, I'm proud of you?"

"I did!"

"And let it go at that? Why do you have to make me feel it takes you by surprise that I should do good work? You always used to make me feel the Living pages were for lightweights, and you would respect me if I wrote on politics or business or the G.N.P. So good, so good for you, you've worked your magic on me once again. Congratulations." Duncan drained his glass and stood.

"No, please," she coaxed, "don't leave, you just misunderstood me. No, I don't even mean that, I don't mean it's your fault at all." She'd been thrown off. "I blew it, Duncan, and I'm sorry. Please."

"You are?" He had been going to use the bathroom, but he guessed he needn't say that. She could think he almost left, no matter that he'd never left a bottle of champagne behind and didn't think he ever would. He sat. "There," Duncan said.

"I'm sorry that I made you feel the Living pages were for lightweights." She remembered telling him once in a fight that if he were a lawyer with a choice between the jobs of orchestrating acquisitions or filling out income tax forms, he'd do tax forms. There was no analogy that fit, that she could think of, and point two was that Living *was* for the living. It was about people, at least.

"I don't believe anymore," Duncan admitted, "that the Bar Association will only admit dead bodies." That's what he'd said in that same fight. "You're looking alive and well, for instance."

"Thanks, you too." So she refilled their glasses.

"I might be a little touchy about Nina. She's in Santa Fe tonight."

"I forget what she does. Did you say she's a painter?" Jessica remembered it was something odd.

"She's at the M.F.A. as an assistant curator."

"Oh. So how long's she there for?"

"The museum?"

"Santa Fe."

"Another four days." Duncan checked his watch and saw that it was still the afternoon where Nina was. "So don't mind me if I get drunk."

"I won't."

"I'm kidding." Then he looked around to catch the waiter's eye. "But why don't we get something to eat," he suggested, "just in case." He saw Amanda and her children getting up and smiled and waved, which brought them over on their way out, which had not been his intention.

"Hello, I'm Amanda Morris." This was the best way to find out who she was.

"Jessica Jones."

"Ah, Duncan's sister?" asked Amanda.

Was he not there? "No, my wife," he answered, "that is—"

"Ah, how nice," Amanda said, "and these are Jason, Gail, and Scotty. Penny, who's the oldest, couldn't come because she's a cheerleader."

"—my ex-wife," amended Duncan.

"Nice to meet you," Jessica said, smiling because Duncan had once introduced her as "my life." She wondered if he now would slip and say "my ex-life."

"You too," said Amanda. "Great to see you, Duncan, please come see us," as if she had made him welcome other times.

"Sure thing," he said absurdly.

"Yes?" the waiter asked. He had been summoned by a nod of Jessica's.

"Shall we get something?" Duncan asked her.

"Not for me yet," Jessica said, "go ahead, though."

Duncan's lunch date with an old friend had been canceled so he could do Carlos Fuentes, and though it had been well worth it—even Bic had grunted grudgingly, though he feigned having been kicked in the balls and said, "The child is father of the man? Hell no! No more, Jones!"—Duncan was a little dizzy. The champagne had made him feel he must be at a family wedding and should fill a plate with food from chafing dishes. "Chicken wings?"

"We don't have chicken wings. We do have mussels, and tonight the sauce is marinière."

"No, never mind. You don't have pigs in blankets, do you?" Duncan winked at Jessica. "Or plain old goldfish?"

"I think I can get you goldfish from the bar," the waiter said with disapproval in his voice. He filled their glasses a last time and set the bottle upside down in the glass cooler.

"Never mind, thanks anyway," said Duncan amiably. To Jessica he said, "We can go wander in the market." There were chafing dishes by the hundreds in the market.

"We can pick up something to take back to my place, if you want."

"And watch my plane come in? OK." He'd have to watch the time, but he had liked it there the other time. He would get Greek, and she Chinese, just watch. He was talking in circles. "Chinese?"

"I was thinking Greek," she said as if she'd read his mind and meant to pull the rug out. "This is mine," she told him, reaching for the check, "remember?"

"Thanks." He couldn't help but notice that her MasterCard was gold, unlike his own.

Before they got to Dionysus, for old time's sake they got tacos they ate standing up at Pepe's. Duncan ate a spring roll from the Lucky Garden booth while Jessica went to pick up the pumpkin pie she'd ordered for Thanksgiving. "Do you sell much Rocky Road?" he asked the Mother's Fudge merchant. Once he had bought a pound of it for Jessica for Valentine's Day.

After a slice of Regina's pizza, they ate baklava from Dionysus and left Quincy Market, walking quickly in the evening now grown chilly. Technically there was no reason any longer to go back to her apartment, but the invitation seemed to stand. Duncan could smell the fresh-ground coffee she had bought and wondered if she meant it for him or the next day's guests.

While she made coffee, he found his way finally to a bathroom. On his way back through the bedroom, Duncan stopped to notice that she too now used a comforter inside an envelope of sheeting. He had thought she was committed to hospital corners for life, and it pleased him to be wrong. What didn't please him was that on the other table by the bed, not her side, or what once was her side, was a glossy magazine. The magazine was called *Success*.

"So who's been sleeping in your bed?" he asked her in a big-bear voice. He didn't stop to recognize that she might now think both were her sides of the bed.

"Not Goldilocks," she answered coyly. "Still take sugar?" She opened the cupboard door behind him and reached over his right shoulder to bring out the lovely sugar bowl her grandmother had bought in Venice and brought to them shortly after they were married.

"No, I gave it up," he said. It was so easy to pull her to him, so easy evidently after she put the bowl on the counter for her to put both her arms around him. Duncan couldn't feel her breathing. He was not sure he was either.

"This is my fault," Jessica said before Duncan kissed her.

"No, it isn't," he replied, "it's mine. We're going to watch my plane leave, is that all right?"

Jessica did not want the responsibility for that. Her plan had been for them to maybe rub each other's feet and talk and reconcile eventually to the extent that they'd be better friends than ever. Wasn't that the latest thing? Then why was she not in the least inclined to draw back from this kissing? Couldn't she admit to herself that all day she'd wanted Duncan on that couch that faced the ocean? She had met two dozen men she'd felt inclined or else obliged to sit with on that same white couch, but none had been successful in upgrading her commitment to perfunctory foreplay. Now, as if her history with Duncan had been any different—when, in fact, if anything it had been worse —there was this passion she could draw on. For no reason she could name, there was this passion.

It was foreign and familiar, but from way back, almost as far back as when they were at Stanford and would pack a picnic of strawberries big as apricots and apricots as big as plums, and plums themselves that were the size of peaches that could have been melons, and would put the top down and drive to the ocean or north to the redwood forest to lie down and let their fingers do the walking. She would play him like a keyboard, he remembered, stirred as much by memory as by the fact that Jessica all these years later hadn't seemed to lose the touch. This was old business they transacted, and, he wondered, how could it be wrong when all it felt to him was overdue?

She thought about the other woman, realizing that's who *she* was, which made no sense. She was the original, the only woman he had married, and their title had been searched and been cleared. She owed him an apology for not having responded to him adequately all those years, and so, with his tongue in her mouth, she said so using the same language. This was once when Jessica would not withhold.

She drew him after her out of the living room and down the hall to where the bed he'd never seen before this night was just as easily unmade as was his own, the down puff in its envelope of Marimekko fabric floating out of their way like a cloud. The window was closed to the cold, but it was open to the sights and to the several thousand lights of Boston harbor and beyond. It made them feel they could be flying through this crisp November night and looking down as eagles do with extrasensory perception more than the mere naked eye. Look, they were naked. They were strangers, they were old friends.

Duncan asked himself the definition of adultery and decided this was it and not it, and he would do better if he thought about it later on. He didn't even know to what extent it was premeditated in this case; all he knew was his blood was circulating in him like Old Faithful. The only direction for the liquid in him to go was out.

It came into Jessica the way their eager champagne had splashed from its bottle into tulips made of glass. It didn't spill, and nothing broke, and soon it settled into still wine. What it was appropriate to do, it seemed to them, was forgo the temptation it was to put into words what might have happened. Journalist and trial lawyer though they were, with words their allies, even co-conspirators, they knew enough now to be not just inarticulate but mute.

The only certain thing was that Duncan should never plan again to take an evening plane to Buffalo. This would make two for two he'd missed.

# Ten

THE HOUSES along Canyon Road stunned Nina, none more than the one in which they were about to have Thanksgiving dinner. It was terraced like a vineyard is in an Italian hill town, balconies that opened out on balconies, and terra-cotta pots on each housed flowers that were so exotic Nina wished she'd brought a camera. No, she wished she had brought Duncan, who would find it as hilarious as she did that she had assumed they would be sitting in a circle on a dirt floor with some Indians and having maize and being thankful just to have survived the crossing.

For someone, supposedly, who was up to her elbows in the misery of the world, Dulcie kept company with elegance so easily that Nina wondered how much time, in fact, Dulcie was spending with the Indians, or if her efforts now were put entirely toward raising funds. And this was not a criticism but a consolation for the next time either of their parents ran on about Dulcie's being the sister of mercy. Nina would enjoy remembering that Dulcie had suggested that they get a pedicure together.

"Something to drink?" one of Dulcie's friends asked Nina. He said "somesing" in the French way, but his Yves Montand face, the much younger Montand, gave away his nationality before that. Nina had been told by Dulcie that old friends from her North Africa days would be mixed in with the new ones. This one held a sweating bottle of chilled wine in a hand banded at the wrist by an enormous turquoise bracelet his shirtsleeve was rolled back to display. They all seemed to be modeling for Ralph Lauren.

Nina contemplated answering in French but thought it would be condescending to be saying in effect, "I guess from the way you say 'somesing' you must be French," so she held her empty glass out and said, "Thank you." And when it appeared he wasn't going to move on to fill other people's glasses, or not right away, she asked him, "Do you live in Santa Fe?"

"I live." He shrugged and said, *"Partout,"* because the word for "everywhere" had slipped his mind. "I am a *pilote.* Pie-lot, you say."

"Your English is very good," said Nina pleasantly.

"No, not for conversation, only for the radio. I listen very well, and I know many numbers. I must to practice." He said "practeyes."

"With what airline are you?" She had translated from French to English, as had he for everything he'd said so far.

"The Air France," he replied. "I fly—you say 'I fly'?—with Morocco as basis. You say 'basis'?"

"I would say 'home base.' I would say 'Morocco is my home base,' or 'I fly in and out of Morocco.' "

"My home base." He left off the *h.*

"That's right."

"Or 'I fly in and out from Marrakech'?"

" 'Of Marrakech,' that's right." There were so many ways to be unidiomatic.

"So. Do you speak French?" The pilot laughed and took a long sip from his wine.

"*Oui,*" Nina answered, adding the absurd, "*un peu.*"

"*Bon,*" he said, "*nous pouvons parler français, d'accord?*" He spoke as slowly as he could.

"*D'accord.*" She smiled.

"*Encore à boire?*" It was his opening sentence in both languages, apparently.

This time Nina said, "*Non, merci,*" and introduced herself to him as Dulcie's sister.

Now he put the bottle down on an exquisitely tiled table, and they shook hands in the way that is so un-American, which is to say more flesh than muscle, and so formal. "*Enchanté*" and *Enchantée,*" they said, zipping right on to the familiar *tu,* the *vous* form inappropriate out here on groovy Canyon Road and on a feast day between people who'd been gathered there by Dulcie, whose style was more style than substance (which, again, was not a criticism so much as a fact). Michel, his name was.

Nina was impressed that Dulcie had persuaded him to come from Marrakech, which was where her blue caftan came from with the little crocheted buttons to the waist that Duncan had undone that first night. He said he had really only come from L.A. for this dinner, though it was so *amusant* to think of having corn and turkey he'd have come a longer distance. Was it true, he asked her, that in the United States they impregnated turkeys with a butter substitute and froze them with imbeded *trucs* that sent a signal they were cooked? She said she didn't think it could be, though she knew they did a lot of shocking things to food, like steroids. She was trying to imagine Duncan here and guessed he would have wandered off, bored. He would know, though, being all-American, about the turkeys.

"Oh, you know the French," she'd have told Duncan later, finding him down on a lower terrace, "how they love to go on about food and politics." She knew he didn't "know the French" in that sense, but it was a figure of speech that would serve to make them feel aligned. She wished she'd asked him to come with her.

Michel asked her with a smirk if Nina had heard about the contraceptives in the birdseed they feed to the pigeons. They were talking about Paris.

She had read ten tons of contraceptives had been fed to pigeons to insure the legacy of André Malraux when he was Minister of Culture and began to scrub the monuments of centuries' worth, bringing Paris back to life once again as the City of Light. Nina felt, involuntarily, a longing to see Paris for a day to see the light and for a night to see the lights. It was true Boston was a small town in the provinces, in these ways.

"Good!" said Dulcie, coming up between them with a plate of crudités, "now you've met my big sister. Have some."

"No, thanks." Michel said it "sanks."

"Thanks," Nina said, helping herself to one of everything, "when do you think we'll eat?" Was it the sun, or wine, or waiting, or all three? She felt a little dizzy.

"I'm sure Michel told you how he flew food down for me into the sub-Sahara, speaking of food." Dulcie kissed him on the cheek but lovingly, as couples do who once were lovers, briefly, innocently, having remained friends.

How typical, when she'd asked how about the here-and-now, that Dulcie had brought up a serious famine. Nina spiked a Brussels sprout with a toothpick and dragged it quickly through the dip.

"The turkey's done, it's resting," Dulcie answered Nina at last. Looking down at Nina's feet, she then asked, "Where's Emilie?" She told Michel in a proprietorial way, *Ma petite nièce.*

"I ought to check on her, she's sleeping," Nina said and went off. She had made a little nest for Emilie of scatter pillows from the suede couch in the room that was a study but had no desk, as if this philanthropist—his name was a Midwestern fortune's—managed to do all his paperwork by phone. All Nina hoped was that her daughter wouldn't drool onto the pillows that appeared to have been made of ancient textiles from the war-torn countries down the way. They would be irreplaceable.

Emilie was awake but resting, as if she'd inherited from Jules-Jacques his contentment to float along in this in-between zone. All she'd need between her fingers was the day's first cigarette to be the perfect imitation, and in fact, because Emilie brought her hand to her mouth just then to explore each with the other, she was perfect. Covering her mouth, which was, as Duncan pointed out, a copy of her mother's, Emilie seemed only to resemble Jules-Jacques. Her eyes, as his had been, were available by virtue of their shallow set, and they were French blue, fringed as his were by dark lashes that were straight and blunt as brushes. Once, one morning way back when, he'd painted Nina's face with his by blinking, and she'd brought him in her and missed classes (and missed getting pregnant, not that she was trying). Nina couldn't help but wonder now *what* her life would be *if* she had a twenty-year-old daughter whose child Emilie could be—what if?—and wonder who or what force was in charge of working things out after all was said and done. Was it that Emilie had tried to be conceived that whole first year but missed her chances, and then taken up the first that came her way? Thank God she had.

And why not think God was the god of second chances? Nina's parents were of course convinced—it was their business to be—God was the God of all creation, which included all things visible and invisible, as the old Creed put it. But what would be the argument for lesser statements of belief when what they turned on was this baby with her father's French blue eyes? And on Thanksgiving! The point of Thanksgiving was thanks for creation, all creation. In spite of the fact that her life hadn't gone as she'd have planned it, and Nina included this day, she was struck by her urge to acknowledge her appreciation, formally, in words of some sort. Nina tried, but all she ended up with was the one word "thanks" and quite an urgent, "Here we are, now please protect us," that brought tears to fill her eyes and spill all over. What a permanent condition Nina's grief was.

She and Dulcie had spent all the afternoon the day before on someone else's patio, another friend in an adobe that opened out to the purple mountain's majesties across the brilliant sky. They'd talked about Jules-Jacques a lot and how when Dulcie visited they'd roamed together from one landmark to another as if they could take the city's pulse and temperature while others merely took her photograph. Dulcie had called Jules-Jacques the dearest man she'd ever, ever met and said she'd always meant to ask him if by chance he had a brother. Nina would have answered if she'd wanted to that yes, he had a pair with whom he had about as much in common as they themselves did, no more than parents, history. Neither brother had found it possible to contact Nina after Jules-Jacques died, not even to inform her of it, even though they'd both met Nina countless times and had no criticism of her or the life she shared with Jules-Jacques. Families weren't born, but made.

Thank God for that too. She and Jules-Jacques had a family of friends who surrounded Nina with concern, beginning that first afternoon with the delivery of the news that lasted well into the night. And someone was there every time she needed not to be alone, especially those first few days when they were free to go to Rouen and believe because they'd seen him he was dead. She'd had to wait the endless time until the funeral mass to see he really truly wasn't there, except perhaps under the domed lid of the casket borne in by that pair of brothers and a couple of those friends, and his sons Philippe and Marcel, whom Nina knew because they were nineteen and sixteen, behind the two younger in front, Roger, fourteen, and Hughes, seven, who would not have understood yet.

Nina realized, telling Dulcie, something about Duncan, which was that he listened when she talked. The edge—the envy he felt hearing her describe her loss, her sorrow—was smoothed by his more impressive love and concern. And there was no edge with Dulcie needing smoothing, but there also wasn't any other form of identification with her. Dulcie didn't bring to listening an imagination that enabled her to put herself in Nina's place, and so the interchange was flat no matter how charged with emotion was the subject. She was either lazy or had never been moved to form any real connection. Once again—for who knew better than did Nina how poorly prepared they'd been with only the example set by Vivian and poor old Mike?—she wasn't blaming Dulcie for this.

Nina could go on forever, never blaming Dulcie. Duncan said he felt the same way about Skip as she did about Dulcie: an essentially benign but bloodless—and this was ironic, since it was the one true thing they had in common—fondness. Nina realized, telling Dulcie about her last year, it was her friends in Paris who were anxious to see her and Emilie, and whom she also longed to visit. This was going through the motions in one of the nicest places she had ever been, but still. It was the motions.

There was even something missing in the grace, which Dulcie offered. Growing up, they would have sung at some point that day the "Prayer of Thanksgiving," and it moved Nina that Dulcie started with the first line, "We gather together to ask the Lord's blessing," and after petitioning on behalf of all the hungry—not that they weren't at that table also hungry—ended with the last, "Thy name be ever prais'd, O Lord, make us free!" Nina tried to catch Dulcie's eye to share the recognition, but apparently there hadn't been one. Dulcie's reference wasn't an intentional one after all but merely part of her routine, delivered with impressive feeling that was somehow also not there.

Now it was time, finally and however, to put that aside in favor of uncompromised praise for the feast that had been served around the table. Contributions to the meal had been made by a few of the guests more to insure including old family favorites—and someone brought mashed canned yams with marshmallows to prove the point—than merely to divide the work. Much was made of the ritual aspects of the only major holiday whose structure didn't depend on gift giving or religion, and they acted more like sociologists than friends. Michel said only, *"Je m'amuse,"* although if pressed he'd have said what amused him was how seriously they took all this, for a meal that was all one color, but how touching it was that this day of thanks was thanks for having left the Old World for the New. And whereas he had his complaints about Americans, as a pilot he knew what that urge to get the hell out was. Here was a culture full of fliers.

Somebody had given Dulcie the occasion to alarm them with statistics, so she told them that the Sahara spreads southward at a rate of eleven kilometers a year. Consider, she encouraged everyone in spite of the fact that their plates were filled with food, that nearly half the earth already is arid or semiarid, and that over the next twenty years one third of what productive land remains will also be lost. Nina had told Duncan so much about Dulcie that she looked around for him to share the perfect illustration Dulcie was of righteousness. They would have winked at one another.

Instead Nina smiled at Emilie, who loved the candied yams, and calculated the time difference. Earlier the line was busy, but she'd try again to reach him, not having had any luck the night before when, trying Buffalo and Boston, he must have been in between.

Misery, and not the lack of sleep it also was, showed in his face, annoying Duncan's mother further. When the phone rang and he didn't sprint this time into the other room to get it, having been discouraged by its being only relatives twice earlier, she sighed and backed her chair away from the dining room table. Next year she would like to be the guest. She was a little sick of this.

It was for him, his mother said, so Duncan left the plate of food he'd only picked at and said he would be right back but they should go ahead without him. When his mother sighed again, he said the turkey was just perfect. She had made a big deal about getting one that had a little gizmo in it that popped up when it was done, so no more guesswork.

"Hello?" What a hypocrite he was.

"Happy Thanksgiving," Nina wished him brightly.

"Same to you," he answered nervously.

Nina was sorry to have caused him the concern she heard in his voice, so she told him right away, "I miss you."

He said, "I miss you too." He'd had eighteen hours to think of what to say but hadn't dared decide it was best to be honest, if it was. "Are you still coming home on Sunday? What about today instead?"

She laughed. "I'm glad you miss me that much."

"I miss Emilie too. How's she doing?"

"It's a whole new world to drool on, so she likes it."

"Do you love me?" he asked.

"Are you all right?"

"Do you?"

"Yes, I love you. Are you asking because—"

"I love you, because I love you, Nina."

She felt badly that he felt left out, with her out there on the frontier and him just back in Buffalo with Mom and Dad. "You're not still worried, are you?"

"About what?"

"Whether some horse will sweep me off my feet."

"I'm sorry I laid that on you." Mortified would be more like it.

"No, I understand, I do, I was scared too. We were exposing what we have to the world for the first time, and it *is* a test. I'm glad it's over." Not that it was over, with three days to go, but she'd found out already what she must have wondered even without knowing it, which was whether her life in Boston was enough. The question wasn't whether she would rather have Jules-Jacques and Paris—since she couldn't—but if Duncan was substantial enough for her. What she'd learned was that he was. "It's helpful, even, having Dulcie represent my past so clearly. I can see it's really over and, for the first time, feel good about the ending. I don't mean feel *good*, but I mean feel secure or something, grateful that I had it, very grateful to have you."

This would have been good news to him except of course the

contrast worked against him. He knew he and Jessica had made
a murky ending that was most unworthy of the breadth and
depth of their relationship, but then he hadn't known it wasn't
over. It was clear, and reaffirmed the night before, that there
were things he didn't like about her—had learned to like even
less than ever since the divorce was made final in the summer—
and it was clear she had her power nonetheless. He'd seen he
would do anything to get her to approve of him. He wished
they'd had their second thoughts before, not after, parting. *Now*
could it be over?

"Are you still there?"

"Sorry, I heard what you said, it's just—" It's just that inca-
pacitation set in like bad weather.

"Just so you know not to worry," Nina said, "and that I love
you."

"I love you more," Duncan said, but what he meant was he
was more afraid to lose her.

"More than I do?"

"More than ever." Saying that seemed to release him to the
possibility of doing better, even if he couldn't yet see how to
start. He had three days. They said goodbye, and he hung up
and went back to the dining room to decide over pumpkin pie if
he had someone in his family he could talk to.

Duncan's mother waited for an explanation, then asked simply, "Long distance?"

The bite of pie seemed to be floating in the juices of his
mouth. He swallowed it with an enforced gulp and reached for
his glass of wine to "wash it down." Under the table, Cathy
nudged him with her knee. "Right." He pushed the dessert
plate toward the center of the table. "Great pie, Mom," he said,
not looking at her.

His mother ignored what she knew wasn't a real compliment
—not that she'd baked it anyway—and went on, "I asked because you had two long-distance calls last night." She might
have meant to tell him but forgotten in the holiday commotion,

or meant not to tell him in order to punish him for not arriving when he should have.

He assumed it was the second and said, "Thanks for telling me."

His mother's eyes filled.

"It happens to have been important," Duncan accused.

She was so tired of her inadequacy as far, obviously, as he was concerned. Why couldn't Duncan be like Skip? "If it was so important, why weren't you here to accept the calls?"

"I missed the fucking plane, all right?"

His mother stood. "I won't allow that word at my Thanksgiving table." She had served the pumpkin pie and, picking up the silver spatula, she asked, "Who wants more pie?" She looked around the table. "Dear?" she asked her husband. "Skip, dear?"

"No thanks, Mom, it was delicious."

"Duncan," said his father sternly, "that was inappropriate. This is a family meal, with children present, and you could apologize not only to your mother but to Skip and Cathy."

"That's OK, Dad, it's not like they've—" Skip attempted.

"That's irrelevant, Skip," Dr. Jones dismissed him. "Duncan?"

"I apologize," said Duncan, looking at his mother.

"That's all right, dear. I hope they weren't *too* important."

Cathy nudged him this time with her elbow. All he'd told her was that Nina was away when she'd asked if he was going to bring Nina home to meet the family. He shifted on his chair to put himself out of Cathy's reach, annoyed by her assumption of complicity. "Not too," he answered. He was fantasizing going on to say, "I was fucking my brains out with my ex-wife, whom you might remember, which is why I wasn't here."

"That's good," his mother said. "Girls, if you'd like to be excused, you may."

"But no TV," said Cathy.

Heidi, Dorothy, and Alice, like the Lennon sisters, sang a note, except it was a protest.

"I already said they could," their grandmother explained, "since it's a special day."

"They brought their crafts, Gamma," said Cathy firmly. She said, "Go ahead, girls," and they did.

It was impressive, Duncan thought, but if she was so much in charge, why did she call his mother "Gamma," like her daughters? She had gone from "Mrs. Jones" to "Mrs. J." to nothing and then fallen on the "Gamma" Heidi uttered one day like an intercepted pass on the ten-yard line. Jessica, at least, had said right off that she would call her "Anne," since that was what her name was.

"Pass the cream and sugar to your father, dear," his mother said to Skip. The cream and sugar were in front of Cathy, who passed them while stifling a giggle. Only rarely did she call him "Gampa," and this wasn't one of those times. Even his own wife always referred to him as "Dr. Jones" and never ever called him "Ray." His name was Raymond. Jessica had called him "Raymond."

"Thank you, Cathy. Wonderful pie, wasn't it?" He gave himself two sugar cubes and poured a rich amount of cream. It wasn't even coffee really anymore because of caffeine interfering with his sleep.

"It was," Cathy agreed absurdly, since like Duncan she had left almost her whole slice, "everything was."

"Everything was wonderful, Mom," Skip repeated.

"Great, Mom," Duncan added, "everything was great, Mom."

"I tried a new kind of turkey this year," she told Cathy, "that's self-basting and says when it's done. It could have been a little moister for my money."

"It was good, though," Cathy answered. She had never gotten up at four to put the turkey in the way Skip's mother and her own did, which was because their mothers before them had in order to fit ten hours' cooking time in before two o'clock, when their extended families would sit down to eat. A turkey that was sized for five adults and three kids and some extra for a sand-

wich was a different bird entirely. It did not need to be put into
the oven in the middle of the night.

"So what's our bet?" asked Skip.

"Who's playing?"

"Don't you even read your own newspaper? Minnesota, with
a three-point spread." The Vikings were the favorites, Skip's
included.

"OK, I'll go for the other team." Now he would have to watch
the game, but what else was there? Get into a heart-to-heart
about his love life?

"I can tell your heart's not in it, but OK. Your bet, Dad?"

"I'll go for Detroit, a dime a point."

"Come on, a *dime?*" complained Skip.

"That's my legal limit," said his father with a chuckle. The
exchange went this way every time.

"It's hardly worth the trouble," Skip said, humoring his father
with a whine.

"You boys can bet your money, you don't have to take your
cue from me." He always said this.

"No, Dad." So did Skip, this.

Duncan had to be reminded of his part in this negotiation, but
he didn't feel like playing, so he didn't.

"I guess we can live with it this time," said Skip for Duncan,
"can't we?"

Duncan merely said, "Excuse me." On top of his slice of pie
he put his cup and saucer and his unused teaspoon. With his
other hand he carried his wineglass and water glass, so that he
disappeared without a trace.

"Dear, is that necessary?" asked his mother. She meant that
he hadn't made two trips, or none; to her it was bad manners to
stack dishes. Then the four adults remaining shared a look that
meant, "*Now* what's his problem?" When she heard the kitchen
door shut and they watched him pass by the far window, Duncan's mother sighed and said, "I'll never understand that boy."
Her pointed look to Skip, then Cathy, meant they were to tell
her what he'd said to them, if anything.

"No, nothing," Skip exaggerated. In fact Duncan had told Skip on the way from the airport next to nothing, which was that he had slept longer on the plane than all the night before. "It's work, is my guess," Skip said.

"I do wish he wouldn't work so hard," eclipsed what Cathy was about to say, which was a good thing. If she'd offered, "I think it's because his girlfriend is in Santa Fe," Duncan's hurt mother would have asked, "What girlfriend?" Cathy took that as a signal of her having had too much wine and reminded herself, for the time she and her mother-in-law would clean up the kitchen and talk intimately, to say nothing at all about Duncan or her disappointment at his getting there at the last minute. She had hoped he'd fill her in and was prepared to ask him, if there really was a baby, if he wanted to take back for her the little pile of special dresses she had saved. How nice, she thought, it was a girl. But never mind.

"I couldn't stand that constant deadline. Awful pressure, if you ask me," Skip defended Duncan. His work was in the insurance field—his father was, in fact, his client and a good one—and his spare time was for his girls and for golf and, when he could, the two together. Skip's dream was to go to Scotland, play St. Andrews as a foursome, and let Cathy knit her sweaters in real Shetland.

"We have the whole weekend for him to relax," said Dr. Jones.

Duncan knew all these buildings better as the streaks they were when he was on a bike and racing home, late, from a friend's house. Now they were—or once again, since he was sure they'd gone down with the sixties—Greek. Above the doorways were the letters that meant so much to so few. The only three he'd learned, he'd always joked, were Kappa, Beta, Phi, or whatever it was he'd graduated as. "Phi Beta Kappa?" That was it, yes. "You're an asshole, Jones, you know that?"

Did he ever. Duncan shuffled through the leaves that once would have been raked and burned and told himself exactly that. He'd gone down with the sixties too, it could be said, but he had yet to make his comeback. His next birthday would be Duncan's fortieth too, for a further challenge he would not be up to.

Kicking leaves piled by the wind, he wondered if they shouldn't have put Boston in the settlement, awarding Boston to one or the other of them and requiring that the other move away. If he'd lost Boston, there at last would have been his excuse for moving back to the Bay Area, and there at least was his assurance, if he were a writer for the *Chronicle*, of not being delivered to her every morning. Could she be prevented by court order from subscribing to the Boston *Globe?* Of course she'd be the first to know the answer to that. All he knew was he had been awake all night in Jessica's bed waiting for Thanksgiving morning to arrive so he could leave her. At the first light he had tried to waken her and half succeeded. Letting himself out, he'd taken off with him her copy of the *Globe* in order to prevent her from reading his Carlos Fuentes and calling him up to say how much she'd liked it. He would get himself a guard dog who would take his calls from now on.

All because he'd seen a copy of a magazine he hadn't ever heard of, called *Success,* on Jessica's "guest" bedside table and reacted like a cuckold, slamming himself home to her not once but twice, until she finally made him feel he had succeeded. He had felt twice cuckolded, in fact, and so there was a logic, and he even thought that Nina could arrive at understanding what he'd done if he described for her the panic his imagination served up when someone's *Success* was by his ex-wife's bed while Nina, so he fantasized, was in a hot tub with some wild and woolly Westerner who had a year-round tan.

He stopped to see that someone's child on someone's lawn had raked the leaves to make a maze, or else the heart with valves and chambers. The big difference between hearts and mazes, Duncan analyzed, is you can't backtrack in the heart, not even to check where you've come from. In the heart, reverse means you could have a clot and you could die. Was that the lesson? Duncan shivered with a chill that came in the wind that picked up a few loose leaves and floated them and dropped them gently in the street. That he could die—that he would die —it was his goal to have avoided dealing with until he'd made his full recovery from the failure of his marriage. How he envied those who these days married knowing their odds were just fifty-fifty, if you could believe statistics. Weren't they lucky, those who seemed to know not to "take personally" a rejection by a spouse.

But Duncan's fall had gone so well he'd thought he might well have recovered. He and Nina seemed to have come out from under the umbrella of their awkward start, and the wide sky seemed open, looked so blue. His day at work was challenging in all the good ways, and he'd come back to relying on the fact that he could do it. He was someone Emilie knew she could count on, so he was investing boldly in the future of a generation other than his own. He had his health.

Whose fault was it, then? What he meant was, could he blame it on one of those categories such as "the perversity of man's existence"—talk about not taking something personally—or was it his fault all alone? Would Nina have been capable of what he'd done, of having let it happen to her to derail her? What a contrast he and she made this Thanksgiving.

Duncan tried imagining, as he turned back and began to walk faster, since he had gone off without a jacket, telling Skip how he had this new woman whom he loved a lot, see, but who'd left town, which he couldn't deal with, see, so he had gone to bed with Jessica—yes, Jessie—and was such a hypocrite he would deserve whatever happened. Skip would answer with a blank look, then would say, "Can you run that one by me again?" Skip would laugh self-consciously, apologizing for the fact that Cathy was his one-and-only, then would say, "You mean that after all this time you finally had sex with your wife?" And he would laugh again. "So tell me what you think your problem is, again. I may not know much about life in the big city, but this new girl sounds like trouble anyways. My own advice is, if you can, you ought to stick with what you know."

It cheered him up to know he wouldn't have to have this conversation with his brother, and to be reminded that he didn't envy Skip precisely, even if he did wish sometimes he had Skip's security. It cheered him to know Nina would laugh if he told her Skip had said you ought to stick with what you know. She would ask, "What did you say then?" Duncan would answer, "What I said was, 'All I know is I love Nina.' "

# Eleven

EMILIE HAD PROFITED from having Nina as her companion night and day, day after day, and had she been a little older she'd have asked if they could stay there, please, forever. Nina too had prospered, having had only to follow Dulcie all around and see the sights designed like sets by Mother Nature. All she'd needed to be able to say was what Emilie could—ooh and aah— and for the first time Nina could have argued from experience in favor of the rough life of the single parent.

In the sky the elements were less fortunate, and the pilot had to leave the seat-belt sign on for the rough air up ahead. But over what must have been Pennsylvania Emilie at last and without benefit of drugs (although Nina vowed to discuss this option with the pediatrician if she ever planned another long flight) went limp, closed her eyes, and was gone. For the rest of the trip Nina's only issue was what she should do about the fact that she'd had a full bladder since the Midwest.

Ah but Boston did look pretty from the sky. The points of land were outlined with lights that from up there looked like

rhinestones, and, since planes come in to land at Logan as if
every one was coming in from overseas, it was like sneaking
down the front of an already plunging neckline.

Duncan waited. If he had felt vulnerable when he put them on
the plane it was nothing compared to the vulnerability he felt
now. It was awful to imagine telling Nina, and the best idea he'd
had was that they stop off at the bar up in the tower for old
time's sake and a stiff drink on their way home. He thought he
could tell her there, it was so dark, but knew it was impractical,
since Emilie would not be the right age again to take such places
for a few years. Should he tell her in the car? It was dark there
too.

Then what, though, just drop her off at her apartment? *Then*
what, though, let time go by and call her up to see if she's
speaking to him yet? Much as he would hate this too, he'd rather
have her kick him out—what melodrama it was easy to imagine
—and toss his things after him into the hallway of her building.
What a fool he was the way he'd gone on about Nina's seeming
to have packed her diaphragm. That would be one he'd hear
about, deservedly, first in a voice ferocious with contempt, next
hurt, then later and forever after their recovery (if there was
one) as a half joke. It was not occurring to him not to tell her.

Until now. He sat by the gate waiting for the plane that had
touched down in Dallas and pretended it meant something that
there was a mean TV hero on the program of the same name.
No, he couldn't model himself after "Dallas" for the stark pri-
meval reason that the city had let an assassin live there who had
killed his real live hero. He had standards.

"Oh?" she'd have the right to say. She'd find out one day,
some way, and she'd say, "You have your standards, do you?
Screw those standards!" Which was what, of course, he'd done,
not that she'd be in a position to appreciate the pun. It wasn't in
him not to tell her. Here came the first passengers from Nina's
plane.

Nina had put Emilie in the umbrella stroller she had brought
aboard, and after dropping all the other carryons down at her

feet, her arms were free to put around him. Then she held him long enough to make his eyes burn, and they stood there in the stream of people like a rock around which water rushes. "How I missed you!" she said. Unless she took Emilie to Paris—and how could she, soon?—she never would go anywhere again without him. Absence made the heart grow fonder, it was true, but so what? The whole point was presence.

Duncan merely held her so tight her eyes burned too.

"So," said Nina as they walked now toward the baggage carousel, "you dropped us off and then what?"

This part was good and safe. "Then I went back to the paper," he replied, "and, let's see. Oh, my series started." This was where the trouble had begun, in fact.

"Great," Nina said, "how does it look?"

"It looks good," Duncan answered, "maybe even great. I saved the papers for you."

"Great," she said again, "and did you get a good response?"

"I did." He stopped. "I wish you'd been here."

"So do I." Of course she'd been aware of how his work had been improving in direct proportion, Duncan said, to the stability she offered him. This series demonstrated his compassion and his outrage. It was right on, in its values and in its tone. "I'm so proud of you," she told him.

He had shot himself in the foot, hadn't he? He half expected to limp as he moved to grab the car seat from the merry-go-round. And forget the tower. There was too much luggage.

She was loading herself to look like a pack mule anyway and evidently wouldn't want to hang out at the airport even for old time's sake. Nina's arms were so tired she wished only to put these things down for the last time that day. It was good she had a job for which she would need her eyes, since her eyes weren't tired in the least, thanks to that restful landscape. In fact, it was as if she'd spent five days gazing at enormous paintings done by Georgia O'Keeffe.

Duncan transferred Emilie into the anchored car seat and remembered that the last time he and Nina had left Logan as a couple, Emilie was in a pouch and rode up front in Nina's seat belt. Nina had been planning to be in the backseat of a taxi and had not been comfortable, he recollected now that he knew why, to have Emilie's soft skull between her and the vast traffic. Jules-Jacques's head, hard as it was, had been squashed like a piece of ripe fruit.

Nina sighed and rearranged herself in her seat as if they were at the movies. Since it was the Sunday of a holiday weekend, whatever progress they made would be slow. They were in line to leave the airport and were silent for a long time before she said, "When I lived in Africa there was so much land that was just land, it never stopped amazing me when I moved to France how every inch of land was either cultivated or it had a building put up on it."

Duncan nodded, then since it was dark, he said, "Mn."

"Out West there's the earth again," she went on, "and now back here it's all tinkered with, and tampered with." She paused. "Here they rework the same square footage, don't they?"

"And a lot of it is fill, too. Not the earth the way you mean it."

"What is fill?" asked Nina.

"What is hamburger?" he said, to mimic A-1 steak sauce advertising.

Nina laughed. "What is it, really?"

"Leftovers," he answered.

"Garbage?"

"Old cars and disposable diapers, is what I've heard."

"You could do a story on it," she suggested. "I'd be interested to know."

"It sounds more like a high school term paper," said Duncan.

"What did they use for the Back Bay? That was before there were Pampers."

"Old cars."

"Before there were cars," she said.

"Dead horses, I've heard."

Nina reached across and messed up Duncan's messed-up hair

more. She had no real need for Duncan to be serious. "Still, the land."

"You want to know what's buried there?" he asked. "Under that tumbling tumbleweed you'll find it's nuclear waste. I'm serious."

She didn't want him to be serious. "And dead horses," Nina added. "Mine, for instance."

What a jerk he'd been his whole life, but especially this past week.

"Tell me about Buffalo," she asked, to change the subject.

"Skip's wife, Cathy, gave me dresses to give you for Emilie. She said to tell you that she smocked them all herself, and that you'd know what that meant."

"How sweet of her! And how generous. I can't imagine smocking."

"I came close once. Smoking."

This made Nina laugh too. It was nice to be with someone silly and irreverent after five days trying to be earnest enough to suit Dulcie and her friends. "That's very sweet." It pleased her that he'd obviously told his family all about her. It would be a relief to exist as far as someone's family was concerned. She hadn't, of course, those five years she was with Jules-Jacques.

"Did I say they're hand-me-downs?"

"But I assumed it." Was he trying now to undercut her pleasure?

"What I mean is they're all sizes, not all will fit Emilie now, is what I mean." He had felt her get defensive in that flash of time.

"That's nice," she said, recovered.

"That's all." He touched Nina's cheek, her neck, her shoulder. Yes, he loved her, he was saying.

Gradually, going back and forth like this as if to compensate for not being able to get from one lane to another in this traffic, they were at the toll and finally through the tunnel. Straight ahead was Quincy Market, which meant they were also close to Jessica's place, which looked out over the water. Duncan took the street less traveled and went through the business district, to escape. The tunnel, added to his situation, had made him so claustrophobic he needed air, even if it was too cold to roll the window down for long. If for no other reason than that she knew what the traffic was like, would she send him back out in it once he told her what he'd done?

Now that they were out of the tunnel, Nina wanted to tell him what she'd been thinking. Once they got to her place they'd be getting there still, rearranging Emilie, unpacking somewhat, taking a shower, getting there still, then relaxing. Now would be as good a time as then, and sooner. "What was best, getting away," she began, "was looking at my life from outside it. There were thousands of small observations I made, and I found, to my surprise, I talked a lot. And what I talked about was you." This was unlike her because Nina was more cautious, usually, but she was not uncomfortable. "I told them all I love my life here: life with you, in Boston, having you to share my daughter with, my work and sharing that with you too, helping you the way I do while you help me recover as well." So cautious had Nina been for so long, it was like trying out new muscles, saying this. She didn't even know she had them. "Out there I felt so expansive I just grinned when someone asked my sign and yours and told me it was in the stars or moons or suns that we would meet and love each other."

Here he could have interrupted, but he didn't.

Nina laughed. "I had a chat with one guy our age, and I thought it was about how we seem to have more than one life, by which I meant you, for instance, had been married for a long time and no longer are, and I the widow, sort of, that I am, and then Amanda, even though her life hasn't changed drastically she's making some important changes. It seems to be symptomatic of our generation, I said, that we do in half a life what once took longer." Nina laughed again, remembering the disappointment she saw in the guy's face. It seemed he was quite prepared to talk about reincarnation—literally, his own!—and found Nina's more abstract observations rather rudimentary.

"I know what you mean," said Duncan blandly. His experi-

ence, however, was that he seemed to take more time than had
been allotted.

"For so long I felt so cramped," she resumed, "because my
life wasn't open-ended. I was in a situation that was finite by its
very definition, by my own design." She turned to Duncan.
"And it's not as difficult as it would be here, honestly it's not,
but it's not easy either, even in France, being someone's other
wife. Since it's accepted more or less, the stress is not so obvious. But years of it," and now she turned away again, "and then
that awful ending to it fifteen months ago, then before I could
catch my breath the baby—" Nina also left her sentence open-
ended.

Duncan heard her "fifteen months" and had to admit how he
hated having her know just exactly how much time had gone by
since the accident. He'd thought perhaps she'd stop at one year.
When does one stop giving babies' ages in months; was it
twenty-four? "I know how hard it was," he told her sympathetically. Or thirty-six? No, it had to be twenty-four. Just nine to go
in that case, if the same rule held.

"I know you do," she told him gratefully, "and this is what I'm
saying. I'm beginning to feel like the great weight's lifting. I'm
beginning to feel as if there's a future." Now she looked at him
again, to say, "That has been missing, you know, not only from
our relationship, but from my life." A pair of tears dropped
down her cheeks like bait on hooks on fishing lines.

There was no way in Chinatown for him to stop the car, so
Duncan took her hand. He otherwise would have pulled over
and burst into tears in her arms, and eclipsed what she was
saying.

"Oh I knew I'd be around, I'd be involved with Emilie. I knew
there was a future that way. But I didn't *welcome* it, I didn't want
it." Nina took a breath and told him, "Now I want it. And I have
it."

At a red light Duncan kissed her, which was a way to avoid
words. What he felt like doing, though, was throwing up. They
were in her old neighborhood now, in the South End she had

left to spend that month out at Amanda's, and he would be taken only for a wino or a junkie if he were to puke in public. No one would think he was just a hypocrite.

"I'm sure it's very difficult for you to take my history in. Yours is much more conventional, and easier to integrate, I'm sure, than mine is. That's what I was saying out there in these conversations, how two people like us nowadays each have our own work on our own lives before we can come together. Then we have to like each other as we are, and *then* find a way to have a diagonal relationship with each other's past. See what I mean?" She could show him back at her place how it was a box with three sides, with a top but not a bottom if you drew lines to connect all the points that could be connected. There was no direct line, this meant, between two pasts, so although it was a dance, it couldn't quite be called a box step. "Do you?"

"It sounds complicated," he said lightly, then responding to her having said he'd made her life worth living, or at least worth looking forward to, "I love you."

Nina laughed. "You once suggested we have pamphlets made up, all of us, remember? All the time that would be saved, you said, if everyone used handouts, as if we were back in school. You were right."

"Was I?" He was glad he was right about something.

She laughed. "But when I told Dulcie and her friends your idea they assumed what you had meant was past *lives.*"

"So their brochures could say something like 'Travel Back Through Time?' I like it." Now he laughed too.

" 'Witness History with a Viking!' "

" 'Meet a Pharaoh!' "

" 'Invent Fire!' Dulcie has no sense of humor, none at all," said Nina, "does she?" This she asked as if he'd met her in some past life.

"Was she someone interesting?"

"Who, Dulcie? I don't know." She paused. "I couldn't bring myself to ask her." Nina yawned. "I'm glad to be back." They were crossing Massachusetts Avenue and would be home soon. "I missed you."

"I missed you too." And wasn't this why it had happened? He hoped to have her believe him when he told her this was why, no matter that it wouldn't seem so. They were close now.

It was only seven o'clock Santa Fe time, but Nina was quite exhausted. She decided all she'd do when they got back was feed the fish and water the plants, then collapse.

He could have said he ought to water his plants too, but even Duncan had finished postponing this. He didn't want to seize the moment, but he didn't want to lose it and be basing his decision not to tell her on default. He made two drinks and sat down on the living room floor on a cushion. Already he ached. "I got a call from Jessica," he said, "about the series, and she asked me for a drink." It didn't matter anymore who had asked whom.

She came and sat. She'd get the plants in the bedroom later.

"That was Wednesday, on my way to Buffalo." He took a sip.

And so did she. She was no good at listening to him tell her about Jessica, who wasn't dead.

"She had a bottle of champagne we drank, and then we went to her place, walking her home, I guess it was." Had he told her that he'd gone there once before, on his way back from Buffalo after his cousin's wedding when there was no answer at Amanda's? He knew he'd deliberated, but he couldn't now recall what he'd decided. Typical. "She lives down on the waterfront," he said.

"I know." He'd told her that he'd gone there, in a conversation about views.

"That's right, I was there once before." To reassure her it was not a habit of his, Duncan meant.

He was so unrelaxed about this, so was she. "And so?" she asked. Instead she could have said, "So what?"

"And so this time I saw her bedroom, going through it to the bathroom. I had never seen her bedroom since she left mine."

Duncan's fingers knotted as if he were knitting without yarn. "And my reaction to it was quite complicated." There was no point keeping Nina in suspense. "It was clear to me what I felt was jealousy, but not clear of whom. That whole day I'd been aware of you, your absence, and I think it frightened me to have you gone, or anyway to realize how much I loved you." He could feel her studying him, so he looked up to say to her, "How I love you. I so love you."

She stayed silent.

"You were gone and Jessica had left me, and I hated feeling like the victim. This is stupid, but I saw on what was my side of the bed a magazine on the night table, one I hadn't ever heard of. Called *Success*. It made me feel like such a failure, then it made me awfully bold. I must have figured what the hell more can I lose." He sighed. "This isn't a defense, just a description. Maybe it's an explanation."

Nina only cared to know whether they had or hadn't, but she wouldn't ask. Eventually he'd have to say. Of course they had.

"I went into the kitchen and brought Jessica, essentially, back to the bedroom. I'm not saying that she wasn't willing, even eager, but it was my impulse, my idea. It was my need."

"Will you stop trying to find the right word? Christ, Duncan!" Needless to say, it was not this that made her mad.

"And I, and we—" got it on? made love? had sex? "—we went to bed. I'm—"

"Sorry?"

"Yes." He was. "I'm sorry."

Nina's voice was shrill with disbelief. "How could you let me say that in the car?" She stood and stumbled on the watering can, which sent up a splash. "How *could you?*"

"It was the best news I think I've ever had, what you were saying in the car."

"Oh sure, oh *sure* it was. Don't you know what I *said?* Why did you let me say those things?"

"You mean they wouldn't have been true if you had known?"

"No, but I never would have said them. *Never!*" Never would she again. *"How* could you have let me go on telling you I love you? What are you, a *sadist?"*

Was she really angrier that he had let her say she loves him than that he'd made love to Jessica? "Because I wanted you to say you love me," Duncan answered.

"You're some victim," Nina challenged, "you're some victim, all right. Sounds to me like you've got things right where you want them. By 'things' I mean people, of course, not that you seem to understand there's a difference."

*"I'm* a person. That's the whole point, that's what happened!"

She felt dizzy, so she sat, three yards away. "I'm tired of being tyrannized by Jessica, I'm sick of it. Don't you plan *ever* to recover?"

"Believe me," said Duncan, "I'm sure it's not worse than being haunted by a ghost." As if it mattered what it meant to Duncan that Jules-Jacques had died. "I'm sorry, never mind that." It was not as if Nina burned incense and lit candles at a shrine she'd built to him. And it *was* worse: if anyone knew tyranny by Jessica, he did.

"Don't bring up Jules-Jacques here. Don't you have *any* standards?"

Well, he'd thought he did have, but, "You're right, I'm sorry," he said.

"What you're saying, bringing him up, is I should be *used to* sharing my man with another woman, right?"

"I didn't mean that, no."

"So say it!"

"No."

"You obviously think it shouldn't *matter* to me after all my practice as the other woman, don't you?"

"No."

"She's used to it, you told yourself, so what the hell, why not? She knows I have a wife, you told yourself, and obligations. *She'll* be a good sport, you said. You shit."

This he could not deny; he was a shit. He hadn't thought of any of this. The truth was, the problem was, he hadn't thought at all of Nina. It was as if he were simply cashing in a saving's bond he'd held for years, that had matured. It was to get back what he'd put in, plus the interest. When he was in Jessica it was to get, not give. It was to pick up what he'd left with her: his self-respect.

"How could you? Have you no imagination at all? Couldn't you *imagine* that this would be a big issue for me? If you'd said you picked up someone in a bar it would be better than your wife."

"My ex-wife."

"No, your *wife*." The anger—it surprised her—cauterized her. Any juice there might have been for tears evaporated. "No, your wife," Nina repeated, staring hard at Duncan.

What a thought. But it was true it was more complicated than what he had told her. He and Jessica made love, then dozed or fell asleep—or at least he did—and at some point, who knew when in the night, he was wakened by sensations that were dreamlike. He was being stroked so lightly it was as if butterflies were carrying him in the sky and he was floating the way they do, being borne on currents of air. He had always wanted to fly— not fly airplanes but have wings—and he thought he was. By the time he came down to earth he was so filled with desire he had to burst, and so he did in Jessica, who'd brought him to her with her two hands. Over time she'd brought him into manhood too, and it was not her fault he'd lost it. This was what kept him awake and waiting for it to get light so he could leave.

"Now you should go."

"But could I tell—"

"I don't want to hear anything more."

She was right. What could be worse than telling her he loved her? He got up on stiff legs and picked up the suitcase she had brought in for him from the car. Remembering, he set it down again and pulled the zipper to him.

"No, don't open it," she warned him.

"But the dresses Cathy sent you for the baby—"

"Don't you take them out of there!" She almost said, "I'll kill you, Duncan, if you take them out of there."

Before he had a chance to think how Cathy would expect some thanks and couldn't Nina please write her a thank-you note, Duncan remembered that's what he had said to Jessica about his mother's pillow. When would he—this was the question—make some progress? When—this was it—would he grow up?

Nina contemplated asking for her key and giving him his, but there were the other things too, and then she'd cry, surely. And he'd ask her if she could forgive him, and she'd try to. "Go," she told him.

He would not ask, "Can I call you?" or say he would be in touch. She'd say no and it wouldn't matter what he said, she'd still say no. He said again, "I'm sorry."

"Just go. Go away." She didn't feel well, not at all, not that she ought to.

Duncan let himself out the door, and Nina opened a window. She felt feverish. As if she were going to faint—she never had and didn't know what it should feel like—she sat down again and put her head between her knees, which made her certain she was going to vomit. She could hear the engine of his Saab start up, then go away as she had asked. She'd never make it to the bathroom. Her saliva became bitter, so she lurched into the kitchen and after a heave brought up what little there was in her stomach. She was standing by the sink and realized both that she'd never vomited except into a toilet bowl and that this was a better place: you didn't have to kneel to throw up in the kitchen and, if you were lucky, as she was, you had a wall switch for your Kitchen-Aid "food waste disposer." In less than a minute it was as if it had never happened.

# Part IV

Part IV

# Twelve

THIS WINTER what it did was snow, voluminously. At first it was very pretty, petticoat on petticoat, but as the layering increased, the city became like a woman in too many heavy skirts, who couldn't function from the waist down.

Duncan's Christmas gave him yet another opportunity to feel estranged. When Buffalo got heavy snowfall after snowfall after snowfall, he got stranded there and overstayed even his mother's welcome. She told Duncan to find some way, even dogsled, to get back to Boston if they were so boring he had to watch television all night long and sleep all day. And who was it he spent so much time on the phone with?

Nina had anticipated Christmas this year as one more in a long series: Jules-Jacques always with his family, she the orphan taken in by friends. Indeed Amanda had invited her and Emilie to Weston for the blessings of the season and some sledding, but they'd spent two nights and three days having the most wonderful time, and Nina had realized the difference Emilie made in her life. She meant that Nina at last had a family.

And Nina agreed when Duncan asked if they could be to-gether New Year's Eve, to get the old thing over with and out of the way before it contaminated January. He arrived at her apart-ment with champagne and a bright woolly hat and mittens for the baby. Both so cautious, they drank little of the champagne, and she didn't ask him to stay much past midnight. What she said was that she knew that fourteen years was fourteen years, and even if it was belated and at her expense a marriage of that length required a proper burial. She told him it reflected well on him that, in spite of the fact that Jessica had hurt him in a big way over the years, he was capable of being careful with her feelings. Who could argue with his living by the Golden Rule instead of the law of the jungle? But he wasn't going to work it out while she stood by and watched. She wasn't going to hold his hand as Duncan terminated what the courts had declared null and void the previous summer.

Duncan said he was resolved to win back her trust in the new year if he didn't before the end of the old one, but he couldn't tell her what she'd hoped to hear, that Jessica had disappeared without a trace.

The facts were that Jessica was not yet ready, and that she'd convinced him it was best to let her try to compensate for all those years of the cold shoulder. It would be important, went her argument, for how they would regard their marriage from the future, looking back, and anyway she felt it would be in-authentic to deny it. What was it to him, she asked, but good news that at last she wanted to be friends?

He didn't say this, though he tried to. What he said instead was what he might have read in a divorce book: people who split up are almost never talking to each other. This did not mean they're not speaking, although some aren't; they're not talking. Something can end, but how can you finish it if you're not talking? Duncan wasn't saying people should be able to talk— isn't it the point of the divorce that they can't?—but people shouldn't then expect to have it over with. Nothing is over, he believed, until it's finished.

Anyway, it got them going, and as if their life was like the jigsaw puzzle Duncan's nieces had picked out for him for Christmas, they had found the straight-edged pieces for the frame. Once it was started, they could work on sections every day until it was put back together. Early January was a consolation too in that there was an evening when she let him stay the night. They were aware that Jessica and Duncan had made love more recently than they had—just one day more recently, in fact—but that had gone unmentioned. There were no words either for the wonderful relief they both felt.

So that when his birthday approached and he said the only present he hoped to get was to wake up on that birthday in his own bed with her with him, she agreed. And since it was his fortieth, Nina thought Emilie could give him a rocking chair for his old age, an antique she'd had refinished and upholstered. She was pleased to have the impulse to give Duncan something large and permanent. It was as if she had concluded that there was to be a future.

She came into Duncan's kitchen after having swiveled Emilie to sleep in Duncan's desk chair. Everything, as far as she could tell, had been left as she'd left it in November, and this made it seem as if it hadn't been that long ago. She figured out, though, that the baby had last been in this crib one fifth of her entire life ago, which put it all back in perspective. The reality was that it had been fall and now was winter. Time was marching on around them. Nina went to stand by the quartz heater shaped like a magic wand, to get warm.

"This place is freezing, isn't it? I should have made red flannel hash and not poached salmon." He had set the table and arranged a centerpiece of daisies. "Skip and Cathy sent me some blue flannel sheets, for thinning blood they said, now that I'm almost older. We can sleep on them tonight." He was so happy, having her there. "Let's go dancing for my birthday," he suggested, turning his head from the parsley he was chopping to see how she was reacting. "I was thinking all day how we've never danced. I hope you like to."

"Yes, I love to," Nina answered, laughing that he'd thought that all day. She went to the telephone to call the sitter to reserve her for the next night and asked Duncan what she could do in the meantime.

"Dry the lettuce? I'll do dressing, then we're ready." Then the phone rang. "Dancing is a good way to turn forty, isn't it?" asked Duncan as he went to answer the phone.

Nina nodded. She was forty-one already by a month, her fortieth having been spent with Rosie Lopez, from downstairs, and Rosie's brother. They went bowling—she for the first time in her life, seven and a half months pregnant—and Rosie brought birthday candles and got them to stand up in the mushrooms on the pizza they went out for, after. It was the best time she'd ever had in Boston, and Nina reminded herself to call Rosie. She had promised before having left for Santa Fe that they would get together, the three of them, and go bowling. Rosie hadn't yet met Duncan.

"Oh hi," Duncan said.

She cleared some counter space by moving aside Duncan's mail and heard him answer, "No, I haven't opened it yet. No, I'm cooking." Nina saw that the return address on the top envelope was what she guessed was Jessica's. If Duncan could say, "Nina is here and we're about to have dinner, so I'll call you back tomorrow," she decided that she wouldn't let it bother her this time. But Duncan didn't. "That's nice, no, I can't, though. No, I'm tied up lunch and dinner, thanks, though. Then too."

Duncan tried to indicate to Nina he was helpless for the moment but would get off right away, but Nina kept her back to him, patting the lettuce. "That's great," he said, "good for you, a raise, that's great." He could see on the counter next to Nina's left hand Jessica's familiar writing. Now she wanted him to open it, to see her jingle to him. "I forgot to bring the mail in, actually," he lied. So then he had to listen to her say it. Why could she not take the hint? "That's cute," Duncan responded feebly, "listen, though, I've got to run, I'll call you back tomorrow. Yeah, thanks. Good for you, about the raise. OK." He hung up and reported, "Jessica was calling to say they gave her a raise."

"I gathered Jessica was calling to see if you got her card."

"That too." Duncan took the phone off the hook, looked for some matches, lit the candles. "Let's forget she called, OK? She doesn't have that many friends. She got a raise and called, that's all."

"Why couldn't you say that you'd call her back tomorrow?"

"But I did," he said, not without accuracy.

" 'Nina's here,' you could have said," protested Nina.

"That's right, but that's not her business. I just try to be polite, no more."

"Here, open it and get it over with."

"Why are you doing this?"

"No, Duncan, why are you?"

"But if I cared, why wouldn't I have opened it while you put Emilie to bed? Yes, it's perverse, as you have said, but do you need to hear me tell her?"

"What's 'cute'?"

"What?"

"You said, 'That's cute.' "

"Nothing's cute, that was a lie too."

"Jesus, Duncan, don't you hear me telling you this threatens me?"

"It shouldn't, though."

"It *does,* though." Nina's voice cracked, and she was embarrassed.

Duncan took the envelope from her and dropped it on the floor and tried to hold her. When she stiffened and pulled back, he said, "You think she doesn't know about you? She knows all about you. She was the first one I told, the day after we met again at Logan. But it wouldn't matter what I said, and not because she's deaf, because she's that self-centered. It's what's going on for her that matters to her, only that. And sure, I guess it flatters me to some extent, all this attention, her belated interest in me, I admit that. Do I trust her? No, I don't, because it isn't really me she cares about, or else it would have mattered when I said I love you. You, I told her, Nina." The sleeve of her sweater had been pushed up for the lettuce, and he stroked her arm. "She's always been one who acts out her feelings without reference to whatever else is going on, it's what she learned to call authentic and still thinks is all that counts. And I'm supposed to care because, she's so important to herself, how could I not? How could I not be sympathetic, even yielding, when she says she has discovered after all, comparing me to other men since me, that I'm not all that bad?" It made him laugh to hear it said, it was so stupid.

"No, you're not," said Nina neutrally.

"I *know* I'm not that bad, I've always known I never was as bad as *that.*" He had to laugh again, though it was more absurd than merely funny.

"Open it."

He stooped and retrieved the envelope he tore open. On the card there was a tall vase of blue roses and a nosegay of red violets. Inside it said, "Violets are red, Roses are blue, We've got it backwards, Me and you."

"You mean she made this?" Nina was impressed but startled to see that the card looked "real" but was, in fact, hand-drawn and hand-lettered.

"She decided as a child, apparently, that she can do at least as well as Hallmark can, and sometimes better."

Nina looked again at the card. "Don't you think you ought to tell her it's just not *appropriate* to spend an evening making this thing?" What was inappropriate was sending it, she meant to say.

"She'd say she finds it necessary to work things out in her own time and that as a lawyer she knows more about divorce than I do, and that it's a tribute to me. What's it to me, she would ask, to open my mail? She has ways of making you doubt everything about yourself, believe me." Duncan left unsaid that Jessica would also bring up the night in November once more, what she called "the smoking-gun night," even if it did ignore his own interpretation, which was, to refresh her memory, that imagining some man in her bed had forced him to feel rejected first by her and then by Nina, whom he was afraid would leave him for a cowboy. That Duncan's initiation had provided Jessica with the long-overdue chance to forgo snubbing him sexually, and that, in *fact*, she had been eager, qualified as a by-product. Jessica had said when he presented reasons, "You don't have to find excuses. I enjoyed it."

"It's true," Nina answered simply, "she has ways of making me doubt everything about myself."

This time she let him hold her. "What will happen, I assure you," he said soothingly, "is it will stop. She's getting bored already—note the sarcasm in her card's jingle—so she'll become indifferent soon and we'll be back to where we started when she brought divorce up in the first place." Duncan sighed. "I'm sorry about all this, but that's where I would like to end up, at indifference. Can you wait this part out with me?"

She could have used reassurance that this was a one-time wait and not a ritual in the making, but her instinct was to trust him. Yes, she trusted Duncan, evidently. Did she want to doubt that now, again? "I can, yes," Nina told him.

"How's the lettuce, dry?" He let her see that his eyes weren't, and was relieved to find that hers weren't either. In the presence of their feelings for each other, they were joined.

"Do you really want me to say whether or not the lettuce is dry?"

Duncan grinned. "Do you know what I want you to say? You're right, it has nothing to do with the lettuce. I want you to say that you think we can live together one day."

Nina closed her eyes as if to stop the pink from spreading from them to her cheeks. She smiled at him then, but apologetically, and answered, "How's the salmon, poached?"

Then later, everything accomplished but the night's sleep, Nina thought about an answer. They'd proceeded with their dinner, entertaining one another with some stories from their childhoods, and made love on Duncan's new blue flannel sheets as slowly and distinctly as their urgency was going to let them. Then when midnight came it brought them Duncan's birthday and more talk of wishes before Duncan drifted out from under her like the tide from a boat aground whose only way off was to wait for an incoming tide to lift her.

Nina waited for sleep, entertaining herself with the fact that Emilie in her ten months already might have had more time alone with Nina than her own mother had given her in forty-one years. Even during this last visit, whenever Nina suggested something they might do together, Vivian told Mike about it and persuaded him to join them; there he would be, waiting for them by the door. And it was not that Nina didn't want him along—in fact she preferred his company to her mother's and might not have known what to do out there alone with a stranger—it was merely principle. In principle she and her mother, having spent so many years in one another's company around the world, should have been able to have lunch. She took her time considering this, trying to discover finally which it was: if Vivian had loved Mike too much or her too little.

All through school and college she had listened to the tales of woe of sons and daughters of those worst-case marriages and envied them their forced alignment with one parent or the other. It would not have been creative if she'd said so, but it was apparent to her that divorce made kids feel useful, let them know how much they mattered, and that she'd wished for that feeling in her own life. (It was good that Duncan was asleep for this, on second thought, to save her having to defend her fervent hopes throughout a long, unprofitable adolescence for her own parents' estrangement and eventual divorce. It wasn't quite as literal as it would sound, and he would not know in the dark that she could stand it if he laughed.) She'd hated having parents who were so dependent on each other there were no needs to be met by their two children, who had waited on the sidelines, as if this were ballroom dancing and not life, for an occasion— serpent bite or scholarship to Wellesley College—to cut in.

She'd promised herself all her life that, if she ever were to marry, she'd refuse to love her husband all that much, especially if they had children. (Duncan would explode with laughter.)

But the truth was she was serious at some level, which was why her primary relationship, twice, was with a man with whom Nina had an ending ready-made, first her commitment to continue on at Wellesley, then his to his wife and children. The truth was she had to unlearn before she would have a chance of ever learning. (Duncan would wish he were there to hear her say how much she wanted to unlearn.) In realizing this, Nina saw she was anxious for this progress, A, and B, as Duncan would say, it was relatively easy to accomplish. All she had to do was let go of a few suitcases. All she had to do was travel light.

Nina had promised Emilie immediately upon her birth that she would only love her more and never less than at that sublime moment; she had actually told that absolutely newborn baby not to worry! But it was exactly what she wanted Emilie to know most, even if it did reveal her own lifelong preoccupation. And it was the truth, and there were worse things to have promised than that this was only the beginning. Nina smiled. If she were telling Duncan this he'd say, "That's right, for instance, 'Kid, it's all downhill from here on in, so here's the house key: good luck to you.'" Her own good luck was this good man and the proof of these eight months since the day they first saw each other at the French Library that their feelings were indeed resilient. Nina hadn't realized it was eight months and wondered if they would be born soon. She would only love him more and never less than at this moment.

It was pity Nina felt now for her mother, who appeared as on a stage, a character purposely drawn larger than life in order that she would seem lifelike. Nina watched her mother tell the audience, soliloquizing, that she knew her daughters held her in contempt for her refusal to allow them access to their father, but it was her *inability*, not her refusal. She would have liked to be bigger, but the fact was she was small. And she was scared. Her mother said, "Why are we gypsies? That way there aren't any standards to fall short of."

Recognition struck Nina like a chord on the organ of the largest church she'd ever been in. It still sounded in the silence following.

And Nina nearly said out loud, "No, that's no actress, that's my *mother!*" That was her real mother pleading (Nina being judge and jury) for a lighter sentence for the crime confessed to. It was not an option to return a verdict of not guilty—the confession was on record—but there was the matter of intent in question and whether or not the malice was aforethought. If it was mere consequence, was that so awful? Nina took a deep breath and released her mother's hold on her and let her go but set her free. And then she slept.

But Emilie, as if noting the change in atmospheric pressure, cried out later in the night in urgent need of reassurance. Soaking wet, and so cold her skin was embossed in a piqué, Nina put a new diaper on her and a long-sleeved shirt under dry, footed "woollies," euphemistically so called despite the tag that said they were fully Acrylic. Holding Emilie in one arm, with the other Nina stripped the crib, remaking it with extras as a nurse does, half by half. She tried convincing Emilie to want to stay there and knew that was silly of her, so they swiveled and Nina sang a song called *"Plaisir d'Amour,"* which didn't do it. They walked to the kitchen and back and brought with them the quartz heater and a bottle of warm water tinted with cranberry juice. This time Nina sang, "Twinkle, Twinkle Little Star."

Now Emilie concentrated less on muscle flexing and more on the reflex of her sucking. Soon there would be pauses, then extended pauses stretching to rests, then there would be rest itself. By the light of the heater, as if she were embers, Nina would watch Emilie cease flickering, grow dim, and go out. She would bring her up in case a bubble wanted out and place her on her stomach for the hours left until morning. There was one less than there had been.

And it had begun to snow, as promised on the early news. She watched it in a streetlight's halo and remembered freshman year when she and someone down the hall who'd lived only in Florida stayed up a good part of the night while their first snow accumulated. Before they could ever sleep they'd needed to go out into it, even if it was against the regulations, and they had. It had amazed them to leave footprints not on sand and not with bare feet, and they'd left them everywhere until at last they were caught up with by the watchman, who escorted them back to their dormitory with assurances that he would not report them. The other young woman—"girl" in those days—transferred at semester break, to Duke.

She wondered how many there might be who were Wellesley '63 and never married. "Not yet," she would answer at her twentieth reunion this year, if she went, when someone passed out questionnaires and asked them to give marital histories for a profile. Others would be on their second or their third, which would make Nina feel young. What would make her feel appropriately old would be the mention of those classmates who were dead already from, as it is awkwardly put, natural or unnatural causes. Nina would feel then that she had better hurry. The thought that she might consider going to her twentieth college reunion was completely unexpected, since all those years she'd assumed her life would be lived out abroad, where she "belonged," not within reach.

She was within reach for the first time in two decades of predicting what her life was going to look like. This was partly the effect a child has, that no matter what, no matter where, in five or six years she'd be ready for first grade; but it was mostly the result of Nina's feeling settled down. She'd lived in Boston fifteen months and voted to elect the governor of Massachusetts. Her job at the Museum of Fine Arts had a future, in that there would always be contemporary acquisitions and, more pointedly, they seemed to like the work she'd done already. And she was in love with Duncan. If she weren't in love with Duncan, would it matter to her that another woman had sent him a birthday card?

Nina unplugged the heater and went back to bed but back to lying there awake. Duncan was such a sound sleeper she knew that she could use his heat to warm her feet and tuck her body in behind his and not wake him. She could ride behind him, holding on at his waist, as if on a motorcycle, not that this was her ambition. If she would permit herself to, Nina could uncover something, and she knew it. She had a routine she called "doing the artichoke," a system of working her way through the leaves past the choke and to the heart of certain problems, one of which had been put on a plate before her in the kitchen.

She'd tried hard to be offended by the card but would admit now it was merely leaves to pull off. If she wanted to be threatened she could get in closer to the truth about it: Jessica was thinking she should have a baby one of these days and was looking into ways.

This came to her in such firm form it didn't seem like speculation, in spite of the fact that she'd heard nothing to suggest it was true. Duncan had, if anything, described Jessica as the sort who wore clothes she was always needing to protect from other people's children's fingers. Duncan's point of view was that she had decided back in law school she believed in only children: namely, herself. Even discounting for bias against Jessica, the case in favor of her wanting children of her own was pretty weak. But Nina meant she could *imagine* Jessica at thirty-seven looking into motherhood and reaching the conclusion that she'd loved Duncan enough at one time in their lives for them to have a child together. She could picture Jessica deciding this and, maybe without telling Duncan, getting pregnant.

Maybe she already was! This was the choke.

Nina counted out on her fingers seven weeks—saw Jessica as that much pregnant!—since Thanksgiving. Now the jingle Jessica sent—"Violets are red, Roses are blue, We've got it backwards, Me and you"—meant something, and this was the choke all right.

Nina tried to remember everything Duncan had told her about what had happened that night, and she saw it as a setup.

Jessica had found the moments of his weakness and her strength
and gotten them to coincide. And gotten pregnant. Nina tried
hard to remember Duncan's mention of what birth control
they'd used, but Duncan hadn't mentioned any. There it was.

She couldn't breathe and had to sit up in the cold to get some
air. Here was the heart, in quarters, in four chambers like a real
heart.

One: if it were true, how could she tolerate it? Nina knew from
the alarm she felt she absolutely couldn't, no, she couldn't tolerate a child of his being conceived and born and raised and her
not being that child's mother.

Two: her eyes filled at the thought that someone would do
that to Duncan, who was innocently sleeping, unsuspecting.
Duncan, being loving, being generous, would only show that he
was happy. He'd never tell Jessica she had no right to interfere
like that in his life. Certainly he'd never show his disappointment to the baby. It wasn't the baby's fault she had been born.

Three: consequently and at last, Nina began to wonder what
Jules-Jacques would have felt if he hadn't died that day. She had
assumed he'd have been thrilled, but what if, for some reason,
he had been upset. And for what reason? Not because he didn't
love her, not because he wouldn't want a child by her, but that
he would have thought he ought to be consulted. He might have
thought Nina shouldn't have decided on her own, even if it was
a decision that was not premeditated but instead one coming as
a child does from an act of love. But *why* not? Well, because men
weren't just walking sperm banks? True, but this would not at all
be Jules-Jacques talking. He was not—had not been—one who
used the liberation's language, men's or women's. So why not,
then?

It was simple. It was because Jules-Jacques would have
thought about what Yvette would feel. It was one thing for a man
to have a mistress, but a child, no. Jules-Jacques would have
cared how she felt.

Four: finally, it was Yvette's turn, the wife who throughout has barely had a name. Now, finally, it was time for Nina to attempt to understand and then to care what she'd been feeling.

Nina left the warm bed, brought the heater from the study back to Duncan's kitchen, and sat down where they'd had dinner. Maybe Nina had begun to. Maybe, starting with her patting lettuce dry in paper towels, she had been feeling what Yvette felt. What was it she had decided about whether she could tolerate a child being conceived and born and raised and her not being that child's mother? Nina was ashamed of herself. Not once had it mattered to her what Yvette felt.

This was not to say she wished or ever would that Emilie did not exist, only that her joy with Jules-Jacques, of which Emilie was the emblem, hadn't been bought with Yvette's pain.

# Thirteen

WHEN IT WORKED, Mark Otis always saw it coming. This allowed him to be ready for what Cartier-Bresson called "the decisive moment," the moment born of all the preparation. At the circus any child could practice with the trapeze acts, could watch them swing the bars just so and hang from them in just such a way as to make the transfer from one to the other bound to happen. Figure skaters too, a child could study their moves easily and know where they will intersect in lift or spin by having noticed how fast they were going in their opposite directions, in their overlapping circles. In real life it was less obvious. You had to work at it to see.

Mark dialed home, and he got his father. It was lunchtime. "Hey, Dad, how come you're home?"

"Sandwich," said his father, chewing audibly, "there. What's up?"

"Since I have to do some printing, I just thought I'd come out after work and do it there."

"Tonight? Your brother has his game, so we'll be eating at five-thirty. Shall I tell Mom to expect you?"

"No, I can't that early. I'll get out there when I can."

"That won't go over very well."

"I can't get out there by five-thirty, Dad," protested Mark, "not that I'd want to eat then anyway."

"Tonight's the game against Beverly, I mean. Our Bobby's doing great, they call him Bobby Bird. You ought to try and catch the game."

"I can't, though, if I've got to print."

"Then use your darkroom at the paper's my advice. I'm not sure Bob would understand. Your mother wouldn't, that's for sure. I thought she asked you to come out and you said you were busy tonight, or am I wrong?" Mr. Otis checked his watch and saw he had to move along.

"Was that tonight? Must have had something that got canceled."

"So what should I tell your mother?" Down to basics.

"Nothing, I guess. If I show up at the game, I show up."

"You won't get a seat unless we save one; don't you read your own newspaper? Beverly's on fire this season. Bobby'd be so happy if you'd say you'll come." He checked his watch again, as if more than a minute had gone by. "I'll say you didn't call, how's that?"

Mark sighed. He knew when he'd lost to his father. If it were his mother he had lost to, he'd be going to the game.

"We haven't seen you in so long, though. Come on out some other time, Son, will you? 'Bye now."

"See you," Mark replied, although he didn't mean it literally. They were the only people who were not sufficiently impressed, in his opinion, even if they had been once, protecting him and his young talent as they were now protecting Bobby's. He could move his darkroom out and go to it whenever he liked, and, Mark thought, maybe he ought to. When he thought about it more, he realized he liked his darkroom in their basement for those years, like this one, when Christmas and New Year's fell on weekends. It was his solution to the problem others solved with Bowl games played by teams they haven't followed. Mark could always disappear and come back squinting and a little stoned on fumes on holidays, and no one minded. He decided not to push it. He even wrote a note to himself to check the next day's paper for the score.

"Yoo hoo, come in please," Duncan kidded, "yoo hoo, Otis! No one can complain about your concentration, at least."

"Yeah?" Mark was surprised to look up and see Duncan Jones, who still seemed to make a point of not starting conversations with him. He said, "Oh hi, happy birthday." Someone had collected money for a sheet cake with a computer keyboard done in frosting, and he'd had some.

"Thanks for the cake."

"Sure, no problem. So how's forty?"

"So far I can recommend it very highly. What are you now, halfway there?" Duncan smiled warmly. He was feeling too expansive for sarcasm.

"Only fifteen years away, I'm gaining on it." What a stupid thing to say, Mark felt.

"Boy genius," Duncan answered.

"Get any good presents?" What a stupid question. Duncan did intimidate him still, no question.

"Bic just gave me his, in fact, an easy story on a guy, a painter, who sounds schizophrenic. Paints the Arctic and the Caribbean both. It will be very short, I'll tell you, so you'd better plan to make the pictures big." He laughed because of course it was neither Mark's nor his own decision what size either of their work was when it went onto the page. And Bic had not said Otis would have the assignment anyway. Duncan was merely trying for coworker loyalty on the occasion of his birthday.

But it worked. Mark said, "No problem. What's he have, two studios? A winter and a summer place?" Mark laughed with Duncan.

"He must have deductions enough for all three of us, travel expenses alone."

"Ask who he submits them to," suggested Mark.

"Or else he's someone who's never been anywhere except on drug trips."

"That would do it," Mark said knowingly. "Ask who he submits *those* expenses to." He laughed some more.

Then so did Duncan. Somehow he'd missed every drug but grass, with the exception, once, of some hashish he couldn't stop believing wasn't mountain goat turds. Probably it was true that the Arctic and the Caribbean were hallucinations. He had not himself hallucinated. Now that he was forty, Duncan had to admit he regretted not having a more misspent youth. Before leaving Mark's desk he said, "Thanks again, for the cake."

"Sure, no problem," Mark replied again. Mark watched him cross the newsroom and was struck by how much Duncan seemed to be part of a team. Mark wondered if that might be true because of Duncan's having been there fourteen and a half years (as opposed to his own three and a half) but decided no, it wasn't. Duncan, like his brother, Bobby, was the teammate sort of person, which he wasn't, being at heart solitary. Also, he liked to be better than the competition and, if colleagues were your competition, this did not make for team spirit. Still, Mark noticed that it did seem to be fun. He guessed he might surprise them after all and show up at five-thirty. Bobby always came to his things.

Duncan's desk was out of sight of Mark's, but Mark stayed in his mind another minute, long enough for Duncan to appreciate that Mark might have a sense of humor after all. He hadn't ever noticed, frankly, any trace of wit or ease and wondered if it was that Mark was getting older, or if he was. He knew *he* was. What else could he think about but this, today? He called the gallery where the show was being hung and said he knew that the reception was the next day, but he'd like to see the paintings without people in the foreground, also interview the artist for a story for the *Globe*. The magic word "publicity" brought someone to the phone who sounded more important and much more accommodating, which was how it worked each time. This wasn't what was meant by the power of the press, he knew, but boy, it sure was power. It would be nice if he had more of it in his personal life, Duncan couldn't help but think.

Lunch at the Ritz Bar was to celebrate his birthday with his oldest friend in Boston and best tennis partner, the man who had told him, when he said about the Club Med travel poster of a woman offering him all she had and a pineapple. The pineapple was by far the more appealing, "You're a pervert, Jones, you know that?"

Duncan went on with his story of the rocking chair's arrival, now that it had been established they had everything they needed from the waiter, telling Eddie, "It was tied with a red ribbon, and she had me cut it with a pair of scissors, not untie it. It was like the opening of a bridge and like I was the mayor."

"And you loved it," Eddie said. He touched his glass to Duncan's, adding, "Here's to you, kid, happy birthday."

"Thanks," said Duncan, touched by the initiative from an unsentimental, almost antisentimental, Eddie. "And it was a bridge, in fact," Duncan continued, "nothing Nina could have given me would have made me so happy. It seemed such an obvious investment in me. And my future. And our future."

Eddie's marriage was what he called two thirds working, which was all it ever had been, but he had enough kids to watch them play doubles and he knew, unless his wife made the move (which she wouldn't), he would never be in Duncan's shoes. He envied Duncan his beginning, now that he had made it out from underneath all the divorce shit, and liked Nina even though he could see what his wife meant when she complained Nina was aloof (by which she meant Nina was not confessional) and quite wrapped up in her career (meaning she had one). "Elaine always asks me if I've asked you," Eddie answered warmly, although indirectly, "so now should I tell her you admitted you and Nina 'have a future'?"

Duncan laughed; it was the phrase his mother would use, an antique. Abruptly Duncan was reminded of the breakfast he

could taste as if it were last Saturday's, when Skip had told his
family he was now "engaged to get engaged" to Cathy, with
whom he was at the time engaged in what he had confessed to
Duncan was "just foreplay, period." Duncan remembered wondering if that meant "things" had "made some progress" or
what. He told Eddie, "Just ask Elaine to ask Nina," then he
paused and finished, "to tell me." He laughed again.

"You could do worse," said Eddie noncommittally, "in fact
you have." His laughter flared up and subsided.

"So you think my taste in women has improved?" Duncan
asked blandly. He had joined in too.

"All I'll say on the record is your game has." Eddie waited for
Duncan to say it, then said, "And as we men know, that's really
all that matters." He meant it to be ironic, but it came out
sounding real. It *was* real, in a way.

"Jessie sent me a card and called me up to get us to have
lunch or dinner."

"You're not seeing her still, are you?"

"Not since that time in November, but she says she's working
on our termination, which, she says, was incomplete. She says
she wants to get a sense of what it is that's over."

"She's just making trouble."

"Do you think so?" Duncan wanted validation.

Eddie put the triangle of his club sandwich on his plate, for
the effect and so the insides wouldn't spring out. "*Sure* she is,
you kidding?" Eddie wiped the mayonnaise from his fingers
with his napkin. He was good at planning sessions, when the talk
can be strategic and the goal is problem solving. "If you didn't
have a girlfriend, do you think she'd follow you around like this?
She didn't when you didn't, did she?"

He admitted, "No."

"She doesn't want you for herself or anyone else either, that's
what I think." Eddie took a sip of beer. His kids were always
doing this, and he was always refereeing.

"What confuses everything is that time at her place, I wish

that hadn't happened. We were really going at it, for whatever reason. She told me she loved me." He had not told Nina this.

"It's true, she loved you. You loved her. So what? Look, I've felt guilty too for having sex I shouldn't have"—this was Eddie's first mention of it—"but you can't be governed by the stuff you say or she says. Ninety-five percent's exaggeration."

Duncan felt like saying, "Not for me, it isn't," but he also wanted to ask, "You've felt guilty too? Who with?"

"Nobody in particular." Eddie picked up his sandwich now and took a bite. "Just women," he said with his mouth full.

"No shit," Duncan said, amazed. "Do you tell Elaine?"

"Once," he answered, not looking at Duncan, "but she still holds it against me, uses it against me, so I never would again."

Duncan sipped from his wineglass, then ate a bite of his omelet. He felt sorrier for Eddie than he did for himself. "I see what you mean, in that case." What a bankrupt system, where sex is for saying what you don't mean. After a pause, Duncan said this.

"I agree," Eddie replied, "I'm not building a case for it, just saying you can spend your whole life feeling guilty. What is it, two months now? Why don't you tell Jessie, 'Look, I'm not excusing it, but it won't ever happen again, so let's just forget it,' and see what she says."

"I think I said that." He had said it several times in several ways these seven weeks.

"Then say, 'Look, don't keep carrying on like we're lovers, we're not lovers.'" Eddie finished off his beer. "You have to *say* things."

Duncan noticed that there was a major inconsistency in his advice—be honest there but not at home—but that Eddie was right, at least, about not letting sex torment him. He was letting having sex with Jessica torment him. "Maybe I'll write her a letter."

Eddie signaled for the waiter and asked for another round. "No, I don't think in terms of letters, but we do have different circumstances. What I'd do is call her up this afternoon and spell it out and get it over with. Remind her you're divorced, for Christ's sake. Sometimes you don't act divorced, you know that?"

"I have hard times with transitions, that's why I don't make too many." Duncan was apologizing, and he saw that.

"Maybe, but you're making one now, unless Nina isn't what you say she is to you."

"She is."

"Then jump across, Jones, fucking jump *across*. Let go. If you want to talk about bridges, talk about a few you should *burn*." Eddie leaned across the small table to avoid being overheard. "So you got your rocks off on Jessie for a change, so what? What's to feel guilty about? So you liked it, what's the problem? You're perverse, you know that, Jones? You'll never run out of ways to torment yourself."

"That's true." He'd just thought of another. Eddie was a pro. It showed.

As if to prove it, Eddie said, "You've got an old abandoned building, arsonist's delight, and there's a fire that guts it, just a couple of the outside walls remain. The site's a given, and besides it's not a bad one, so you're hired to build the new one. Do you follow me?"

This was exactly what he meant, a pro. Eddie's long training and apprenticeship were over long ago. He was the real thing now and had all the authority he needed. Duncan nodded.

"Would your first plan be to keep the old walls standing?" Eddie revised, "Never mind, yours *would*, that's the point, isn't it?" He smiled. "Mine wouldn't, and yours *shouldn't*. You're not being hired to reconstruct, as if you were a plastic surgeon fixing up a smashed-up face, you're being hired to build it new, to start again. You get it yet?"

What Duncan understood was why he envied Eddie, and it was because of Eddie's steady growth, his steady progress, gathering experience and building on it. Even if he was a hot-shot architecture student, as he was, he couldn't build a building until he had earned a license, unlike Duncan—this was his point

—who could come fresh out of grad school and write anything he wanted, anything the hell he wanted. Duncan had come on with all four burners going, and instead of having one and lighting more he'd had to watch the first three go out one by one, and the fourth flicker. Or, even if he'd managed to keep them all going more or less, as some would argue on his behalf, he was now no better off—and this was his point—than when he had started out. And look at Eddie. Eddie was one of the city's most successful architects and would be twenty years from now, and would be even better then. And what would *he* be? Only older, only farther from his promising beginning. Duncan let the waiter take away his plate with nearly half the omelet left. "Just fine," he answered, asked, "Was everything all right, sir?"

Eddie said fraternally, "Forget all this, I mean it. Her, but also me, forget my lecture. Screw it, Jones, you're doing fine. I have no business lecturing you." Eddie's look was sheepish. "Talk about not letting go of the old; shit, just look at Elaine and me."

Now the waiter brought two cups and from a small pot poured their coffee. Then he went away and came back with dessert plates. From a platter he lifted onto the plates before them, with a fork and spoon that cradled the Napoleons they hadn't ordered, rectangles of cream-filled, frosted, layered pastry. Duncan's had a candle in it, which the waiter lit with matches from his pocket. He did not sing.

"Elaine wishes you a happy birthday," explained Eddie. He did not sing either. "Make a wish."

So Duncan did.

He hadn't known where they should go to dance, but the brand-new hotel attracted their attention every time they went next door to the Aquarium with Emilie. From the outside it was a ship, and they'd kept meaning to go see what it was like on the inside. Now they had found the occasion. Inside, it was like a ship.

They rode the gangplank escalator up to go aboard, expecting to see streamers of confetti and finding an evocation in the

many trailing plants up near the railings along exposed corri-
dors. The railings were white, as they would be. They followed
the sound of music to the left but ended up with cocktail pop
tunes on piano with a bass, so Duncan asked a waiter in such
whites he could have been a sailor where was Rachel's. Half
expecting the young man to tell them to go aft and starboard or
whatever, Duncan smiled when he was told to go back there
around that corner, make a left.

Since it was just a Tuesday night, there was no line, as there
would be on weekends, since there also was no cover charge,
but there was no room either. He'd imagined they would get a
bottle of champagne and keep it in a cooler at a corner table.
They had to make do with one and a half places at the bar.

The band was on extended break because as many people
liked to dance to records as to live music. The emphasis was
"poppy-rock" for both, or so Duncan had been told by a colleague of his at the *Globe* who was, he said, "deep into nightlife."
So far so good, though: the voice of Donna Summer.

They got drinks to save their places at the bar, then went to
dance and made it through the awkwardness of exposing their
dancing styles to one another by means of the greater awkwardness of crowding. Neither one of them appeared to be much
good, which Duncan knew, at least about himself, was untrue.
One thing he could do was dance, so they kept at it.

Nina's dancing was too subtle for the space, so she began to
let her arms go to claim more. She had been taught to dance by
blacks and even all her years in Paris was more at home in clubs
where the emphasis was on the footwork. "White folks" her age
always seemed to do the Lindy and look like they needed to take
swimming lessons. She thought Duncan wasn't bad, though. He
had rhythm.

When the band came back, it came on loud and clear and
brought the pace, as well as the involvement level, up. A number of dancers who were only checking out the scene, and
wanted to avoid a sweat until they'd first made a connection,
drew back to their sideline posts and resumed sipping on their

Brandy Alexanders. Duncan took advantage of the energy, also the space, and so did Nina, and, though they were quite mismatched as partners go, they made a fairly fancy couple. People even gave them room.

"Did I know that you like to dance?" asked Duncan when their thirst brought them back to their drinks. It felt like a discovery, as if of life as we would know it on the moon.

"I guess not. Did you tell me you did?"

"No, I guess not. But I do."

"I see," said Nina, "so do I."

"I see," he said delightedly, "so why haven't we ever done this?" Duncan took her hand and led her back to where the music was. He didn't mean she should answer him, but she did, "Well, first I was still nursing Emilie, and then we kept on going out to dinner so that we could talk, next we saw all those movies, then we didn't see each other for a while, and, let's see, that brings us to this month. You know, we just haven't known each other very long, is what I think it is." He couldn't hear a word she said.

Nina admired him, how it was so obvious that he was well coordinated, even though the way he danced wasn't what you would call athletic. He just *danced,* and she admired it. He was that way making love. She hoped the next would be a slow dance. When it was, she put her arms around his neck to keep him there.

They both had breath to catch and so they leaned into each other and liked feeling their hips stationary and as if joined while they shifted weight together from one straight leg to the other. Duncan pressed the middle of her back to make the contact overall and constant, and they rocked now, staying in one place but bending one knee and the other to tip pelvises, always together. Nina would have laughed to see herself so earnest, had she been outside herself in any way observing, and so might have Duncan, who could hear the sound of her blood like the ocean in his ear. Oblivious, was what they were. The song was an accomplice in the sense that it repeated itself many times before it ended.

It was just as well the farthest thing from this was conversation, or they might have found out they had traded places. Duncan would have had a chance to tell her about lunch with Eddie and the promises he'd made to Eddie and to himself to call Jessica and tell her he would not wait any longer for her to be finished finishing, so it was over. Over. He'd decided, since this was his birthday after all, he could say anything he wanted, so he'd called her. She was out sick, he'd been told, but never mind, he'd call tomorrow and tomorrow and tomorrow. What he'd say was it was time for her to get a therapist to be his stand-in. If she needed to resolve things, she could do it in his absence, in the presence of a person who was trained, and paid, to be there. Let her play out these few last tunes on a couch in someone's office, and let her pay for a change, instead of him. He would have sacrificed his present and his future for this past and almost had. If Nina hadn't been there waiting still, he could have. He held Nina even tighter. During all those years of marriage all he'd asked from her was this warmth Jessica was offering him now. And Nina was correct to call it inappropriate. Two other words that came to mind to describe Duncan's situation were that it was either perverse or that it was merely absurd.

And it would have been absurd as well as perverse if Nina had told him that she'd been awake almost the whole night and was finally sensitive to Jessica's position and hoped they would make a place for her and find a way to meet her needs. If she had said this, he would not have found it funny. If she'd then gone on to explain all she'd realized she felt about Yvette, and how she now identified with her and wished to be forgiven, Duncan would have been discouraged beyond ready reclamation. So what if she sympathized with Jessica? He wasn't going to get caught in it, not at this late date or ever. He was ready to be cut loose, not entangled in a new way in the net made up of loose ends. If they'd talked they would have fought and ruined Duncan's birthday.

As it was, they never went back to their drinks. Instead they found their coats and put them on and rode the escalator down to the ground level. Neither one spoke, but they smiled and gave themselves away as lovers by this grinning. Rachel's band had fallen as if off a cliff into the smithereens of music that was fast again and frantic, loud enough to rock the boat the building was. It made them glad to have escaped in time, intact, and this made them smile all the more. They looked like models—for what, toothpaste?—gliding down two stories on the escalator made of chrome and stainless steel. They didn't even feel the cold air. In a way they were still dancing.

Duncan's Saab was brought to them by an attendant who was fast if not attentive to the fact that many owners aren't impressed at seeing how fast their cars can go in how few seconds. If it were another and less special day he would have found an eloquent way—verbal or nonverbal, either—of responding, but he didn't even try to. He was only interested in avoiding contact with the world at large, which meant for Duncan everyone in it but Nina. He hoped, for example, that the baby-sitter was one of the ones who lived in Nina's building and could get herself home without having him accompany her. There had been already enough *interruptus* to this *coitus*.

# Fourteen

THE NEXT MORNING Duncan tried again to reach her, but Jessica's secretary said she wasn't in the office. He chose to assume she must be out of town and not at home, sick, because in all their years married Jessica had never missed a day of work. He didn't think she could have been sick twice in two days.

He was struggling with a piece whose subject he was not able to locate, and though this was not an impulse Duncan could afford to have each time a story didn't write itself, he'd promised himself he would make it worthy of being the first thing he had written as a forty-year-old. What it was supposed to be about was this young artist whose paintings reflected the light in the Caribbean and the Arctic. Duncan worked at it until it was time to leave for the warm-up before that night's Celtics game, but even so it needed something. He would almost never bring work home now that composing on computers had begun to seem a natural act; nevertheless he printed out what he had and put it into an envelope for later on. Perhaps the body heat at the

game and the fact that his place would be freezing cold when he
got back there would inspire him.

Nina, meanwhile, was enjoying Emilie's discovery that the red
sauce on her spaghetti was a kind of finger paint. Then when she
saw the same was true of chocolate pudding, it was as if she had
found the *raison d'être* to last her whole life. She was so thrilled
she nearly propelled herself out of her high chair. In the tub she
was so squirmy she again seemed motorized like some mad
dervish. Nina knew that Emilie would pop out like a light bulb
after all this, and that she would need to wash the red and brown
streaks from her own hair before going to the French film that
had just arrived from New York with an entire set of rave re-
views. The student who came once a week in exchange for a few
hours without roommates had arrived as well.

Nina had her coat and hat on when the phone rang, so she
said to say she was out. What the student said instead was, "Just
a minute, please, and I'll see." She told Nina, "It's for Duncan."
She knew Duncan from the fall and knew he'd been around
again these past few weeks.

"It *is?*" He'd never had a phone call here. In fact the telephone rang very little even over at his own place. Nina said
she'd take it, and she answered, "No, he isn't here, but I'd be
glad to take a message."

"Is this Nina?" she was asked.

"Yes."

"This is Jessica. Do you know where he is?"

She was about to give Jessica Duncan's number when it struck
her that if this was *Jessica,* unless he'd had it changed his number
would have been *hers* for a long time. She would have it. Anyway,
he wasn't home, as Jessica no doubt already knew. "He's at the
Celtics game." In the short silence Nina used for thinking what
on earth to say next, she heard Jessica take in the sort of breath
that is a gasp. What she said then was, "Is it an emergency?" Of
course it was. Why else would Jessica be calling? Not because,
two nights before, Nina had found it in her to be charitable for a

change. There was no way for Jessica to know of Nina's change of heart, since even Duncan didn't know about it.

"I just—hoped—to tell him—something." Jessica was talking in these little puffs of speech designed to postpone the inevitable tears. "But—thank you—anyway."

Nina had not heard Jessica speak, but she knew enough to know that no one trained to litigate could speak like this and win a case. No jury ever reached a verdict of not guilty out of pity for the lawyer. "How can I help?" she asked without stopping to ask herself if she wanted to help.

"But I'm so—upset I—can't think—what to—*say!*" This last word was a little shriek of its own.

Obviously, Nina could see, Jessica would not have called unless she'd already tried everywhere else and still needed to find Duncan. Nina at once felt unthreatened, as if Jessica the viper had become, before her very eyes, an earthworm. There was no mistaking honest need, not even in a person known as a manipulator. "Would it help at all, do you think, if I listened? I don't think there's any way to reach him until after the game."

"I feel—so—"

"I know." She would have guessed "embarrassed" was the word.

"Alone!"

"I know." She did, in fact, know what alone was.

"It's this—bleeding—I—I'm—scared." Jessica took a breath and said, "I know it's—normal, but—"

"You're *bleeding!* Oh my God—" She'd not herself felt so alone she'd contemplated—doing something—but she could imagine it, and had. She said, "I'll be right there," and was about to hang up when she asked, "Where are you?" Probably because Jessica had called there two nights before, she pictured, incorrectly, Duncan's, and that Jessica had gone there for whatever reason and let herself in with her old key—you see?—and slit her wrists or something. "Are you there at Duncan's? I'll be right there." Nina had her key to Duncan's too. This was ridiculous.

"No, really, no." Nina's alarm had helped her to recover. "No, I'm here, I'm home. And now I'm so—" it was the right word suddenly "—embarrassed."

Nina asked herself what she was doing standing in her coat and hat and talking to a stranger who was saying she was bleeding and was so *embarrassed*. This was what must go on in romances you can buy in six-packs at convenience stores. It wasn't real life.

"I appreciate your offer of help, I sincerely do, and your concern." Now she was fine. But did she need to talk, or not? The point was that she had not anticipated finding Duncan not there, which was what had thrown her off and close to tears. And here they were, the two of them, however it had been achieved. It had been proved that Nina could be sympathetic, so she ventured to explain to Nina, "I've had a miscarriage." It was a word she used rather often, although always speaking about justice, never herself. It was also the first time she'd said the word. It made her cry now openly.

"I'll be right there," said Nina without hesitation, without, in fact, really hearing what it was or what it meant. She heard it, that is, and rejected absolutely having heard it. "You wait right there, will you?"

"OK," Jessica replied.

Nina already had the phone book open. She had looked it up before, after Thanksgiving, and she knew there was a listing for a Jessica Jones who was an attorney and who lived on Union Wharf. She'd need to leave the number for the baby-sitter too, she realized at the same time as she realized Jessica had hung up without saying goodbye. She remembered Duncan calling that an affectation of hers, which did not seem to excuse it. Nina cut off all these thoughts except the one about leaving the number for the baby-sitter—"And for Duncan, if he calls," she called over her shoulder as she left—and left.

There was a taxi as if waiting for her, and a driver who kept up the steady stream of chatter necessary to avoid deciding in advance what she felt about what might—or might not!—have happened to her, not that it had happened to her (which was the point). When she got there she was like an egg that was broken but hadn't yet been scrambled. Her shell was right there in two halves.

Jessica had changed her bathrobe from an old one to a good one, but she had retained the battered look. Her face was pale with grief and streaked from weeping. Nina, with her freshly washed hair and soft gray velour shirt given her by Duncan for the way it matched her eyes, contrasted. It would be important for them both to keep in mind which one of them was at the greater disadvantage.

Nevertheless, Nina found herself remembering, for instance, what he'd said about the view—it was a great one—and she couldn't help comparing their encounter in the airport tower just across the harbor with what she imagined now it was like that night in November when these two had watched his plane take off without him. Nina knew, before she knew for sure, it was appropriate to think of that night.

There was tea to steep and pour, which occupied the first few minutes, and then they went to sit on the two white couches to consider how to start.

Jessica came right to the point by asking, "Have you had a miscarriage?"

"No, never," Nina answered. It did not seem relevant that most unmarried women didn't.

"The kind I had is what's called a missed abortion."

"I didn't know there were several kinds to have." Or was Jessica saying it was not entirely natural, that she had intervened?

"What happens is that you have it in stages. Just at the point I began to wonder if I could be pregnant, all those symptoms stopped. I had a half a day of cramps I took to be my period, just late, and I relaxed. I had to go on business to St. Louis, and so I made an appointment for a check-up for the next week and went. And I felt awful, worse than would be usual, and longer, but I still considered it was normal. Yesterday it came out."

Yesterday it had been Duncan's birthday. When she called the night before it, Nina tried to calculate, what had she thought? And when she made that birthday card—"We've got it backwards, Me and you."—what had she thought? Had Jessica said there was a point when she thought she must be pregnant, or that there was not that moment? She would have to figure that out later on. Now Jessica was starting to cry.

"I was getting dressed for work and had, I thought, the kind of stomach cramps you get with an intestinal flu. But instead this —thing—this tissue came out. It looks like an—eyeball." And she shivered.

Nina shivered too.

"I got a jar and scooped it out and took it right in to my doctor. I had no idea if she'd say it was a malignant tumor, or what she'd say."

"And what did she say?" asked Nina.

Jessica blew her nose and stuffed the used Kleenex in the pocket of her bathrobe. "She said that it was a perfect casing of the uterus."

"So what does that mean?"

"It was a blank. She used that word." It had not seemed the right word then, nor did it now. They used blanks to start off races, didn't they? Not for the finish.

"So what happened?"

"I'm not sure, I have to find out. What she said was I was pregnant briefly, but it didn't take or wasn't right or something. Then instead of having a miscarriage in the regular way I had it in stages." She could not believe, even now as she said it, she was pregnant without knowing she was pregnant. And now there was all this bleeding to confirm she was no longer.

As if this were of importance, Nina said, "I've never heard of it—did you call it a missed abortion?—but how awful it sounds. No, I've never heard of it." As if this mattered. "Could she tell how pregnant you were?" She herself had gone three months and not suspected she was pregnant, not that there weren't mitigating circumstances.

"Just a few weeks, five or six." Her shoulders shook. "I can't believe it's over before I ever knew I was pregnant." Now she covered her face with her hands and said, "I was awake all last night, and I couldn't face it. But I'm sorry. I should never have called you. I left a desperate message on his phone machine, I was so scared. Not scared exactly, just alone. You must think I'm so—"

"No, I don't."

"So selfish."

"No, don't worry."

"I'd have tried to call my parents, but they're on a cruise ship in the Mediterranean." It was not clear whether she'd have really told her parents even if she'd had the option. They'd supported first the marriage, then the divorce and would think of Jessica as going backward, or in circles.

"No, it's fine, I'm glad you called me." It had given her a chance to see it was more complicated than a simple matter of identifying with Yvette. And anyway, it hadn't been established yet if it was Duncan or the man who read *Success,* or some third party, had it?

"Is he going home, do you know, after the game?" What she meant was, would he get her message still? She'd called back with a countermessage but knew Duncan wasn't the type to listen to his whole tape before responding to a plea. She wanted him to come to help her deal with this, since it was his too.

"Yes, he should be. Even if he doesn't, though, I asked my baby-sitter to tell him to call here."

Jessica had not been told there was a child. Her look revealed this.

Nina felt accused and couldn't think what to say.

"He never said."

He would have told Nina it was not Jessica's business, and in a way he'd have been correct, she understood now. Why, then, did she feel indicted?

"This is not what could be called a case of perfect timing, is it?" Was it Duncan's? Had they known each other long enough for her to have his child? She counted backward to last summer —June? July?—although he'd said then he had really met her sooner, hadn't he?

She was reprieved. Nina admitted freely that she had a baby eleven months old. She'd seen Jessica counting and had realized it as what she'd done, back to that night at Thanksgiving. Nina nearly laughed out loud.

"So—"

"Emilie was three months old when I met Duncan." Nina smiled.

"Yes, thank you." Jessica smiled back. "I don't think I'd have handled that one very well. The way you are." Jessica hadn't yet tried to imagine what it must be like for Nina, all this, so she tried now. But she couldn't.

"I can still have the illusion that it was somebody else's," Nina replied. What she didn't also say, except to herself to remember it was true, was that it was over. Jessica might have been pregnant, but she wasn't any longer. "Was it?" she asked.

"No."

"Of course. Why would you have called Duncan if it wasn't his?"

Jessica knew what Nina meant, although she also realized she'd have called Duncan to the rescue even if it hadn't been his. "That's right," she said, "and I'm sorry. This must be hard." She'd achieved a minimal appreciation, at any rate. "Had he told you, at least?" For the first time Jessica saw there was another side to her thinking there was nothing wrong with what had happened in November.

"It was the occasion for a separation."

"He never says anything," said Jessica. To her, she meant.

"It's not the sort of thing to not say." Now what? Nina wanted out of there. A buzzer sounded, as if she was hooked up to a timer that had gone off.

"Here he is." Jessica confirmed it was Duncan with the intercom before she buzzed him in. "Before he gets here," she said, "thank you." Jessica went over to where Nina was—she'd stood up and looked as if she were about to jump out the window—and embraced her. It was a risk in so charged a moment, but she was that grateful.

Nina remained rather stiff but said, "You're welcome," and she meant it. *Now* what, though?

He was still out of breath from running back from the illegal parking space he'd settled for, and at first—why should he have looked around?—he didn't see that Nina was there. "What's the *matter?*" he asked Jessica, "What *happened?*" He had only heard the message that something awful had happened and that he must come right over.

"Nina's here," was what she said.

This seemed both awful and not at all awful. Duncan looked around for her and asked, *"My* Nina?" It was cute, the way he said it, but still he could not believe in such a crazy overlapping. He had been determined they would not be modern and all have brunch once a month. It never had occurred to him that Jessica and Nina would be in the same room, except maybe if it was his funeral. "Is this my funeral, or what?" Where was his mother, in that case? He looked around. When Nina laughed—he'd told her she'd see Jessica when he was dead, the same way she had seen Yvette for the first time when Jules-Jacques died, and that this was the way to do it—Duncan laughed too and asked, "Am I dead? No, really, am I?" He fell down dead then for the effect and said, "So this is what it's like. I've always wondered."

"Good old Duncan," Jessica said, walking to him from the doorway. "Would you like a cup of tea?"

Now it was Wonderland he'd come to: he was Alice. "Tea?" He'd had enough beer at the basketball game but had sobered up abruptly and still skidded along on the effects of adrenaline. "No, scotch," he answered, pulling himself up and asking Nina in a whisper what the hell was going on.

She whispered back that he'd have to ask Jessica, and then she asked about the game.

"The Celtics, you mean?" Why not? Wasn't he so full of what a genius Larry Bird was that he'd been about to burst with what an utter *genius* Bird was? "The best play not just of the game, of the *season,* took place right in front of me. The best damn play of the whole season." Even if she'd asked him to, he knew better than to try and describe for Nina what, on the late news he'd raced back home for, even the sportscaster couldn't seem to narrate. All he said was, "Only seeing is believing."

Jessica came back with glasses and a crystal bowl of ice, and since the scotch was still unpoured, Nina determined she should leave and that she would leave. She did not use the excuse of having to get home because the baby-sitter had to get home.

Duncan urged her to wait long enough for him to leave with her, but Nina indicated that it would be better if he stayed and if she didn't. Jessica walked Nina to the door and promised to return the favor one day, to which Nina replied that it was a gift and not a loan. She couldn't help but wonder what Yvette would have said.

Duncan told Jessica, "Well, I thought your father must have died, the way you sounded." He could tell it wasn't that, whatever it was. He'd decided, rushing here, that it would have to be really bad or he'd tell her face to face what he'd been trying to get through to her to say. The first chance he got he would seize as by the wrist, and he would tell her it was over.

"It was lucky I called Nina's looking for you. I should say that *I* was lucky. She was good to me. I can see why you like her."

"Love her," he corrected.

"Yes, I can see why."

"You could have made things easier for us," said Duncan.

"And I could have made things easier for myself too, if I'd ignored you when you came on to me, for example."

"Jessie, won't you let that *go?* That's old, and we have all recovered."

"That's the difference between men and women," she said.

"Jesus, Jessie, everything with you has got to be a point of law!"

"What I mean is that men can walk away and women can't."

"That's bullshit!"

"What I mean is that she can get pregnant." And this was how she announced it.

Duncan had so many simultaneous reactions all he heard was static between stations. He had trouble tuning one in.

"That's a major difference, I think."

"So do I," Duncan admitted. What he said next was self-serving, he knew, but he had to ask her, "Is it mine? Or don't you know?" He had to ask, he had to know. Should he have had to ask? Why was she taking so long?

"I know it was," Jessica said, her eyes filling, hurt that he had not assumed it, "or you wouldn't be here, would you?"

"If you asked me to, I would be." Duncan meant he was her friend but wasn't sure it sounded like that. "Aren't I your friend?" he then asked. He wanted to ask how she knew for sure it was his. Wasn't it the point that she had someone else, who read *Success?*

"So do you want to hear about it?"

"Yes," he answered. What he meant was yes and no. He wanted it not to have happened.

"It was that time at Thanksgiving," she said as if there were other times to choose from, "even though of course I used my diaphragm."

"I thought you had," he added. He'd have asked, or checked.

"But then you have to reapply the stuff."

He'd been asleep for that part.

"And I didn't. I must have thought it was soon enough after the first, that second time, because I didn't think about it."

Even he knew that you had to reapply the jelly, not that he had learned about it with her. Were they really people married for a decade and a half? They were so inexperienced. "When did you find out you were pregnant?" he asked.

"Not until today, for certain."

You see? What else was there neither of them knew enough to know?

She said, "I felt I might be, but the symptoms stopped and I assumed I couldn't have been. I was wrong, though."

"Symptoms stopped?" He didn't think they were supposed to, the whole nine months.

"I miscarried." Once again she began to cry.

"Jessie, oh, dear Jessie," he soothed. Duncan put his arms around her and she clutched him, sobbing now. He didn't think she'd ever done this in their marriage, not like this. She'd obviously waited so long.

It subsided after some time with no effort on her part, as if she'd emptied herself of it and was after all a bucket, not a well. "So it's all over," Jessica said.

"Are you all right now?" he asked. "I mean, what did the doctor tell you?"

"I guess I am," was the reply. "She said she would keep an eye on me until I'm regular again and so forth. She told me a couple things I shouldn't do right now, like sex." Jessica laughed.

"Don't worry." He could laugh too.

"There's a lot of bleeding, though, and other than the fact that I feel awful, I'm just fine."

He leaned back now and stared into space out the window. It was not exactly black because of all the city lights, but there were no stars. He could feel the sadness coming up on him and entering him like a virus. Pretty soon he would be having his own symptoms.

"But it's maudlin," interrupted Jessica, "because the truth is that I've never been the type. I'm not the type. I honestly would rather be a daughter than a mother." She admitted this with what seemed, even to her, a cheer that was inappropriate. "But it's true," she insisted, not to apologize, just to explain.

Now she'd carried him away from whatever he might have said, and he said nothing.

"I did think about it when I wondered if I might be pregnant. You'll be glad to know, I'm sure, that I couldn't see having it."

"And what if I'm not glad?" he asked her.

Now it was she who said nothing.

"What if it might matter to me?" he persisted. "What if I might feel *responsibility?* Is that so unimaginable?" He got up to get the distance he required. "I see how it affects you," he said, stepping away, "to miscarry, but you are remarkably unmoved by your having been pregnant with my child."

"I never said it was a child. The doctor said it was a *blank.* That's why miscarriage happens, Duncan! And don't tell me you would want a child of mine now. Yes, before, I know, but not now." Even sitting down she was the prosecutor, he the witness.

"Who are you to tell me if I want a child or not?" He did, of course he did. He always had.

"With me, I'm saying."

"Jessie, I spent ten years thinking if we only had a child our marriage would work."

"That's not how it works," she answered, and was correct.

"Sure, I know that, but I'm saying I spent *ten years* wishing you would have my baby!"

"But you don't *now,* is all I mean." And she was right.

"Is that the point?"

"Isn't it?" She let it hang there, pointed, like an icicle.

It was his strong urge to go home to Nina after what he'd been through—and he knew she'd understand and sympathize and be available to him even before dawn, way before dawn—but he forced himself to go back to his own place. What he had experienced with Jessica should have its own night. After all, they could have ended up as enemies. Instead they'd come away as friends at last.

The city was dead as a doornail, whatever that meant, and he would have been tempted also just to drive around until it was light going from one Dunkin' Donuts to another, filling himself up with yeast and powdered sugar, drinking coffee with nocturnal animals not unlike himself. He resisted because it sounded like a *Globe* story about Boston in the middle of a winter night. And he already had a story.

Duncan's story was the old one about adolescence and adulthood, about growing up. (He hadn't turned the heat up, had he, when he got back from the game? His place was freezing: talk about the Arctic Circle in that story he was writing!) As if to become an adult, Duncan spun the thermostat and built a fire. And then he took a very hot shower and poured himself a brandy. It would have been adolescent to pretend there was no way to take back his apartment from the January zero degrees. He had no desire or need to hibernate under the covers when he could get rid of the cold. He was feeling powerful. It was a new experience.

Because the copy was right there and he was filled with good intention, Duncan read his own descriptions of the outsize canvases spread with paint colored tangerine and turquoise for the Caribbean and aqua and salmon for the Arctic Circle. Somehow you could feel the difference when you saw them, and he had been moved, in fact, by how the painter showed him the way one was warm and one was cold, but he had done a lousy job conveying that. "These pastel rainbows," he began a paragraph, "evoke two vastly different worlds. It is the sun's slant that—" that what? "—distinguishes the ice world from the other, which is also water." It was meaningless to say it was the sun unless he knew how to explain it. And he didn't.

He wrote in the margin, "These paired pastel rainbows reflect two times of day: high noon in the Caribbean and dawn in the Arctic." But what was the time of day if not the sun? All Duncan knew about the sun was it had shone in Martinique the week he was at Club Med and recuperating from his marriage. He thought of the free-form pool behind the bougainvillea hedge there, clogged with rafts of Styrofoam on which dozed naked oily bathers lying on their backs wide open to that sun. To Duncan they'd resembled waxy water lilies inside out, all reproductive organ, and he'd noticed the way on the surface of the pool and catching light was rainbow proof that oil and water cannot mix.

The rainbow proof. He read the sentence again and decided "These paired pastel rainbows reflect two times of day" meant he should look up the word "reflect," at least, in Oxford. There were many definitions, as there always are, but two meant something to him: one was "to throw back (light or heat or sound)," since it seemed to be the painter's challenge; and the other, since it had to do with him, was "to think deeply, to consider, to remind oneself of past events."

*That* was the story. Duncan had so many past events about which to think deeply, was it any wonder that he didn't understand the sun? Perhaps it would be worth it after all to learn about the sun and why the light is what it is at the top of the world and how white is a color without hue and what that means. It seemed the least he could do to begin to get his life in order.

Wasn't he also a color without hue? He had shown promise early on, but even *he* admitted he had not fulfilled it. Jessica of course had told him all along he would be sorry if he didn't make more of an effort to outgrow his boyhood, but it was hard to believe her when the times demanded so much that it certainly seemed it was his innocence that had been lost along with so much else. In 1968, the year he married, the two candidates for president of Stanford's student body were a topless dancer and a one-armed Communist, who won; the president of the U.S. was Lyndon Johnson, who withdrew; they murdered Martin Luther King and Bobby Kennedy and, meanwhile, Southeast Asia; Mayor Daley called the cops and gave the victory to Nixon. Duncan would not trivialize that year by saying it had been all downhill since (though Watergate was up, or down, there), but in his own life it had been.

He'd shown promise early on but hadn't ripened; wasn't this it? It was summer in his life—even if it was winter, really—and if he could not mature now, he would have missed his only chance. In autumn he'd have to fall off the branch like the other apples. How was that for motivation?

Duncan put another big log on the fire and took a sip. There was the good news too. Even though it had not developed into anything, a seed of his had begun to sprout. He was capable of being someone's father. How was *that* for motivation?

If he wanted to be serious with this first assignment of his forty-first year, he'd ask Nina her advice. It was her field, it was her very purpose in life to know about darkness and light. If he were to take this painter seriously—and, more important, *Nina* seriously, and himself—weren't the resources already within reach? He'd ask her tomorrow if he could come out to the museum for her lunch hour, and if she would teach him what she knew about art.

"These paired pastel rainbows," Duncan read again. He crossed it out. Come on, do you write Silhouette Romances for a living? Look: you are a decent guy, he told himself, or you would not be in an interpersonal mess most of the time, and you do have talent—tell me Bic's opinion of you counts for nothing—so come off it, will you? So *come off it!* Claim your life, for God's sake, *claim* it! Let's get going. Let's talk physics. Let's talk art!

"The painter functions as a prism," Duncan wrote on a new piece of paper, "to break up light into all the colors of the rainbow. The artist's imagination breaks up light so that the rest of us can see it."

# Part V

# Fifteen

...ST DAY of April, Nina had loaded her entire inven-
...lly goods into a U-Haul van Duncan drove to Irving
...nbridge. He'd put flowers everywhere for them the
...when a new business opens up and had made shelf
...ace for Nina, more than she could use. He'd left his
...e's room because it was too big to move, but he'd
...from the walls the awards and photographs he
...the office if he had an office. They were boxed now
...nt, ready for the move they'd make together when
...ed her to let go and trust him enough to look into
...'d never had the urge before to buy a house the
...w. He even looked forward to becoming handy.
...en wooed and won, as if he were a candidate for
...he the voters. He'd worked hard to prove to her
...orthy of her trust, and she had overcome her
...lly. She'd never lived with anyone but Jules-
...me, and had reason to be nervous quite beyond
...had Emilie to think about and wanted to avoid a

false move for her sake. She liked it, though, when they arrived by U-Haul and the first thing she saw was a paper banner that could have been in a supermarket. GRAND RE-OPENING, it said in red, UNDER NEW MANAGEMENT, in bright blue. Nina felt she'd voted for the right man, at least.

The next morning, Sunday, May Day, Duncan woke not having slept as well as that night for as long as he remembered. He got up with Emilie and started breakfast as if, the way Gerald Ford toasted his English muffins for the press, he would be on the front page of the *Globe* for having scrambled their eggs. When she came into the kitchen—never having slept so poorly, but requiring herself not to say so—he had squeezed a dozen of the sweetest oranges and had a glass for her all ready, having thought ahead enough to have used one of Nina's glasses to let her know she was at home. She forced herself not to say, the juice glass notwithstanding, what it was that had kept her awake that all her stuff had disappeared.

Right there in Duncan's kitchen, for example—poof!—four boxes of things she had lived with for ten years, in Paris and the South End before Huntington Avenue, had evaporated. Nina's books were only few among his many now, the only other trace of her in the living room being lots of cushions she had used on chairs and couches, and of course the birthday rocker. She had not known how much more substantial Duncan's household was until combining them and seeing. Practically the only aspect she would call improved in an important sense by her arrival were the paintings she'd collected over the years. One replaced a Club Med poster in the bathroom right away.

But she knew she'd recover from the night's sleep, as from the loss of her minimal environment, with time. There was a cleaning woman who'd been coming once a week for ten years, and she thought she could make that adjustment all right. Cambridge would be so much better a place to live in the summer even if it did mean driving now to get to the museum and the daycare center. It would happen, and before she knew it they'd be hunting for a house together out in Brookline, down

Green Line from her job and everything else, and be on their merry way the happy couple. What else had she learned in her life from their moves all over the world, if not for the first few days to keep to herself what she thought about a place? And what else than that adaptation, once she figured out what language they were speaking and learned it was one of hers, was one of the things she was good at?

He had never been so happy, he kept saying, never ever. When his mother telephoned that Sunday, and Nina made herself answer it because it was supposed to be her phone too now and she was closer when it rang, he'd told his mother, "That was Nina; she and I and Emilie, her baby daughter, live together here now. Would you like to meet her?" He'd held the receiver out to Nina, and she'd taken it to take him up on his not having said, "Oh, just a friend," in spite of the fact that she hadn't wanted to meet Duncan's mother on the telephone and had no idea what to say except for what Amanda would have, which was, "I can't think of anything to say," to which his mother replied, "Neither can I," and they'd laughed together, nervously, and said goodbye. "So far, she said, she likes you," he'd told Nina when the call was over, which was very shortly after it began. He'd never ever been so happy, he insisted. It was easy to believe him.

The next morning at work, after the anticipated phone call from his mother to ask all the questions she could not ask knowing Nina was right there—all of which Duncan answered breezily enough to have been termed oblivious when in three other rapid phone calls Duncan's mother told his father, Skip, and Cathy everything he'd said—he'd been called in to chat with Bic about what Living ought to do for Mother's Day the following Sunday. Perfect timing. His proposal—just a thought, less than a thought in the strict sense—that Living do something on metamorphosis for Mother's Day appealed to Bic, even after Duncan said he was only kidding; he knew nothing about bugs and wasn't anxious to learn more. Bic had told Duncan to remember Kafka and his novel of the same name, and to come up with a mere five hundred words by Friday morning.

This may not seem like many words to a talker, and in fact it isn't many for a talker, but a writer can spend days on what amounts to fifty lines, two pages. As opposed to talking, writers tend to need to think first what to say, and this takes time. They sometimes have to look the word up to get going—from the Greek, meaning "transform"—and make it mealtime conversation with their unsuspecting, not to say uninterested, partners. Often help arrives in some form; only rarely does it happen dinner that night can include a dozen different sets of pictures of moths metamorphosing under the lens of Nina's mother's portrait camera. If she'd mentioned that her mother had a moth collection, he'd forgotten.

But the piece was finished, and Duncan felt better about nature and himself. It turned out he was right that he'd known nothing, and wrong about his not being anxious to learn more. It may have been that it was spring and he himself had been transformed, but Duncan could have spent a month alone in research. He found himself jotting down on three-by-five cards answers to the sorts of questions Emilie would ask one day about how things work in the natural world, where there are explanations if you know them. One day he'd get her a tadpole and they'd watch it change into a frog before their very eyes, and he'd get out the note card on which he had written, "On the water surface in late spring at night the female bullfrog lays 10–20,000 eggs."

He'd get a microscope and show her the tiniest vegetables, infinitesimals with still smaller dancing daughter cells inside them, and, thrilled, she would tell him how they look like emeralds, so that from his cards he could explain how photosynthesis works.

He'd show her a picture of a dragonfly nymph and teach her about the molting process, since the dragonfly molts up to fifteen times, the compound eye developing new lenses, and antennae joints, the wing pads forming for the final transformation into its short-lived but brilliant adult form. He'd tell her all about those wings that take up to five hours to pump with blood after the metamorphosis, and all he could about those miraculous wraparound eyes with their twenty-five thousand hexagonal lenses that view the world as a mosaic. Emilie would understand he wasn't the magician, but still it was magic.

He was ready to leave early to make sure to be on time to pick up Nina on this Friday, the end of their first work week together, but he was delayed by Bic and photographs Mark Otis took in some lab over at Northeastern. Since they were pictures of nature at her best, he couldn't just flip through them quickly and be gone. In most of them you couldn't be sure what it was unless you worked.

"I see now where spring got its name," Duncan observed to Bic and Mark, "the world springs open." He felt this about his own life, this year, as opposed to last, when Duncan was out of the country as the buds burst, ducklings hatched, and ferns unfurled. Last year he went to Martinique and missed the rebirth altogether.

"That's a caption," answered Mark.

" 'The World Springs Open'?" Duncan joked, "Yes, yes! I love it!"

Mark missed the intended fun and said, "No, that's too corny, but I like something like 'Where Spring Got Its Name,' don't you?"

"I guess so." Duncan chuckled.

Bic too was still laughing.

"Christ," said Mark, "I'm trying to be serious. I hate ninety percent of what you so-called wordsmiths attach to my photographs."

"Slow down now, Otis," Bic suggested gently.

"Really, ninety-five percent of it is shit!"

"Hey, do yourself a favor, pal, and relax, will you? And do us a favor and shut up about it. There's an art to caption writing, and there's someone out there trying for that extra five percent to get a perfect score with you. Don't let them know they're getting close." Bic patted Otis on the shoulder. "Watch it, too, kid. I had ulcers in a previous life, and I don't recommend them." He knew what it was with Mark beyond the rudeness caused by youth, some of which he would doubtless outgrow, and was sympathetic. He himself had spent years having jitters every spring before the prizes were announced. The rumor was Mark wouldn't win it, and even though Bic wanted it for the paper, and certainly for Mark too, he would be glad for Duncan's sake if Nina wasn't front-page news another time. He'd met her, and he'd seen the baby for that matter, and was grateful to them both for bringing Duncan back to life. The rumor was that Duncan might win.

Duncan had been made aware that his November series growing out of interviews with interracial couples was a source of some annoyance to those of his colleagues here and elsewhere who were looking for the Pulitzer and may have thought by mid-November it was safe to assume they had the advantage. Duncan was the dark horse journalist of last year in that sense, and it was hard to argue that he hadn't put his finger on it about Boston's racial climate. Duncan, naturally, was pleased, but what he most looked forward to would be the update in a year. He had decided to reinterview those people he had done the story on, and to report how many more, if any, than the sixty-nine black employees the *Globe* had back then—just 2.9 percent—it might have a year later. He was glad to have his articles referred to by some of the liberal candidates for mayor and sincerely hoped to have an impact on the city payroll if it helped to have shown how much worse things were in Boston than, for instance, in New York, that truly "world-class" city. But to win a Pulitzer Prize for the year of his divorce? He hadn't dared hope. He merely excused himself and left Bic's office to go pick up Nina and get on with his life. One thing he did not think he would get—or else he'd have them now—was ulcers.

Nina had grown restless, then frustrated, waiting for him. She could not wait on the street now that Emilie seemed to insist on

her right to run around but was reluctant, since the daycare
center had been open for eleven hours, to keep a staff member
beyond the five forty-five closing time. It was a chance for her to
hear what Emilie had done all day, in more detail than usual, but
still. Unless he could convince her in five seconds his delay was
unavoidable, she was afraid it all would tumble out, about all her
things disappearing among his and the fact that there was no
mail addressed to her, and how she didn't like not living closer
to the subway system. She had known it would be harder not to
walk to work and back home, stopping on the way to drop off or
to pick up Emilie, but not how much. Nina did not want to tell
Duncan any of this, because she was smart enough to know from
past experience that every move included a brief period of in-
tense nostalgia for the place she'd left behind, no matter how
unhappy, in fact, she had been there.

And anyway Duncan spent his first two minutes so successfully, apologizing, she let go of that annoyance altogether and
decided she would concentrate instead on how welcome it was
(putting the bright side on the stop-and-go of rush-hour traffic)
to be in his car together, self-contained. Emilie was so glad to
see not only him but the contraption he'd attached to the bar of
her car seat so that she could "drive" too that Nina chose to be
content and stayed that way until they got to Irving Street.

Duncan went first into the kitchen with the few groceries
they'd stopped for, and Nina followed with Emilie, who strug-
gled to get down. He read the note left by the cleaning woman
and told Nina she said she was sorry, but she broke the sugar
bowl by accident. It didn't register at first with Nina she might
have meant *her* bowl, when there were so many things to break
of Duncan's, but she must have glanced involuntarily at the
place on the counter where she'd put it after breakfast, because
she saw it was not there. It was a ceramic bowl she'd made when
she was twelve and managed to save ever since, and hadn't
brought to work to keep on her desk to put paper clips in
because of the cleaning crews that hurried through the offices
each evening. Nina asked to see the pieces, as if the bowl weren't

simply an artifact but someone she'd loved who had died. Her
mother had recognized the bowl in the guest room at Amanda's
as an old friend; even her unsentimental mother knew it represented Nina's childhood. She could cry.

Duncan sensed the alarm in her and rushed around to see if
for the first time in ten years the garbage was still somewhere.
She was saying she would glue it back together and asking what
kind of person would have just *discarded* what was not hers to get
rid of. He found himself saying, not really remembering the
bowl, were he to tell the truth, it must have smashed into a
million pieces, or else it would be there. Would she like him to
call up and verify that was what happened?

"You don't have to be sarcastic," Nina accused.

"I'm sincere," protested Duncan, "I'd be glad to call her up.
The trouble is, she's always here in time to get the garbage
picked up."

"It's not garbage," Nina said melodramatically.

"I know." He held up to her the kitchen wastebasket with its
new white tall-size plastic bag and stuck an arm down to the
bottom. "But it's either on the truck or here. It's not here."

"Can't you at least say you're sorry?"

He felt he'd apologized enough for one hour and said, "*She* is,
read the note!" He pointed to the kitchen table as a lawyer
would a witness.

Nina did, and was embarrassed. "Please say to the lady I was
putting sugar in my coffee," it said, "when I heard the truck
come early. I was in a big rush, so the bowl fell off. Very sorrily
yours, Mrs. M." Nina said, "Now *I'm* sorry," and moved to
where Duncan stood with the wastebasket, which he put down.

" 'Very sorrily mine'?" he asked, putting his arms around her,
"I *am* sorry it happened."

"I know." She let herself be soothed.

"But you're not sorry you're here, are you?"

She answered, "No." In the quiet created by kisses, Emilie
could be heard having fun, and though Nina was aware that
probably Mrs. M. had left the lid up and Emilie was engaged in

what the books call water play, in the toilet, she knew she meant
she was glad to be there. Emilie squealed with delight.

"Could I make the suggestion of an overnight away from
here?" Duncan would have proposed it in any case, the weather
forecast was so good, the week so tiring. Now it seemed a great
idea. Nina agreed.

They finished dinner with a guidebook of New England inns
and picked one that was said to have fine food and feather
pillows. Duncan called and made the next night's reservation
for a double with a crib, and he was told they were all set. It
seemed that way to him too.

Then Amanda phoned to say what a momentous week it had
been, as if they didn't already know that. Duncan passed her on
to Nina after these few pleasant words and went into the living
room to see the week's *New Yorker* cartoons.

"Hi," said Nina, "how've you been?"

Amanda thought the answer should be obvious. "Terrific!
God, how could I not be? Hasn't this week been *stupendous?*"

Nina didn't want to have to ask, "How so?" but did.

"I must be calling at a bad time, am I?" How could anyone
who wasn't in the middle of an argument ask how? But how
could anybody argue, this week?

"No, we've finished dinner, it's a good time. What have I
missed?"

"*Missed?* Have you been in the Soviet Union this week?"

Nina laughed. "No, I've been here, we moved."

"I guessed that, since your number's disconnected. Good.
But how about the Catholic bishops' pastoral letter, Tuesday?
I'm so *proud* of them! And the next day the vote in Congress on
the nuclear freeze resolution, two hundred and seventy-eight to
one forty-nine, and wasn't that *fabulous?*"

Nina was glad she hadn't been too preoccupied to miss those
events altogether, but she certainly hadn't absorbed their im-
port adequately. "Yes, it really was," said Nina, "fabulous."

"It makes us feel we're having an impact!"

"Sure, it should." She'd intended to get to one of their meetings but had never been able to make it, not for lack of interest in the issue, she believed, but just because it would slip her mind between Amanda's invitations. Maybe with Amanda as involved as she could be, Nina believed they were all safer and she wasn't needed in the fight. No matter how she worked it out, it was a rationalization. Dr. Helen Caldicott said the war would take thirty minutes and leave 90 percent of all Russians and Americans dead. The ultimate qualification Amanda had for helping educate the world about the dangers of nuclear weaponry—she was a mother!—was as true of Nina.

It had started for Amanda with a request to donate both time and money to Physicians for Social Responsibility, and quickly she had found she had a new identity, and not as a physician's wife, although she was one, but as what she'd always been, which was a mother to four children. She'd gone on to start a group of mothers organizing mothers. "Aren't the bishops bold!" she exclaimed now to Nina. As a contemporary Catholic, she didn't always think so. "I went to mass just to thank them. Now I hope attendance is way up this weekend so people will get the message. Isn't it great! And what timing for the march tomorrow. Tell Duncan to make them give it a huge headline, Sunday."

"What march?" asked Nina dumbly.

"What *march?* You know, Nina, you really should *care* about the threat we're under of nuclear war, you of all people: you have a child, an innocent baby you should be trying to protect."

"I do try and protect her," Nina answered.

"Then listen to this: of the forty-five nations currently engaged in war, *all but two* have received U.S. military equipment over the past nine years. Not every weapon was a nuclear one, true, but still." Amanda took a breath and interrupted herself with another recently acquired statistic. "Did you know plutonium has a half-life of twenty-four thousand, eight hundred years?"

"I didn't." She knew nothing.

"Don't you think if you were told that Emilie would die at the

age of fifteen of a certain disease, you would do everything you
could to see that the cure was discovered?" This was a tactic
Amanda used at meetings in her presentations. "Well, this situation's worse, since there's *no cure* for the disease of nuclear war.
What that means is we've simply got to prevent it. You and I and
other mothers have to bring the pressure to bear on those in
authority. We have to tell them *we* want the authority on this
crucial issue, because if *we* don't care enough, who will?"

Who could argue?

"I don't think you care enough about it," accused Amanda.

"I'm sure I don't care enough, but I do care."

"Good, demonstrate it. The march begins at the Christian
Science Plaza at ten and will end with a rally in the Common.
You can march with us, which is why I called in the first place."
Let Nina just try and say no to her now.

"But I'm not free tomorrow," said Nina, "we'll be out of town
and have a reservation and everything. I can't make it this time."
This was what she'd answered every time, but it was true, and so
what else could she say?

"Cancel it, Nina, I'm talking about the future of the human
race! You can't tell me you've got other *plans!*"

"I know, but I do. We're tired and need to get away, so don't
make me apologize, please. I'm making my own small world safe
this weekend."

Amanda knew how to hit this one over the wall with the bases
loaded. "In Germany, you know, there were six million victims
of this kind of concentration on, supposedly, making your own
small world safe. Where's your concern, your *outrage?* Are you
going to let it happen and let *everybody* die this time? I don't see
how you can think you have an excuse."

"It's not a fair comparison," Nina said angrily.

"Then march," Amanda answered sweetly.

"You're exhausting."

"No, I'm tireless, though."

"Can't you leave me alone this week, of all weeks? I need time
to settle in here. We need time to be alone, away. And I already

have a conscience of my own, all right?" She now knew it was working. "Damn you."

"Can't you do the march and then go? Where is it you're going?"

"Maine," she answered glumly.

"Maine's not very far. It's so important," coaxed Amanda. "Just remember you're the daughter of a pacifist. Don't you think Mike would be there demonstrating? Or what about Dulcie, what would you tell Dulcie, you're too busy? You don't care? Even *my* mother's going to march, and she's never marched in her life! She even sewed a banner for our group of mothers. My kids are all coming. Anyway," Amanda argued, "how can you say 'this week, of all weeks,' when it should *be* this week, of all weeks: the freeze resolution vote, the bishops' letter, what more reason could you need?"

"OK, you're right."

"I know I'm *right.* Just say you'll march."

"OK, I'll march."

Amanda refrained from some piety such as "I know you won't regret it" and said, merely, "Thanks." She rapidly went on, suggesting where they meet and when, then mentioned an idea. "If you and Duncan want to leave right from the rally—just to show you I wasn't ignoring what you said completely about what you two need—why don't we keep Emilie with us? And she can spend the night, and you can pick her up sometime on Sunday?"

For all fifteen months of Emilie's life Nina had been there for her to wake up to each morning, and whereas there would be a first time, to which Nina could admit she looked forward increasingly, how could she let Mother's Day be that first morning? "Mother's Day?"

"You think she knows that?" asked Amanda.

"How would I feel?"

"To wake up with Duncan in some charming inn after a wonderful night's sleep, to fresh orange juice and blueberry pancakes, and to roam around and browse or trespass, and when you feel like it to get in the car and not have to plan when you drive to coincide with Emilie's nap?"

Nina smiled. She was right on about the car part, but that didn't make it less of a matter of conscience for her, now that conscience was an issue.

"Should I be a travel agent?" asked Amanda.

"I'll call you back, I don't know yet."

What began as an idea was now something Amanda wanted and believed in like a cause, so she began to lobby for it. "You can profit from the time alone," she argued. She was right about that also.

Duncan wouldn't have suggested this plan this soon, though he had been looking forward to outlasting the time-sharing plan they'd been on since their meeting. Much as he loved Emilie, in other words, he had been waiting for the morning when they'd wake up to each other's music for once, not the baby's. He told Nina, trying to make it sound like not very many, what a gift it would be to have twenty-four hours on their own. He would let her bring up the fact that half of them were Mother's Day hours.

Which she did.

"It's up to you," he said, and meant it.

Nina stretched out on the couch to contemplate her situation but encouraged Duncan to go back to his *New Yorker* until she had something to say out loud. Very soon she did. "It's not how I had pictured it," she began, "how I pictured it was that the student from downstairs would spend the night in my apartment one night while we went away. Now that we've missed that chance, though only barely, I have to decide if there's a remote chance the next best thing would be for me to leave her in the Common. I can't picture going off and leaving her, to the background music of protest songs."

Duncan assured her they'd have many other opportunities. He left to her the fact that there would never be a better time than in the first week of this new life.

Nina said it.

He admitted he agreed but said again, "It's up to you."

"Help me imagine it," she asked.

Duncan had been to many marches on the Common, starting with the spring of 1970, after the killings at the Kent State demonstration against the war in Cambodia, when the student population swelled the Boston ranks so that there was practically no one *not* there. He would not have left a baby in that crowd and hoped to find her the next day, and Duncan said so, adding however that this crowd would be smaller and benign. It was a group of mothers and grandmothers, he reminded Nina, and their children.

She decided she could always wait and see, and then concluded she could always make a choice and change her mind at the last minute. Knowing this seemed to allow her to accept as due, as past due, time together as a couple (rather than as the trio they also were), so she decided to determine how she finally felt the next day, but to *plan* to go away and celebrate the second half of Mother's Day with Emilie. And she told Duncan.

He sprang from the rocking chair as if it were a catapult and landed on her on the couch. He didn't want to overdo it and find himself disappointed in the end, but Duncan risked it anyway and told her how much he'd looked forward all his life to Mother's Day with someone who was not his mother—Nina would know he was signaling the difference between her and Jessica—"Or anybody's mother, frankly," Duncan added.

Nina laughed, then groaned and shifted one of Duncan's misplaced elbows.

"Even though you *are* my favorite mother," he teased. What she needed him to say was that she was a good one. "And a very good one," Duncan tagged on solemnly.

In her view, one of the best things about Duncan was how seriously he took her role as the mother of a baby who would never know her father. He had helped her be a better mother by his own experience of loss, which had confirmed his own desire to be a father. It had not been easy, but it had been helpful, having to work through the winter's lessons about death and rebirth. It had been this promise, finally, of the seasons that had carried them both forward into spring. Some years it came late and was short, but there had never been a year without a spring.

"I knew about you, before anything else, that you're a good mother," Duncan said, "and, in fact, one of the first feelings generated by you in me was the wish that someone would hold me and look at me the way you did your baby. I remember thinking that if this was what you did in public, there at the French Library, how intimate, how exquisite, how *perfect* it must be. How perfect you must be for me. I knew that." He also remembered wishing her the mother of his child, as abstract—and as pointless—a wish as that was. He wanted her, or somebody, to love him that much.

Nina understood about involuntary love and knew her voluntary love for him would never equal what she had for Emilie. She wasn't sure whether the difference was merely that Emilie was a child and he was an adult or, from her point of view if not in fact, that Emilie could die. Nina understood that of course Duncan could too, but that didn't seem as likely. Emilie, she feared in some dark space within her, might decide death was a way to know her father.

Duncan took his glasses off and put them on the oak cube of a coffee table that was once half of a pair. He didn't want to see this look on Nina's face. "I love you," he said, understanding, holding her. It would be quite sufficient for him if tonight and every night, afraid that he might die, Nina would hold him tightly.

# Sixteen

ALTHOUGH it wasn't "just" a women's march, the fact that Nina would be with Amanda and her mother's group permitted Duncan to suggest he'd rather spend the two hours at the Laundromat and have that chore done. He would also get a lidded basket that was big enough to hold the vastly increased volume of their week's worth. If Amanda asked where he was, Duncan told Nina to avoid answering. He wasn't performing business as usual—there was much more to launder than was usual—but it would seem that to Amanda, and he didn't want to have to answer to her.

Nina took the subway to the Symphony Hall stop near what had been her own neighborhood the week before and found the children and Amanda's mother at their rendezvous spot. Emilie was in the backpack but was brought out for admiring, and Amanda's mother told the baby she should call her Nana and helped her to practice saying, "Na-na, Na-na." She told Nina how from the beginning she'd considered herself Emilie's extra grandmother and she was so glad she and Emilie would share a

room for the night. When she told Nina not to worry, Nina
thought she maybe wouldn't.

And the premarch festive air helped Nina to feel good about
it. Most of them were people her age, veterans of two decades of
this, who greeted each other warmly, as old friends. They
seemed to wear a lot of buttons in favor of whales and gay rights
and against U.S. involvement in El Salvador and the Cruise
missile, and their beards were graying, but Nina found herself
asking, Where was hope, if not in these embraces of theirs?

And it was a glorious spring Saturday, when the trees' leaves
are still chartreuse and daffodils up from the winter hibernation
sway in breezes, when it appears everybody has a baby to wear
on proud chests like badges or display in fancy strollers as a
waiter would a platter for a special presentation. Emilie was
loving it. No one was too preoccupied to make room for her as
she toddled in among them at below knee level, and she didn't
seem to mind that they were talking only to each other about
what they'd planted so far in their gardens. The environment
was so benevolent that Nina could not believe that along Massachusetts Avenue on luggage racks on cars and vans parked in
front of the Mother Church of Christian Science were replicas of
the ground-launch Cruise missile the President was partial to.
They looked like twenty-foot-long bullets and were warheads
yielding fifty kilotons of nuclear power. A sign said Reagan
would be spending $3.7 billion for an initial 560 of these babies.
Just in time, loudspeakers asked them to assemble for the
march.

She had expected, somehow, bands and Sousa music, like the
Macy's Day parade she'd watched with Rosie Lopez her first
Thanksgiving Day back here; she was not prepared for chanting
slogans, but she did it. "Freeze Now," she called out to those
who lined the way, holding their boutique shopping bags and
looking curious but too busy, "Freeze Forever!"

Mike and Vivian and Dulcie would be glad their blood was out
their circulating "No Nukes" flyers and singing the venerable
"We Shall Overcome," and that their baby was one of two

hundred children holding hands and representing, as the hand-
made banner proclaimed, MOTHER POWER. Nina wondered
whether this was what Amanda's mother made and hoped it
was, it was so big and looked so strong. There was a light bulb at
each corner. That was power.

Nine city blocks went by too quickly, but it was enough to
grow in, and when they massed at the Common there seemed to
be many more than had gathered back at the Mother Church.
More men, Duncan now among them, were contributing their
bulk, and other compatible interest groups had booths that
would be manned all afternoon to promote issues and sell buttons. There were upward of five thousand, Duncan said he'd
heard on the car radio on the way over, which seemed like a lot
to Nina until he reminded her to picture the Prudential the day
of the Boston Marathon two weeks before and wonder where all
*those* hundreds of thousands were. Still, she was very glad to see
him, since he was the one person besides Amanda's children she
had seen before. Amanda had been back and forth all morning
with her politicking.

Duncan had tried hard to park close to the Common so that
he could leave the car seat in the car and not seem to be pressing
Nina not to change her mind about leaving Emilie with Amanda,
but there wasn't even an illegal space on Beacon Hill. The one
he found was so far from the Common he decided he should
bring the car seat just in case, or they would spend their travel
time collecting it. It was out of the question that Emilie could
ride on a lap the dozen or so miles to Weston. Jules-Jacques
hadn't used his seat belt that bright Sunday, which meant Emilie
would never be without one.

Duncan's favorite time to walk through Beacon Hill was dusk,
when the gas streetlights going night and day took on the personality of tapers, and when through front windows before
draperies are pulled one can see hanging from the ceilings
chandeliers of brass or crystal lit by small transparent flame-
shaped bulbs. The business-suited men and women who walked
brand-name dogs—it was as if generic weren't allowed—stood

chatting as they waited to pick up with a gloved hand—the glove
a plastic bag they'd turn inside out around the stuff—the day's
digestion. Children came home sweaty after baseball in the
Common wearing Izod clothes Duncan would have been told to
change from after school. Men with good bodies and short
haircuts walked in pairs or couples, having stopped on their
ways home, as had their counterparts whose bodies weren't
displayed as well, to pick up wine, a great cheese, bread baked in
the afternoon, and paper funnels of fresh flowers. Runners
jogged in place on corners waiting for the light to change, then
sprinted off to race their pulses.

Runners jogged in place on corners now this Saturday late
morning, in designer running clothes Duncan would change
from if he were to go out jogging. Tulips bloomed in window
boxes that, when summer came, would house geraniums until
the fall's chrysanthemums and winter's greens. The orderliness
of the life, not just the neatness but the structure, was appealing. Cambridge had its own commitment to an architecture that
was also copycat but trying, emblematic of the culture, to get
younger, then stay youthful. Beacon Hill liked being older. One
could tell its residents believed—and they may have invented
the sentiment—wisdom and age went together. All they needed
then, but most of them had it already, was cash.

Money maybe couldn't buy you happiness, thought Duncan,
but it sure could buy a few nice things. A woman sat on someone's front steps rearranging her belongings. As she clucked
and twittered to herself she unpacked and refolded all the
clothes she'd worn all winter. Dangling from her wrists like
dance cards she might have once worn were mittens clipped on
with a pair of those elastic things you see on children. Cleaned
up, she could pass for someone's Great-Aunt Agnes, who would
live around the corner with her help but chirp and tweet and like
this woman endlessly arrange her feathers. Money could buy
better nests, and privacy.

The homeless of the Common for whom a discarded newspaper was shelter had been budged this morning from the sleep

that often took them well into the afternoon. They wandered in this last block before Beacon Street like teenagers, rumpled and squinty-eyed and not yet ready to begin the day's panhandling activity. They had been routed by the crowd of people of all sorts who wanted more than to outlive the day, who wanted to outlive this present century, whose guardians were almost all men who were almost all, insanely, weapon lovers. Duncan was glad he had come but wished he hadn't done the laundry. Doing laundry was one way to help out, but the clearer message would have been to be here with them demonstrating, marching down a main street singing, "We Shall Overcome." He'd heard them singing only on the radio on his way over.

The speeches had been preceded by more singing, warm-ups in the form of protest songs with choruses, and then appeared a big gun of the peace movement, a local hero with an international following. In a voice made shrill by the sound system, she brought the crowd from their blankets to their feet acknowledging how early on she began warning the world that the casualty of the next war would be the earth itself and upward of six hundred million people. In a gruesome but effective metaphor, she called the superpowers' plan to arm themselves with nuclear weapons a murder-suicide pact they were trying to make look like a legal contract. "Murder!" she cried. "Suicide!" Her words interpreted vigorously for the deaf in sign language, the speaker went on to describe the methods. Amanda returned from making rounds to sit with them and listen.

Emilie, having enjoyed the picnic provided by Nina and Amanda for the children, drank only part of a bottle and dropped into her own world in Nina's arms. And while she slept the speaker went on cataloging the disaster and imploring—yes, obliging—everyone there to win converts. Nina could see how Amanda got her start, and she admitted to being glad Amanda had been effective enough to have brought them there to hear the bad news in detail. The part about innocent babies being born in an unsafe world, when her own was in her arms *sans peur et sans reproche*, made her weep. Her world in contemporary

acquisitions at the Fine Arts and the one she shared with
Duncan, however real, weren't "the real world." In both places
she had tenure, which was more than you could say for the
world these days.

Duncan asked if she'd decided, and as if declaring that she
hadn't changed her mind about what she was ready to affirm,
she transferred Emilie into Amanda's mother's spacious lap.
She would wait for the end of the speech and to see if Emilie
seemed happy with the prospect of Amanda's family's waiting in
line to adore her, then she'd leave the overnight bag packed full
with a fifteen-month-old's many costume changes and the paper
on which she'd written the name and number of the inn, and
they would take off for their first full twenty-four hours on their
own. If the speaker was right, the future wouldn't hold that
many opportunities for an escape.

Immediately the tone changed then to one of reassurance, as
the speaker introduced the triumphs of the week and the crowd
interrupted as if with applause with an impromptu round of
"Freeze Now!" Promises were made that representatives of
both the bishops and of Congress would be coming up to speak,
and that there would be both more music and more cause for
celebration. The mushroom cloud lifted, and it was still the
beginning of the same Saturday afternoon. The sun was even
shining on them from above. Nina and Duncan promised to call
when they got there.

They were aware as they crossed the bridge from Portsmouth
into Maine that both the Air Force and the Navy occupied what
waterfront New Hampshire had with nuclear matériel and men
and women at the ready, and that they could leave that behind,
along with all the statistics and the grim scenarios. They didn't
want to die from dread, and certainly not while the rest of the
world was getting the baseball season going. Nina looked into
the backseat and at Portsmouth disappearing and thanked
Duncan for remembering to make the transfer of Emilie's car
seat. She read as a healthy sign the fact that she regarded as the

more real and more present danger not death by incineration as the world goes up in smoke, but a bad traffic accident.

At Portland, by which time they had relaxed some, they rolled up the windows to close out, though unsuccessfully, the pulp stench, and Duncan told Nina of the childhood pilgrimages he'd made in the form of family trips to Hershey, Pennsylvania, a town that had the unsweetened smell of bitter chocolate that made you sick on arrival but to which you could adjust by the immediate administration of a bag of Kisses. Nina said she'd wondered where he picked up the habit of kisses by the bagful, not that this was a complaint, and he pulled over into the breakdown lane once they were upwind of the mills for as many of them as she wanted. Then they went up the coast and made good time.

The innkeeper, who called himself that, introduced them to the chef, with whom he was consulting about fresh-caught trout and freshly flown asparagus for that night's dinner. Not wanting to interrupt the ritual deliberation, and assuming rightly his guests would be happy with a sherry by the fire, the innkeeper settled them down and went back to discussing, in their hearing, mussels, scallops, lobster, shad, and salmon. They were quite content to get into the spirit gradually, as if this time off were a hot bath scented with exotic oils and followed by a full massage. They both relaxed into the mere anticipation, warmed within by the strong syrup of the sherry and all over by the fire, and they agreed that it was not a bad beginning.

In the room shown them by the innkeeper was the crib that reminded him to ask where the baby was and them to explain how at the last minute, as if it had been her decision, she'd stayed home. He asked if they would like him to remove it for them in that case, and Nina said yes, please, to spare her the confusion it would be to look into an empty crib last thing tonight and first tomorrow. He said, "Gladly," and withdrew in time to miss the glances that commented on his mannered ways, and their own in response to him. They loved it here. They checked the pillows, which, as advertised, were feather, as was the pink satin comforter at the foot of the bed, but thought they better not lie down there just quite yet or they would miss seeing the village they could walk to and would want to see before dark. There was time enough to stroll around the picture-perfect harbor and still see if both of them could fit in what looked like a large enough tub, and make love before or after, or both, and be right on time for dinner.

They walked the rest of the way downhill to the harbor that was no more filled by lobster boats than fields are ever filled by cows, to watch the last light from the sun setting behind them turn the freshly painted white boats a pale golden. As the water was receding, being dark, the boats seemed to be coming toward them, glowing like so many eyes. No longer cows, now they were deer. There were no fences.

Opening more to the event, as sightseers do abroad, they watched the lights around the harbor come on as these few went out, and talked about what life would be like on the water and found it imaginable. She would weave, Nina suggested, and put up the winter's food in freezer bags and Mason jars, and he'd split wood six months a year. They'd have more babies, maybe three more with nice rich Old Testament names. The Maine Yankee power plant would be a menace, but they'd work to see that it did not reopen when it closed for chronic violations of NRC regulations, and they'd never worry again about how plutonium was going to get them one way or another. Maybe they'd have four more, to prove how much they believed there was a future to be part of.

"We will, won't we?" Duncan asked, now seriously.

"Not four, I hope," she answered, "or I'd be a senior citizen. And not three either, I don't think." She laughed.

"But one?" They hadn't had this conversation in any form, and he hoped they would be able to achieve it.

"Oh yes, one, at least, or two," she reassured him, "I would like that. We could be a one-room schoolhouse."

"Maybe make cheese from our goats' milk and tap trees for maple syrup."

"Would you fish?" she asked, concerned. "You wouldn't, would you?"

Why introduce into this sweet fantasy the danger of the elements? "Oh no," he replied, "or if I did, just in streams for trout for dinner." In midsummer Duncan bet you'd have an hour in the water to be rescued before dying of exposure, in the winter only moments. Hell, maybe they had a small-town newspaper for which he could write local color.

"I could have a gallery," suggested Nina. This part of the fantasy was quite familiar, being several decades old and having been brought out and tried on periodically, like an old tux from college, to see if it had grown too small or had moth holes. It fit just right and looked "like new" in this light. "One day I will have," Nina added.

"I can help you," he promised her. He was relieved she seemed to feel she'd made the right choice in picking him to love her.

"One year ago I was looking for work in the galleries on Newbury Street. I had at that point less than a thousand dollars to my name and hadn't finished paying for Emilie's birth. I think I owed them seven something for a phone bill they forgot to charge me for then." Nina felt a sadness growing. "I called Dulcie, only Dulcie. One call to announce the news of Emilie's birth, isn't that sad?" At the time it hadn't seemed at all sad. What *was* was that she had not found Rosie Lopez yet, although she'd reached her brother up in Lynn and learned from him that Rosie had gone to the Dominican Republic, where their father had just died, but would be back soon.

"Dulcie wasn't with you for it? I thought she was." It was how he'd chosen to remember her description to him.

"Rosie," she reminded him, "my downstairs neighbor. We lost touch when I moved to Amanda's, although in another sense we didn't and we never will, not after what we did together." What a triumph it was for them both when Emilie was born. Rosie had helped her *breathe!* "I feel awful that Rosie's father died, and that I didn't know," Nina said softly. She leaned into Duncan and drew his arm more tightly around her. His hand was so chilled she rubbed it with her own and suggested they walk back. The last thing Nina said about Rosie was that Duncan would adore her.

They went back a different way and past a shop they went into to look around at the "Maine Wool" the store was named for. They admired the knitting machines set up in view of the customers, though not in operation now that it was closing time, and all the very lovely sweaters last year's shearing had become, in every size and various colors that could have been drawn from berries and, thought Nina, might well have been. The designs were fresh arrangements of old standbys—hearts and reindeer, evergreens—but the snowflake patterns appealed to Nina because, as in nature, no two were alike. This was an engineering feat achieved by the proprietor, whose absent partner was the knitter, who told them when he asked where they were from and they answered Cambridge he had an advanced degree from M.I.T. Duncan wondered if he'd been profiled in the local paper yet and found himself looking on as it wrote itself: computers come to midcoast knitting. Nina stopped herself from thinking that these sweaters ought to be on Newbury Street and bought by Amanda Morris on her way from therapy, where they'd be triple what they cost here, and decided which to bring home, selecting for Emilie all-over hearts on a background of wild blueberry, for herself the laciest of all the snowflake sweaters, and for Duncan what he'd tried on and was wearing still, where the buck's antlers stretched from one of Duncan's shoulders to the other. Nina wrote a check—Maine Wool was not set up yet to take credit cards, though it would be so by Memorial Day's start of the tourist season—and corrected her address on it, though she was told that wasn't really necessary and no, he would not need some form of identification. When they left there they were warmer for their sweaters, the wood stove, and exposure to the calm life of the refugee from Route 128's high-tech alternative, but had reached the conclu-

sion simultaneously that their fantasy back there on the dock
was just that.

The innkeeper greeted them again and managed to compliment their choices without making them feel that every single
guest came through his door at six o'clock in new Maine wool.
From the room where the bar was came the sound the news
makes coming on—though it was not their Boston news, the
music was a copycat—and they stood in the doorway to catch
what the lead was. When it turned out to be charges by environ-
mentalists that more moose had been killed than permits had
been won in the televised lottery held on the front steps of the
capitol last summer to anticipate the first moose hunting season
in a decade, they went up to make their own news. There would
always be more things to care about than there was care.

The next two hours, the fact that they were theirs alone, made
them know they were on vacation. Duncan pulled the shades
down and brought from his bag a half bottle of red he opened,
and Nina filled up the tub way past the depth of Emilie's bath. It
was good to know from having telephoned that everything was
going smoothly; it was great to not know more. She climbed in
and called out to Duncan to come join her. How it was the tub
was so big Nina couldn't figure out, since all she'd ever heard
about early Americans was that they were all short, but they
both fit the way they would on a toboggan, and they coasted for
a long time before Duncan pulled the plug and said he'd rather
talk in bed.

In bed they talked the way the woman off to the side of the
podium during the speeches had, by signing; everything meant
something. Duncan was surprised to find himself elated by the
possibility—he didn't know, since she'd come from the bathroom second—of Nina's not having worn her diaphragm for the
first time. She had, he soon discovered when he reached inside
her, but the feeling somehow wasn't altered by that fact of life.
He so looked forward to that first time in his life of not shooting
his sperm into a vessel with its lid on he began to try pretending
this was it, and found it was, at least, a dress rehearsal, as it

would be every time now that he'd gotten the idea, from Nina's having given it, that they could one day have a baby.

Jessica had learned from their experience she had no inclination toward maternity, to the extent—what better illustration was there than to have been pregnant briefly—of inquiring into methods less imperfect than what she'd already tried, which was by now quite all there was that didn't represent a health risk for a woman of her age. More permanent was what she wanted.

Duncan had been relieved after having had this conversation with her, because, needless to say, if her pregnancy was not good news to her it didn't have to be for him, and he could be excused from feeling guilty about feeling it was "just as well" and even finally "for the best" for everyone, especially the future baby. Jessica had been able to say that, though it pleased her normally to take bold action on her own behalf—initiating a divorce, for instance—she had not had the heart or stomach for the terminated pregnancy it almost surely would have been if nature, or whatever, hadn't intervened to terminate it. She could not have told her parents what she'd done, and this would have discouraged her in this phase of her life when she was so enjoying pleasing them and having them please her, for a change. It would have been complicated. Now it wasn't.

It was not *un*complicated, but it seemed appropriate to Jessica and Duncan too, the way it ended. If Amanda had been asked to call it something, she'd have told them it was either what spared them having had to invent a way to end their marriage, or it was what they'd invented. She was both by training and by intuition opposed to miscarriage as a substitute for birth control, not that she'd been taught birth control at a school named after the Blessed Virgin Mary, but she would have been in favor of this outcome. Having raised four children and been good at it and happy, she was sympathetic to those who were not so lucky. All she'd lost along the way was herself—and her self had been reclaimable—while others she knew had lost their minds.

This moment of his readiness at last to fertilize an egg came after years and years of counterpreparation, ever since his first

tux rental when the pants were at his ankles and his sword was in
its sheath—God, how he'd practiced getting one on in the dark
he knew it would be prom night in the backseat of his father's
car—with Nancy Churchill in enough tulle to have outfitted an
entire corps de ballet, and him hurrying before she changed her
mind, as she had several times before. That was his blast-off into
inner space and the first of his worries about quality control.
The rumor was that in Russia condoms came with pinpricks in
them when it was your turn to have a baby.

Now if systems failed it wouldn't be disastrous, so it was
proper to begin thinking of his sperm as seed, the way the Bible
did, along with Norman Mailer. He tried to imagine himself as a
Norman Mailer type, and when he asked her if she noticed
anything different about him, Nina asked why he was laughing at
his own jokes when they could be making love. When he could
be appreciating her, she meant.

Beginning with her inventory of his parts back in the airport
cocktail lounge—when she made it so obvious he asked, "So
would you like to see my legs?" and she said yes—Nina treated
him as her treasure when they made love, counting toes and
fingers as if they were coins and polishing him so he shined.
There was so much in him of such worth that she wanted to have
him insured against theft, or so she joked. Aside from Jules-
Jacques, Duncan was the first in twenty years who wasn't easy
come and easy go. He was both worth his weight and her wait,
she also joked.

Not that it was easy, but it did seem to be easier. Nina's having
imagined Jessica as pregnant, even if the circumstances weren't
as she'd imagined them, had not only permitted but *required* her
to be sympathetic. She had hated hearing all about it, and yet
she'd pressed Duncan for the details. If she'd learned to be alert
to what Yvette would have been feeling, she had also recognized
that Jessica was in *her* place and, therefore, she could understand her better than she'd been willing to.

Always part of Nina's definition of herself was that she was the
victim one way or the other of an accident, and Jules-Jacques's

death was as if proof. The way life worked was to bounce off the wall life was and be both player *and* the ball, which made the issue of control much more important. If, as she believed, one wasn't in charge in an absolute sense, all you had was all there was. You had to know to bounce the ball, and be the ball, that bounced back at you. She'd met Duncan because of a frame of film Mark Otis froze, but all the rest was up to them.

And she'd survived their first week as a couple, even with the loss of her old sugar bowl and her first separation from her child. It had surprised her, the way she was able to leave Emilie behind and climb into the front seat of his Saab as if cars wouldn't always be the enemy, to get away and into neutral territory, and to be for the first time alone together. Nina had accomplished so well the difficult task of being someone's mother and somebody else's woman at the same time, she hadn't remembered the relief it was to be just one thing or the other in addition to what it took to be herself. She was only Duncan's woman at this moment and was eager now to give it all she had. She was a woman, not a mother, even if she cradled Duncan inside and out.

And he'd seen how idiotic it was to plan for a baby the first opportunity they'd had for sex without one in the next room sleeping. Duncan had seen Nina come to life in his hands in a new way and found himself stroking her inside and out and lighting fires and fanning them with his own wind until they flamed. It was the fire that melts and cleanses, burning to the ash from which the phoenix rises: it consumed them and it gave them new life. In this guest room on the water far away and on their own, they made each other tremble, understanding that, as if this were their wedding night, it was an act of consummation.

# Seventeen

MARK'S LAST-MINUTE ASSIGNMENT had been to cover for a colleague who was too sick with a flu to walk a half mile and then stand around a half day covering the march and rally, and he'd had no choice but to agree to do it. He had promised to go to Salem Friday night to be there the first time his brother brought his girl to meet the family over dinner, and he'd kept it. What did not go according to plan was the next morning, when his old Dodge couldn't seem to be roused for the trip back.

Since he knew his car better than a mechanic ever could, he'd gone in under the hood and eliminated first one problem as the cause and then the next, and then the next, until the bright spring Saturday was almost half gone and he still sat in his parents' driveway, fuming. Both his mother and his father offered to let him take their cars, but Mark saw it as involving principle to get his own car on the road. When finally he found the malfunction was one he could fix, as he'd suspected, he fixed it and then degreased himself with heavy-duty cleanup paste his mother had first bought for him when he was ten and took apart the lawnmower to tune it up in honor of their yard's first robin, and he'd headed down to Boston to catch something he could enlarge, more to prove he'd made it there than anything else. He knew from the number of these he had covered that events like this one, like the cause of peace itself, never seemed to have endings or beginnings, only middles.

Mark had parked near where the mounted cops sat in a cluster on the horses they were letting strip the lower branches of a tree of its new leaves, and asked the cop in charge—he made a point to identify the honcho in any hierarchy—if it was OK to leave his car there while he only ran in to grab a quick photo for the paper. Mark found it worked better to let everyone assume which paper, in this case, for instance, not to make it clear it was the so-called liberal newspaper he was representing, since one of the *Globe*'s strengths was to not mince words, or images, when it came to police corruption. Mark was answered with a wink, and a snort horses could have made, that he should hurry because meter maids were revolutionaries no less than the nukenik faggots in there crying out their eyes and dancing barefoot in the dog shit.

Inside, in fact, decent-looking people were what Mark had seen. There were the few odd casualties, such as the woman with shaved head who looked unnervingly like a Charles Manson groupie, who was doing warm-up exercises for one of those forms of self-defense and had a sign pinned on her back saying she was looking for a ride to New Hampshire, but only a few odd of them. Mostly, Mark was aware, they'd looked to be what he'd have to call employable if not employed. They were all white, though not surprisingly so, since it was a luxury to worry about nuclear war for those without either job prospects or food or housing, and all ages, he would say, but looking as if they were forty. Many of them, men and women, carried babies on their backs or fronts or toddlers on their shoulders. Some with grown kids held them, as, in any other context, adolescents will not let themselves be embraced, even by each other. It was clear they were all worried and suspicious in one sense, and free and trusting in another. It was not these people whose profits would decline if instead of warheads engineers devised ways to wage peace. They surely wouldn't sing the refrain "When will they ever learn?" if they were stockholders in Dow or Lockheed. Mark had hoped to capture in wide-angle language what their message was. It helped, and was as if at his request, that everyone was saying, "Freeze."

He'd managed to climb up behind the speaker, who was promising the crowd a bishop and a congressman, and taken a few shots of lots of people feeling good about themselves and, more importantly, their cause. The victory V that came to mean peace in the sixties had been brought back for the eighties by, as it was clever to say, popular demand, and there were dozens of hands pressing peace signs on a world in whose saddle there sat a cowboy who had vowed to be the fastest gun in the West. What Mark liked about the shot was that there was a banner in it with a light bulb in each corner, as if somebody or other had come up with a good idea. And a breeze had come up from behind the banner to puff it out as if with pride.

Nina woke up and enjoyed the luxury it was for her to be awake and still in bed. There wasn't any small voice bleating *maaa-maaa* from the other room, so she could take her time with this and come into the Sunday morning slowly, the way people walk down aisles in churches. There was music. It was birdsong.

What she could see of the sky, the thinnest stripe down both sides of the shade like piping, was enough to let her know it was her favorite color blue. It was called French blue, she had always said, because it was the color Jules-Jacques's eyes were and what Emilie had brought back in her own. It was so true a blue it was hard to believe in it as a recessive gene, but so it was. Each visit to the pediatrician for a check-up was an opportunity for reassurance that eye color only changes if it's going to in the first year. Emilie was older than that now by three months.

Nina stretched her legs and pressed her feet against the vertical brass bars that made the bed a crib. She'd thought of cribs as playpens—as incarceration—but could now see that was wrong, that cribs could offer in protection what the womb could. Hadn't she just wakened from one of the best sleeps of her life? All she could tell of the time was that it was late enough for Duncan to have gone out for the papers and fresh bagels, following what they thought of as the tradition he began that August Sunday when he showed up at Amanda's after their first twenty-four hour separation. No, in Maine it would be muffins.

Duncan came in from a walk but empty-handed. He'd been going to ask about the feasibility of having breakfast in bed until he saw it being served on a sunny little porch with three round tables covered with cloths that matched the geraniums in window boxes on the railing. There were no pastels, except perhaps the butter, and the color seemed to be a celebration of having survived the monotones of winter. He brought from behind his back a purple lupine from the field behind the inn and said, "Good morning."

It was ten, she could see from his watch because he raised the shades on his way over to the bed to put the flower in her hand. She looked again. It couldn't be ten. She'd slept thirteen hours.

He sat on the bed. "They will stop serving breakfast in a half hour," he said as if he'd been up since sunrise rather than the short time it had been. "Awake, arise," he more or less sang.

Nina put her feet on the floor, signifying good intentions, but she wasn't ready to put down the lupine. Driving up, she'd noticed them wherever there were open spaces between forests, ribboning along in swatches, country cousins to snapdragons. For a wildflower, lupines have a sturdy personality, she thought with an appreciation for the kind of close attention to detail Mother Nature was famous for. Nina half thought the bells would ring, as if they were more than just seed pods.

"Happy Mother's Day," he wished her.

"Mother Nature gets the credit," Nina answered.

"Happy Mother's Day," Duncan said, bending down and speaking into the top of the lupine as though it could be a microphone. He kissed the top of Nina's head, encouraging her to get going. "You won't want to miss this breakfast," he said with the implication there was no way in hell he would, not even if she were to have pulled him down on top of her. He would have the blueberry pancakes, he'd decided.

She pushed herself up and went into the bathroom, assuring him she'd be ready in time. In the shower she realized that though, in fact, she was still digesting dinner she was famished. Lean and hungry was the look she'd left in Boston, trading it in on the buttery of country overnights in little inns that took in just a dozen travelers. Now she hurried. If they had two kinds of muffins, she would have both.

It was only hard to keep in mind that this was Sunday morning, with no bulky papers for proof. Duncan said he'd asked and been told he'd have to wait for the noon bus down from Portland for the *Globe* and *Times* to get there, as if they were relatives from out of state coming to visit. This was the best news he'd had since moving back East after Stanford and resuming the annoying habit of using up good daylight on what he'd really rather read at night. It wasn't as though he had all the daylight he would want in his life, although he admitted he was looking forward to seeing how "Metamorphosis" had come out.

Nina nodded when he told her about the bus even though she'd never herself sacrificed her mornings to this ritual. She'd read *Time*'s international edition every week and given it whatever time she had in order to read each page, ads included, but it hadn't ever seemed a duty. No, *Time* had been, as they say about time, of the essence. *Time* had been one way to know if she felt left out. She still read it, even now that she was an American and watched a lot of television.

On the table in the hall was a brochure about the scenic coastal route, and Nina took one as they checked out and suggested they meander as a means of transportation back to Boston. Maybe in an antique store they'd find a treasure that could be, if not their first joint purchase, at least something by which to remember this beginning they were making. It could be a present, she said, to each other. She did not say wedding present, though he would have been glad to know that's what she meant.

Yes, a bed, a big brass crib was what she meant, although it was a few stops before Nina knew it. In one shop she almost said yes to the footstool he suggested, but she waited long enough to find the right thing. They were using Duncan's bed, which wasn't good from a symbolic point of view but was a better quality one than her own. A bed of their own was so clearly what they needed that when she saw it propped against the far wall Nina called him over and said, "Here." It was in pieces but complete, and for mere money it was theirs. It took a while to tie it on—no tin cans on the bumper, this—but with the purchase of a quilt to rest it on and the gift of about a quarter mile of twine, they made it stay there on the roof. The quilt was actually nice too and could be for Emilie's bed, he suggested, or somebody's. It was nice to know already where that child would be conceived.

Eventually they tired of Route 1 and went west to find the turnpike they could ride on, though it went by different names, right out to Weston. Duncan hadn't been there since the day she moved back into town to start her job at the museum, but he did remember the way. He remembered getting lost too that first time when he drove Nina back from Logan and it was clear she had no sense of direction.

"What makes you smile," Nina asked him, "everything?"

"Yes, everything," he answered even though it was their getting lost. He'd almost never wanted to get anywhere as badly as he'd wanted to arrive that night.

"I was just thinking about all the snow at Christmas."

"Oh?"

"There was a lot of snow," she said unnecessarily. It was what he'd been stranded in and also what had liberated her to say yes to his urgent request that they be together New Year's Eve. They'd come some distance into spring from all that snow.

He hadn't been to Buffalo since, and he said so.

"Freshman year," Nina explained, "was the first snow I'd ever seen, so snow is emblematic of my independence from my family."

"No, for me it means entrapment. Sun was my snow."

"Christmas night I walked around the neighborhood in snow so fresh there were no tire tracks, the way it was that first night all over campus. Both times it collected so fast it hadn't had time to settle down enough to be attached, and it behaved like powdered sugar sifted onto fancy pastries, hard not to inhale." The memory too was fresh. She hadn't necessarily meant to describe it but proceeded. "That night out in Weston I was thankful for my time alone, for all the time I'd had alone. Walking around there it was so clear to me that I wouldn't have wanted to trade it for, for instance, one of those nice Weston houses with the perfect landscaping and Schumacher print draperies and two-car garage, this one having been worked up to with another smaller one a little closer in to town. And I would not have wanted to trade in my thirties for two fifteen-year-old children—that was clear too—although, God, how glad I was, how glad I am that I have Emilie, and you, and now at last the feeling of belonging somewhere." Even though, in fact, at that point she'd not taken Duncan back, it felt to her as if she had. The snow had made things quiet enough so that she could hear that message.

Duncan reached out for her hand and held it until a toll booth required him to use both his hands to drive the car. And then he held it for another fifty miles, it seemed to him, until they hit some stop-and-go, and he downshifted. What could he add, feeling, as he did, the same way?

In other words, when Duncan and Nina arrived at Amanda's they were not in need of having it confirmed by anyone or anything that they had both made the right choices in their lives (to the extent one can make choices in one's life, they would each add, each knowing from experience about those things one can't affect), yet there it was, more confirmation.

Emilie was up from her nap practicing the stunts she'd learned, which were both verbal and athletic. She was wearing a pearl necklace of those plastic pop-it beads Club Med used for its currency, though not in pearl, but which came from Amanda's mother's jewelry box. Eight-year-old Jason had taught Emilie to dance like Michael Jackson, so he claimed, and Scotty swore she had what it took to be the world's greatest goalie, which was the ability to fall on the ball without fail. Out of her baby-sitting money, and this had impressed Amanda, Penny had bought Emilie a tiny little pair of rubber-soled black canvas Mary Janes that had been freighted all the way to Harvard Square from China and that matched her own. Gail had taught Emilie to sing, and then of course to clap her hands. Nina would not have been surprised if Jeremy had said he'd helped her fill out her application for medical school, but it seemed another baby had decided to be born and he had just been called away. There was no evidence at all that Emilie's experience had shown her anything but slavish adoration, which was not exactly, good as daycare was, the attitude professionals had toward the children for whom they provided not just daycare but day-in-and-out care. Emilie was looking, no two ways about it, like a winner.

When they went into the living room Duncan tried to remember where it was, and where exactly, they'd made love. He wondered if the coffee table had been moved to mark the spot and looked to Nina with the question. What he didn't understand was that it had been radically redecorated and was not the same room at all. Now it was entirely white and looked as if it had been bleached.

What she remembered from that time was not the furniture now replaced, nor the carpet also now gone, but the sliding glass door that was open to the whole wide world. And it was still there. Nina thought about the breeze that rustled leaves and brought the outside in to them, and how it was the next best thing to doing splendor in the grass, especially since the sprinkler system had been off and on all evening.

Every now and then even Amanda laughed at herself by apologizing for the fact that the hors d'oeuvres weren't white because nobody in the family liked raw mushrooms. "What an oversight on my part not to tell the decorator this important fact

about us," she'd lament. Her mother was the sort who had the
same couch against the same wall on which hung the same print
of maple trees in autumn, and Amanda knew enough to be
embarrassed. She could give the money to the Home for Little
Wanderers if she had so much. This was what her mother had
said when she heard what therapy costs. After yesterday her
feeling was that Amanda ought to give it to the movement, as no
doubt Amanda had in generous sums.

Her mother came into the living room now, saying, "So how
did you like us on the television? We made all the local news." It
was as if she were a veteran after one march. What she meant by
"we" and "us" was "everybody."

Amanda congratulated Duncan, thanking him for how the
*Globe* had covered the event. Who was the other friend they had
there on the staff? she asked, thinking the name could certainly
be useful for the future.

"Was it good? I'm glad," he answered. He was more concerned about the Mother's Day piece. "Oh, and happy Mother's
Day," he wished them both.

"That's right," said Nina.

Amanda looked from one to the other of them and declared,
"You two aren't back yet, are you?" They were as distracted as a
pair of honeymooners. "Or is it as simple as you maybe haven't
seen the paper?"

"Not today's, no. We could have been here by the time it
arrived there," Duncan explained, still surprised by the fact that
the paper came up on the bus along with tourists.

"*That* explains it," cried Amanda, satisfied that something
had. "It's good I got some extras, isn't it? You see?" she called
across the room to Scotty, who had laughed when Jeremy said
he'd never seen anybody buy a bale of Sunday papers for one
page (or was she going into the recycling business?) "Run and
get two copies for me, Scotty, please."

The boy ran back in and displayed the two front sections like
two banners. In the center of the picture was the banner with the

light bulb in each corner: MOTHER POWER. "This is the one Nana made," said Scotty proudly, "see how well it photographs?"

"Now aren't you *proud?*" shouted Amanda. "Aren't you *glad* I dragged you there? See? We made *history!*" Then Amanda pointed to the square that was no bigger than a postage stamp but showed up more than all the others. "See the light bulbs?"

Duncan checked the photo credit and was surprised. He hadn't been aware of anyone from the *Globe* and had concluded this was due to his having arrived so late. It wouldn't have occurred to Duncan to have looked up into the trees, although he admired the sort of aerial effect achieved. The headline— MOTHER'S DAY MARCH BY SIX THOUSAND INCIDENT FREE—and the photo caption, which identified the speaker and reported that the mothers from all the New England states were part of a rapidly growing movement, bracketed the picture. The whole thing took up the top half of the front page.

Since their paper would be on the front porch back in Cambridge, for the moment Duncan was content with verifying that his effort had been printed. He pulled out the Living section and was pleased. He scanned the text and thought it was what he had written, in spite of the fact that it looked better than he had remembered. This was due in large part to Mark Otis and the minor miracle of modern photographic techniques, but the credit was his too. It seemed he'd managed to make meaningful to motherhood the major miracle the transformation was from wingless into winged insects. "Where Spring Gets Its Name," it was called. Duncan loved it.

And because they had the bed to put together, and because it was time now for the big kids to do their homework unassisted by a toddler, and because their present to the Morrises was a double bag full of lobsters for their dinner, Nina began putting on what Emilie had taken off and putting back what she had pulled down. Duncan went to put the car seat into his backseat so he could reattach at the same time the steering wheel that made Emilie an official backseat driver. The brass bed frame looked like antlers, as if his old trusty Saab had mated with one of those Maine moose they had not stayed to see on the evening news. What more could he want?

But there was more.

Nina found this time that his place felt like home. Her own things didn't seem so few and far between, and their purchase would redefine what badly needed redefining. It was fine now that the mattress and the box spring dated from the month or two—a sale, an act of desperation on Duncan's part—before Jessica had left and never returned. Now that the old was not just framed but supported by the new, it wasn't any longer threatening. What it was called now was continuity.

It was almost a year exactly to the day since their encounter, if it was that, at the French Library, and as Nina rocked her baby to sleep in the chair she'd given Duncan, she remembered, vaguely as if from the farther distant past, what her concerns were then. She'd been afraid, and even said so to this perfect stranger Duncan at the *Globe* the next day, that her past life would find out about her present. At that point, her present hadn't even been achieved, though she was working at it, so the fear she'd had was really that there might not be one. There had been such an explosion in her life at Jules-Jacques's death, Nina compared it to the day Vesuvius came down on Herculaneum and finished history for all time there.

Jules-Jacques once had given her a dragonfly wing. They were on a bridge, and she was rotating the iridescent wing at his instruction. At one angle it was blue, another clear, and at a third it was a rainbow. She was holding it just barely, so as not to damage it, but so that when Jules-Jacques blew on the wing it flew. It didn't really fly of course; it only coasted, glided, fluttered, landed on the Seine below them and disappeared under the barge coming out from under the bridge. Nina told him he was cruel—You don't just blow a dragonfly wing out of some-one's hands! she cried—and he replied he wasn't cruel, no, he was merely unromantic. Dragonflies only live for a summer anyway, and the wing showed that some die prematurely, Jules-Jacques told her. It seemed funny to her now that, compared to Jules-Jacques, she had been a romantic. Now, compared to her, she would say Duncan was one.

Still, the fact remained that Jules-Jacques died just as that summer's dragonflies were hitting middle age. There was no way to make it seem appropriate, his dying like that. Was it nature who was cruel? At this time of year when the earth was literally bursting at the seams with new life it was hard to know what to think.

Emilie was so big now she sprawled across Nina's lap like a teenager across a bed. Her face was losing its full-moon shape, and she had what would be called a haircut. She'd been walking for two months and talked in three-word sentences with subjects, verbs, and objects. Emilie thought Duncan was her father.

Duncan opened the manila envelope pushed through the mail slot. In it was a clipping and a note that read, "I knew you'd want an extra copy." It was Jessica's handwriting, and the "you" was all three of them:

Emilie was asleep in her lap, Duncan in profile looking at her, and Nina stared into the camera once again, as if she hadn't learned a thing in the year since she'd posed for Otis with her baby in her lap. They made a perfect triangle.

He looked until he found the photograph in that day's *Globe*—in Focus—and he brought it in to Nina. "Look at the gift from Mark Otis," he announced it. Of all the six thousand people, there were all those other thousands to have taken for a portrait of a nucleus concerned about the health and safety of the body in which it was a cell. Mark was giving them a present.

This time it made Nina happy. Already, short though it was, she had a history here in Boston. It was fixed in print—no matter that the ink came off on her hands—that though she and Duncan had the disadvantage of late start they had the advantage also of a late start. And in this picture the only politicians shaking hands above her head were other women, holding hands.

He gathered Emilie from Nina's lap and carried her into the other room. She slept, unaware of the transfer except for the registration of a little sigh, a hum.

## ABOUT THE AUTHOR

Alexandra Marshall is the author of *Gus in Bronze* and *Tender Offer,* novels, and *Still Waters,* a book about a pond. She was born in 1944 in Pennsylvania, grew up in suburban New York, and was graduated with degrees in French from Wheaton College and Columbia University. She is married to novelist James Carroll, and they live in Boston with their two children.